REBA STANLEY

A SECOND
Chance

WestBow
PRESS®
A DIVISION OF THOMAS NELSON
& ZONDERVAN

KJV: Unless otherwise specified, all scripture quotations
are from the King James Version of the Bible.

NIV: THE HOLY BIBLE, NEW INTERNATIONAL
VERSION®, NIV® Copyright © 1973, 1978, 1984, 2011 by Biblica,
Inc.® Used by permission. All rights reserved worldwide.

WestBow Press books may be ordered through booksellers or by contacting:

WestBow Press
A Division of Thomas Nelson & Zondervan
1663 Liberty Drive
Bloomington, IN 47403
www.westbowpress.com
1 (866) 928-1240

ISBN: 978-1-5127-9189-1 (sc)
ISBN: 978-1-5127-9190-7 (hc)
ISBN: 978-1-5127-9188-4 (e)

Library of Congress Control Number: 2017909444

Print information available on the last page.

WestBow Press rev. date: 07/19/2017

Dedication:
To The Great I AM

One

It had been a tiring day at North Side Christian Academy where Maddie worked as a teacher's aide. It was her day to not only do car patrol, but also to straighten up the classroom and ready things for the next day. As she pushed open the outside door to the school, she heard her name being called.

"Ms. Abbott, can I talk to you in my office for a moment please?" Mrs. Reeves, the elementary principal, spoke as Maddie handed the last child she was responsible for over to their parent. Maddie went straight to Mrs. Reeves's office hoping this wouldn't take too long. She was tired, hungry and ready to go home.

"Maddie, I'm glad I caught you before you left. This won't take long. I'm sure you're eager to get home. I certainly am at the end of each day," she said with a kind smile.

Mrs. Reeves was a kind soul. She loved her job and the kids, and Maddie didn't know of a single person who would be better suited for this job than Mrs. Reeves. She ran a tight, well organized ship and treated everyone fairly with kindness and respect even while disciplining those who broke the rules.

"Maddie, I know you were hoping to be a full-time teacher here at North Side. And believe me I would like that as well. Your work and your interaction with the children is excellent.

Last evening Mr. Carson, Mr. Stewart, and I had a meeting to go over contracts and found it very surprising to see all of our teachers in the elementary returning next year. As you are aware that rarely happens," she said pausing briefly. "At the beginning of the school year, Mrs. Tyndale told us more than likely she would not be returning next year, and it was our plan to put you in her place. Earlier this week, she conveyed to me there has been a change in her situation and she will be returning after all. Maddie, I regret having to tell you we do not have an opening for you as a teacher." Mrs. Reeves could see the disappointment on Maddie's face, which saddened her. "We would hate to lose you, and you are certainly welcome to stay on as an aide."

Maddie sat listening to Mrs. Reeves speak. *This can't be happening. I don't want to do another year as a teacher's aide!* "I know when we hired you we promised you an elementary teaching position when one became available. Unfortunately, there still aren't any available. It was out of my hands when Mr. Carson hired Mrs. Daniels. He chose her instead of you because she previously taught here and has more experience." The words tasted sour in her mouth. She was very unhappy with the way this was turning out. "I still believe you are right for teaching elementary children here at North Side. Would you consider staying with us as a teacher's aide again this year? I assure you that I will continue to work to get you a teaching position as soon as one becomes available."

Maddie appreciated Mrs. Reeves' words of encouragement, but words didn't pay the bills. Sadly, living on an aide's salary left much to be desired. She didn't want Mrs. Reeves to see the disappointment that was surely in her heart, but didn't think she could keep from it.

Pulling her car into the entrance of her apartment building on Star Boulevard, Maddie saw several of her neighbors coming home from work just as she was on this cold March evening. Some drove expensive cars, while others were driving vehicles with character much like her own. She didn't judge a person by their clothes, home or vehicle and expected that no one judged her by the same. Her 1999 Toyota Camry wasn't much to look at, but it wasn't the looks of a vehicle that got you down the road.

Slipping her shoes off as soon as she stepped inside her apartment, she let out a sigh as her petite feet touched the thick carpet. Maddie walked to the couch and plopped on her back. Every bit of her one hundred ten pounds laid there happy to be done with the day. But she was frustrated by the news she had received an hour ago. Her mind wandered back to her childhood when she would line her dolls up and play school for hours on end. Maddie worked hard at her studies all through school, she earned the right to be a teacher, not an aide. It was her desire to work at a Christian school. She could have gotten a job at a public school with better pay, but that was not her heart.

Maddie was twenty-three years old, and had seventy-four dollars in her checking account. With payday two weeks away, she had to stretch that as far as she could. Continuing as a teacher's aide would not be enough. The income was just too small. As Maddie floated between sleep and awake, the rattling of keys followed by the opening door slowly brought her back into her surroundings. Her roommate was home.

Meagan Givens and Maddie had graduated college at the same time and became good friends while attending the same church. They had shared their apartment for the past two years. Meagan was a paralegal at a local law firm. She had worked hard to earn her degree and acquire her current job, just like

Maddie. But Maddie's profession didn't pay as well as Meagan's. She did not begrudge her friend's good fortune. It just simply irritated her at times. To Maddie, educating a child is one of the most important jobs a person could have, but it paid so poorly and left her scrambling from paycheck to paycheck.

As Meagan opened the door with her hands full of bags, her purse fell off her shoulder as she stepped over the threshold. She quickly walked to the kitchen to put everything down on their small kitchen table letting out a puff of air causing her light brown bangs to fly upward. Turning, she noticed Maddie on the sofa. She let her lie there undisturbed and began to unload the bags' contents as quietly as possible. Unfortunately, her cell phone didn't have the same courtesy.

Maddie got up and joined Meagan in the kitchen to help her put the groceries away while Meagan finished her call. The girls always split the grocery bill in half, but when Meagan shopped, she tended to forget her roommate's shoestring budget. She often bought items unaffordable to Maddie who sought out the store brand and sale items. With this it was certain the remaining balance in her checking account just got a lot smaller.

Maddie heard her cell ringing and struggled to find it. Frantically searching toward the sound she found it lodged between the couch cushions.

"Hello."

"Hi, Maddie, I'm close to your apartment. Is it okay if I stop by?"

"Aah, yeah, sure that's fine."

"Be there in ten." Ethan ended the call and laid his phone in the cup holder of his car. As he looked up seeing the upcoming light, he accelerated the gas a bit more hoping to make it through it before it changed not wanting to waste any time getting to his destination.

Ethan Price was a very bright and handsome young man with nearly black brown hair and sky colored eyes. He spent his days working as a bank teller at the Bank of Tennessee in Nashville. He loved working at the bank, but he hated going to work each day. What he loved most was riding around in his red Chevy Camaro and sitting around a table with friends playing poker. Ethan too had a small budget, but you would never know it by the way he dressed and lived. His car took up most of his income, but his pockets usually had a few dollars due to his luck at the poker table. Like most gamblers, losing streaks happen. And Ethan had had his share, but today he was doing well. Last night's game had added fifty bucks to his pocket.

Maddie met Ethan at a movie a few months ago. She and Meagan were at Opry Mills mall movie theater when he sat down right next to her with his friend Trevor next to him. Ethan had a huge popcorn in one hand and a large drink in the other. Before the movie started, he began talking to Maddie as if he had known her forever and, having some manners, offered her some of his popcorn. "No, thank you," she kindly replied.

When the movie ended, Ethan and his friend followed the girls out of the theater. "Great movie huh?"

Turning to see who was speaking, Maddie recognized him as the guy with the popcorn. "Yeah, it was."

"I love spy movies. They are fast paced and you never know which way they are going to turn. That and the really cool cars."

Ethan was very personable and somehow kept the two young ladies standing outside the theater talking. "Oh, I'm sorry. My name is Ethan, and this is my buddy Trevor."

Maddie knew she should be more cautious, but she was having trouble focusing on anything other than his handsome face. "I'm Maddie Abbott, and this is Meagan Givens."

"Well, Maddie and Meagan, would you two ladies care to join us for a burger or a drink?"

With a soft chuckle Maddie answered, "How can you eat a burger after putting away that huge tub of popcorn?" Trevor laughed out loud at her response. She wasn't sure what he meant by drink, but it didn't really matter. She and Meagan were not going out with two guys they had literally just met no matter how handsome and likable they were.

"Thank you, but no thank you." The two girls turned and walked toward their car leaving Ethan and Trevor standing in disbelief.

A few days later, bored at work Ethan logged on the computer to check his Facebook. Doing this made him look busy to his fellow employees as well as to his supervisor. Then he remembered the pretty girl he met Saturday night. *Let's see, what was her name again. Oh yes, Maddie, Maddie Abbott.* It was a good thing he got her last name while standing outside the theater, otherwise he would have no way of contacting her. *There she is. I'll just send her a little message.* Suddenly a customer appeared at his window forcing him to stop what he was doing and help the customer with their transaction. Four customers later, he finished his message.

Shocked to see Ethan's message, Maddie was curious and looked at his Facebook page. His profile picture didn't do him justice at all -- the man was gorgeous! A small smile came to her face from the memory of that evening standing outside of the theater. Still, he was a stranger, and she would be cautious.

"Hi Maddie, just wanted to say hello, and tell you I enjoyed sitting by you at the movie the other night. Hope to see you again, soon. ~ Ethan."

After weeks of talking to each other they finally met for dinner, but she insisted that Trevor and Meagan come along. Meagan went, but not with a happy heart.

The sound of his knock on the door brought Maddie out of her musing. Opening the door, she couldn't miss the sheepish grin he often wore.

"Hey, Maddie."

"Hi, Come on in."

Normally, Maddie was happy to see Ethan, but today unfortunately was the exception. She was tired, frustrated, and she had a lot of work to do. There were papers to grade and put in the correct folders for two K-5 classes, and several loads of laundry needed her attention. She and Meagan traded off chores. This week she was in charge of laundry, sweeping and dishes, and it was Meagan's week to do the grocery shopping, cooking and cleaning the bathroom.

"You look sleepy. You okay?"

"Yes, I dozed off for a few minutes. That's all."

"Want to go for a ride?"

"Oh, I would love to, but I'm swamped with work, and Meagan is cooking supper as we speak."

"Seriously? What does a kindergarten teacher's aide need to do that takes up so much time?" he asked taking hold of her hand and kissing the back of it. "Isn't all the real work supposed to be done by the real teacher?"

A piercing twinge ran through her with his comment. *Did he just say I was not a real teacher? And why did he think I didn't do any real work?* His words stung a little, but the kiss on the back of her hand seemed to soothe.

7

It was eight-fifteen before Ethan left, and Maddie still had papers to grade and laundry to get started. Feeling a bit put out about not having the whole evening with her, Ethan drove around downtown Nashville before going home.

⸺⸺◈⸺⸺

Pulling into the North Side Christian Academy parking lot, Maddie just didn't have that lovin' feelin' she usually had at the beginning of each day. It depressed her knowing how hard she worked to get through college and student teaching with high hopes of having her own classroom, only to have the rug pulled out from under her again. She had rent to cover and student loans to pay off; she didn't see how she could stay at North Side.

Struggling to smile and say hello to Mrs. Tyndale as they passed each other in the hallway, Maddie reeled in her negative attitude. *Let it go right now, Madeline. She didn't set out to ruin your plans. She has issues of her own. Now suck it up, do your job, and get over it.* Hoping her little pep talk would kick in any minute now, Maddie headed for her classroom. One of the kids in her kindergarten class ran up to her and gave her a big hug.

"I'm glad you are here today, Miss Abbott. You're fun. I love you."

"Awww, sweetie, and I love you. You make my day wonderful."

As the little girl skipped off to the assembly room to sit with her little friends before going to their classroom, Maddie held back the tears. *Thank you, Lord. You know just what I need and when I need it.*

Maddie's attitude may have changed, but her situation had not. She still had to figure out what she was going to do about her future. Not being in a social mood, she mostly listened to the other teachers talking during their lunch break. As she ate her tuna salad sandwich, she overheard two teachers sitting nearby talk about their summer jobs. Maddie's ears perked up. *Yes, that's it! I need a better summer job, one with serious pay. Then my summer earnings will carry me through, and I can stay at North Side.*

The day had been busy, as most kindergarten days were, and Maddie found herself in much better spirits after overhearing the conversation about summer jobs. With a plan of action and a new energy, she was back to her sweet self. While walking back from the office with a stack of freshly copied coloring papers, she saw Paula the second-grade teacher with her class at the water fountain.

"Hey, Paula, are you going to the game tonight?"

"Yes, Amy and I are working the concession stand. Pam has after school duty too, so we're all meeting at Sonic after work to grab a burger before the game. Want to join us?"

"Sure, count me in."

She too had after school duties to go along with manning the door for the game. Thankfully, she had found a coupon for a half off meal deal in the paper. Otherwise she would have had to decline and swing by the apartment for tomato soup before the game.

Maddie came to most of North Side's games. She loved basketball and being a staff member allowed her to get in free. She wasn't very athletic, so she never played the game herself, but loved to watch it. She was a diehard Tennessee Volunteer fan, and her favorite professional team was the Boston Celtics. Her dad was a Celtics fan since his youth, and she inherited her love for the game and that team from him.

Scurrying to finish straightening up the classroom and other last minute duties, Maddie arrived just a few minutes ahead of her co-workers. She stood looking at the menu board when suddenly there was a presence directly behind her. She sensed a much larger person than either of her friends. Turning just enough to see who was invading her space, she saw two males standing very close to her. Fear almost gripped her when one spoke. "Excuse me, are you about to order?"

"Aah, go ahead." *How rude, of course I was about to order. Otherwise why would I be standing here?* She no longer felt fearful, just put out.

After the two guys sat down, Maddie took a second look at the menu board contemplating her order, which was silly, since she usually ordered the same thing: a number one with cheese, fries and a Sprite, since Pepsi was not an option.

Amy and Pam walked up right before Maddie ordered. They too were looking at the menu as if they had never eaten at this establishment before. "If it were a few degrees warmer I would order a shake, but it's still too cold," Pam said while rubbing the top of her arms.

"Not for me," chimed Amy. "I'll have a Coney dog, large tots, small water, and a medium strawberry shake, please."

Paula pulled her car into one of the stalls, found her friends and joined in. The four women ate their food and enjoyed conversation that had nothing to do with teaching or children. Maddie couldn't help but notice the two rude guys sitting at the table adjacent to them and the amount of food they had ordered. *Big guys, big appetite, I guess.*

Maddie had gotten a little chilled while eating outside, so the warmth of the gym was welcoming as she stepped inside. Taking her chair at the table right inside the door, she readied the money box and stamp for those entering the gym. She didn't like manning the door because that meant missing most of the game, but each teacher had to take their turn working the door and at the concession stand during school events, and tonight was her night.

The bleachers began filling up while the players were on the floor taking practice shots. A line was forming at the door.

"Caroline, hi. I didn't know you were calling tonight's game."

"Yeah, and I see you have door duty."

Frowning, she looked like a child who had just been told to do her chores. "I don't like door duty, but I had no other choice. I'd rather sweep the floor afterwards. At least that way I could see all of the game." Caroline chuckled at Maddie's comment.

Caroline Dunning had been a referee for the local Christian high schools in the Nashville area for over fifteen years. She began refereeing after the loss of her first husband Craig Martin to earn extra money to help support herself and her son Joshua. Though she had recently remarried and didn't need the extra income, she kept it up for the exercise and the love of the game.

North Side was playing the Davidson Academy Bears, and the gym was filling up quickly.

"Two please," someone said handing her a twenty dollar bill. She could feel him staring at her, although she had no clue why. Holding out his hand waiting for his change, they made eye contact, and for a brief instant Maddie couldn't look away. It was if his brown eyes were holding her captive. Then she recognized him as one of the rude guys earlier from Sonic.

"Miss, you didn't give me the correct change."

11

"Oh, didn't I?" Maddie asked. Looking at the bills in his hand and recounting, she quickly recognized her mistake. This blunder was so unlike her.

"I'm so sorry."

"No problem…" he responded as he started to turn and leave. "Oh, and you forgot to stamp my hand," he pointed out trying to hide a grin.

"Sorry." *I didn't forget. You just didn't give me time.* Stamping his hand and his buddy's also beside him, Maddie wished they would leave already.

"Thank you," he said looking straight at her and giving her his best smile. As they walked away and began looking for a seat, he revealed what was on his mind. "Dude, did you see that girl?"

"You mean the girl at the door? How could I miss her… she took our money…and stamped our hands," Ryan answered sarcastically. "We can look at girls after we find a seat."

Nathan couldn't keep from looking back. He turned and saw this beautiful girl with dark brown hair and the most amazing brown eyes.

Nathan and Ryan sat about mid-way up on the visiting team's side. Nathan's youngest brother played for the Bears, but he was more interested in watching the door attendant than watching his brother play the game.

North Side and Davidson Academy gave the fans a good game to watch. The two teams were pretty much equal in their skills. What little time Nathan watched his brother play brought back memories of his own basketball years. And for a brief moment he longed to be running up and down the court making three pointers and hearing the roar of the crowd again.

During halftime of the boy's varsity game, Maddie took the money box and gave it to the correct person at the concession stand. "Let me guess, Pepsi and peanut M&M's," chuckled Amy.

"Yes, ma'am," Maddie answered with a smile.

A soft drink and a snack was her compensation for tending the door. It wasn't much, but it made her happy. Turning to make her way to the bleachers to find her seat with her friends, someone suddenly bumped into her causing her to drop her candy. "Oh, I'm sorry," the person apologized quickly bending over to pick up the bag from the floor. As he arose, his shoulder bumped into her hand that held her drink, causing her to spill Pepsi down her blouse. Peering into the face of the candy owner, he saw it was the beautiful door attendant.

Gazing down at her Pepsi-soaked blouse, she couldn't believe this had happened. Maddie felt her face turn red as she realized she was looking into the same brown eyes that had caught her attention earlier when she gave the incorrect change.

"I am soooo… sorry," he said with shock.

Him again.

"Here's your candy. Please let me buy you another drink."

Her mouth hung open, and she looked a bit in shock herself.

"What's your name?" he looked at her with apologetic eyes that pierced right through to her very soul.

She had no clue as to why this man was everywhere she turned this evening, but she was in no mood for formal introductions.

Grabbing her M&M's from his grip somewhat roughly, the bag ripped and candy went flying. She held back her words, but the anger on her face could not be missed. Amy had seen what had happened and quickly went looking for a towel.

"I….I really am sorry…aah, what is your name?" he asked again. Looking into her wide eyes, he was sure she wanted to slap his face.

"My name is none of your business," she snapped, yanking the half empty bag from his large hands.

"I need to know your name if I am to properly apologize to you. I mean I don't want to just say 'hey, sorry, lady'."

"Apology accepted. Now will you please go?" Maddie sensed all eyes on the two of them and this embarrassing scene. She hated being the center of attention, especially in a negative situation.

"Please let me buy you another drink and bag of candy," he begged.

Trying to keep her temper at bay, she replied through gritted teeth, "No, thank you. Please, just go." It never occurred to her that she could have turned and left him standing there all alone. Instead, the two of them stood there staring at each other, him sorry, and her furious. Unsure what to do, she decided that retreating to the ladies room would be the best choice.

Looking at her heated face and her wet blouse in the mirror, she didn't know which she wanted to do most, cry or scream.

That jerk! She was furiously grabbing paper towels to blot her blouse, as if the paper towel dispenser were the one responsible for her being upset.

Suddenly the door opened. "Are you alright?" Amy asked, handing her a towel. After seeing the look on her friend's face, there was no doubt of the answer. Turning on the cold water, Maddie washed her hands and patted her warm pink cheeks to cool down.

"Yes, I'm fine," she said, forcing herself to sound much calmer than she was. She took the towel and began to dry herself.

"That guy bought these for you and asked me to give them to you. He feels really bad," Amy explained, handing her another bag of M&M's and a cold Pepsi.

"Thank you, but that wasn't necessary." Fighting back tears, she just wanted to be alone to collect herself.

"Oh, and here, you can put this on. One of our girls saw what happened and said she had an extra t-shirt in her bag."

Thankful for the extra shirt, Maddie didn't think she could walk out there with Pepsi all down her blouse.

"Which one?"

"Number twelve; I think her name is Candice."

"I'll be sure and tell her thank you."

The two ladies heard the buzzer sound announcing the beginning of the last half of the game. Maddie straightened her clothes, let out a cleansing breath, and the two walked out together. Finding a seat with her other two friends, she tried her best to enjoy the remainder of the game, but those brown eyes kept showing up on the screen of her mind keeping her from it.

As the game ended, Maddie joined the crowd hurrying to their cars. Stepping outside, she didn't even notice the temperatures had dropped about fifteen degrees since they first went inside. It wasn't until she reached her car that she sensed the need to pull her coat closer to her body.

"Oh nooo! Now what?" she exclaimed as the engine moaned and refused to turn over. Trying again and again, she begged, "Oh please start, please start."

She popped the hood, got out and slammed the door. And then she began looking around for someone that could give her some assistance. Suddenly a truck stopped right behind her car. Sure enough, help arrived.

"Having a little car trouble?"

"Yes, for some reeee..." *Seriously! This cannot be happening!*

Nathan was positive this was where he could make up for spilling Pepsi on this girl. He took charge and began to look under the hood. He quickly made the decision to act like nothing had happened earlier and just help the girl with her car. "Coop, bring me my flashlight will ya." Ryan Cooper, also known as Coop to his friends, jogged to the truck to do as asked.

"Please don't touch my car. This car has to last me until... forever, now please don't touch my car," Maddie begged with frustration.

Wanting to redeem himself, he continued. Sticking his head and flashlight under the hood, he wiggled a few wires and tightened a few things before giving more instructions.

"Get in and try to turn it over."

Irritated, she got in and tried to start the car. It refused.

"You do have gas in the tank, don't you?"

"I have plenty of gas in my tank," she sarcastically responded in a sing-song voice.

"Pull my truck up beside hers and let's try jumping the battery. I think that's the problem," he instructed his friend.

"If you think that's the problem, why did you ask me if I had gas in the tank?" she shot back at him. *Why won't he go away? Lord, please make him go awaaayy.*

Within a few minutes her car started right up. *Ahhh, thank you Lord! Now I can get away from this irritating man.*

"Like I figured, it was the battery. Where do you live?"

"I'm not telling you where I live."

"I just want to make sure you get home safely. I wouldn't want you to be stranded on the side of the road. I'll give you my cell number so you can call me if it stalls on you."

"I don't need your number."

Ryan was doing all he could to keep from laughing. This girl had shot Nathan down at every opportunity.

"Thank you for starting my car. Now you can be on your way, and I will be on mine," she said as kindly as she could.

"Suit yourself... but you need to drive it at least twenty minutes before turning it off or it may not start again."

Maddie quickly put the car in gear and took off.

"Nate, man, I think she hates you." He then began laughing.

———❧———◉———❧———

Arriving at her apartment, Maddie walked quickly inside. *Who did he think he was anyway?* Stepping through the doorway, she roughly took off her coat and tossed her keys on the end table a little harder than intended.

"How was the game?" Meagan asked, seeing her friend was a bit out of sorts.

"Fine."

"Why are you upset?"

"What makes you think I'm upset?"

"Well, for starters the look on your face."

"Oh, there was this jerk of a guy that kept bumping into me all evening. First he was at the Sonic being rude, then at the game he...I innocently gave him the wrong change...he took off before I could stamp his hand, then later he bumped into me and spilled my soft drink all down my blouse. And as if *that* weren't enough my car wouldn't start, and there he was again. I asked him to leave my car alone, but did he? Nooo! He kept right on."

"Did he get your car started?"

"Yes." Seeing her friend's quizzical look on her face, she quickly added, "But that's not the point. I asked him to leave it alone."

Meagan could tell it was best to let the matter drop.

"I'm going to take a hot shower and just go to bed."

———————————

Ryan sat on the passenger side of Nathan's truck once again trying to hold his laughter. He found it so entertaining that every time Nathan tried to get near that girl it was a disaster.

"Nate, maaan, you better be glad you fixed that girl's car, or she would have exploded all over you. I mean she was mad at you to start with." Shaking his head he continued, "She didn't want you to touch her car."

Nathan's love for cars and trade school education landed him a job as an auto mechanic in Goodlettsville. His boss John quickly found out he was an exceptionally good one and wanted to keep him around as long as possible. Nathan enjoyed working on cars, but what he really loved was taking an old heap and making it look and run like brand new. Unfortunately, restoring cars was an expensive hobby, so he mainly helped others with their projects. Since his teens, it had been his dream to one day have his own repair and restoration shop.

"Yeah, well, I fixed it, didn't I? And in what...about ten minutes? That may be a record for me." With the event fresh on his mind as he drove, Nathan asked, "Why was she so upset at me? I was just trying to help."

"Dude, you spilled her soft drink all over her, and then you made her drop her candy. Women don't like that."

"I didn't mean to do any of that."

"You held the bag in your hand. And when she tried to get it back, candy went all over the place. It looked like it was raining M&M's," he said laughing.

"It wasn't my fault. She grabbed the bag out of my hand causing it to rip. Besides, I bought her another one, and another drink too....and I didn't even hear a thank you."

Nathan and Ryan stopped in at Steak 'n Shake. Even though it was after ten p.m., it was fairly common for them to grab a late meal. Sometimes they were joined by other friends, but tonight Nathan was glad it was just the two of them.

"May I take you order, please?" a young lady asked.

"Yes, I'll have a strawberry shake and a large fry."

"And I'll have a large fry and a large peanut butter shake."

"Alright, I'll get this right out for you guys."

Nathan sat with his back to the small partition wall with one leg stretched out toward the aisle. He was not in the cheeriest of moods. "Sometimes, man, it just doesn't pay to be helpful."

"I think she would have responded totally different without the Pepsi incident."

After about ten minutes, their waitress returned. "Here you go, gentlemen. Fries and a strawberry shake and fries and a peanut butter shake. Can I get you anything else?"

"No, thank you," Ryan answered.

Due to his mood, Nathan didn't enjoy his food as much as he usually did. Ryan, however, dove right into his pile of fries.

Arriving at his house around midnight, Nathan tried to not disturb the others. As the door opened, he discovered instead one of his roommates had guests. He could hear their voices coming from the kitchen. It sounded as if they were enjoying a game of some sort.

Nathan Baxter, Nate to his close friends, was twenty-four years old and had recently begun sharing a four bedroom house with reasonable rent with three other guys. The house rules were simple. Rent was due on the first of each month, no exceptions. Everyone was expected to pick up after themselves.

And overnight guests were prohibited. These conditions were working out well for the past four months. Since it had been a rough evening and the hour was late, Nathan went on to his room to call it a night.

Two

Caroline touched the alarm clock to make the awful noise stop. Sunday mornings were the hardest days for her to get out of bed. But if she and Richard were going to make it to church on time, she would need to get up and get moving, now. Cold mornings like this one made the effort even harder.

Caroline and Richard Dunning had been married a little over a year. She had first met Richard at Ace Hardware and then formally at her front door when he came to repair her clogged sink. They kept running into each other in the oddest places. It took Caroline a while before she would consider more than polite conversation, but he finally won her heart. After their wedding, Richard insisted Caroline resign her job from Vanderbilt University Medical Center and be a stay-at-home housewife and mom. She gladly agreed. And despite never wanting to work for his father, Richard now helped run Dunning Plumbing with his brother Brian.

As Caroline slowly walked into the kitchen to get the coffee started, she noticed it looking awfully bright outside and was taken aback by what she saw. "Well, look at that." Those in Middle Tennessee were waking to a thin blanket of snow. "Nothing like being ready for spring and waking up to snow," she commented to no one.

Richard walked in the kitchen where the smell of bacon hovered in the room. Pouring himself a cup of coffee and taking his seat at the table, he remembered a time not too long ago when he spent his Sunday mornings at the Krispy Kreme Doughnuts shop eating his breakfast and reading the Sunday paper. The rest of the day would be filled with watching one ballgame after another. Now he ate a homemade meal prepared by his lovely wife before they headed off to church to worship the Lord. At times he was still amazed at the complete turnaround his life had taken since meeting this woman.

"The weather man said we might get a dusting, but that looks like more than a dusting."

"It'll be gone by noon," Richard predicted reaching for the coffee pot.

As most people did, Maddie usually sat in the same area in the auditorium at church, and today was no exception. The Dunnings typically sat in a pew near her. And within minutes of her reaching her seat Richard walked in and sat down right behind her.

"Hi, Maddie, how are you?"

"Hi, Richard, I'm fine, and you?"

"Oh, I'm good. My wife told me she saw you at the game the other night. She also said it was a close one."

Nathan's face flashed before her mind's eye at just the mention of that evening.

"Yes, we did see each other, but, unfortunately, I didn't see much of the game. I had to work the door...you know, take the money and stamp hands. We didn't win by much, but a win nonetheless. I must admit, I enjoy a close game like that one over one where one team dominates the other."

"I agree that does make for a better game."

Though Maddie enjoyed talking with Richard about the game, she wasn't fond of remembering the guy who ruined her evening. She took comfort in knowing that neither Caroline nor Richard was aware of what had happened.

The music began softly playing which cued that the service was about to start. Caroline scurried in to sit beside her husband glad that she wasn't the only one hurrying to get seated.

"Good morning, everyone. It is so good to see you here. Join me, please, as we sing praises to our God and King," David the church's music director instructed.

Maddie had been attending the Marydale Bible Church for several years now. The church congregation wasn't necessarily small or large, but was a comfortable size preventing being lost in the crowd and had a nice mix with young and old. Brother George Whitehurst may have been up in years compared to her, but the man preached with a passion and boldness that spoke of his love and commitment to the Lord.

Brother Whitehurst walked up to the pulpit and made his welcoming comments to the congregation, then took off his suit jacket and laid it on the small pew that sat between the choir loft and pulpit.

"Have you noticed how much talk there has been this morning about our little snow?" he chuckled. "We would be beside ourselves if we got about five feet of snow, wouldn't we?" The congregation laughed in agreement. "We would all be home, huddled inside eating and watching television." The congregation laughed again at his words, as he did, knowing it was a true statement.

"Would you please open your Bibles to the Book of Esther? This is not a book that gets preached out of a lot, but it has some golden truths in its pages that you would be wise to not miss."

"I was doing my daily reading this past week, and I found myself in the book of Esther and the Lord laid this sermon heavily on my heart. As I was reading, it hit me that the Jewish people of that time were facing a serious, or you might even say hopeless situation." Maddie had her Bible on her lap ready to turn when Brother Whitehurst gave the address, but swiftly found herself daydreaming. She wiggled to snap herself out of it and returned her attention back to the pastor.

"Then I remembered our own nation, and how we are facing some serious and some may say, hopeless issues as well. But don't fear. God is still in control in the here and now just like He was in days of Esther and Mordecai. Turn with me, please, to Esther the third chapter. Now, Haman had his plan all figured out. He was sending out an edict to have the Jewish people annihilated. He had already been given permission to do with the people as he wished by King Xerxes. Things looked hopeless for the Jews at that time, didn't they? When the edict was given out, God's chosen people were preparing their tables for the Passover meal. Funny how God does things in His own timing, isn't it? He is never late, and He is never early. He is always right on time." As Brother Whitehurst spoke about God being on time, Maddie thought about her situation with her job. She wished the Lord's timing on fixing her current job situation was at this very moment. She loved teaching the little kids, but she was barely getting by on the meager income. She couldn't continue to wait for a real teaching position. A nearby movement caught her attention and brought her back to the sermon. "As the destruction was imminent, God's people were reminded of what He had done for them and how He led them out of slavery. Now is a good time for us to sit back and remember what God has done for us."

When the service was over, she got up and visited with a few people as everyone did. A few young adults were going out for lunch and had invited her, but she politely turned them down due to the lack of funds. Not wanting to tell them the truth, she gave the excuse that she had too many things to do today, which wasn't really a lie. She did need to hang up her clothes, make her bed, and do the rest of the things that she had ignored for the past few days and probably would again today.

Driving home, it was quiet in her little car, because for some reason she didn't have the radio on like she normally did. At the stop light at Old Hickory and Dickerson, she sat waiting for the light to change and her mind wandered back to Brother Whitehurst's sermon. Suddenly she remembered how God had given her jobs every summer during college, scholarships to help pay her tuition, a student teaching opportunity, and her current job. It suddenly became clear to her that God had provided for her all along when needed.

———◦———

The forecast was almost right. There was sleet, but it came later in the evening instead of afternoon and with more snow than predicted. Before heading to bed that night, Maddie heard on the news that schools in their area were closed the next day which made her happy like a little kid. There are some things that are never outgrown.

The next morning Maddie awoke well rested and excited to have the whole day to herself to do whatever she pleased. By nine o'clock she finished her breakfast and then took the opportunity to check out the job listings. Suddenly Ethan sprang to mind. She tapped his number on her phone finding out he wasn't so lucky. He had to work. Having snow days was definitely a bonus to working at a school.

"Maybe I can meet you for lunch today since the snow is already melting."

"Okay. Unfortunately today, I only get thirty minutes. That's not enough time to go anywhere, but if you don't mind freezing, we can eat in the car."

"Ethan, I can't tell you how inviting that is," she teased. "I'll try to bring something warm… like soup."

Maddie spent the rest of her morning getting her résumé ready, which made her feel like she was one step ahead of the game. As usual, there were tons of restaurants looking for help, but she wasn't interested in working ridiculous hours and standing on her feet all day dealing with hungry and sometimes rude people. She had had her share of that during high school and college. Last year, she worked at a fabric store which bored her, and didn't provide her with enough hours or enough pay. However, she would call them if she had no other choice.

While driving to the bank to have a quick lunch with Ethan, she passed a few upscale hotels. *That may be a possibility. I'll stop in on my way back.*

Sitting in her car, Ethan ate his sandwich and chips while Maddie drank her soup from her thermos. "This was nice," Ethan said taking her hand. She smiled at him. "What are your plans for the rest of the day?" After sharing her agenda, she was not surprised by his response.

"Maddie, if I worked at a school, I would be enjoying the whole summer off just like the kids do. What other job gives you the opportunity to do that?" She just looked at him saying nothing. "Well, unfortunately, I need to get back inside. I don't get snow days or the summer off. Nope it's Monday through

Friday eight 'til four." Giving her a quick kiss, he went back inside.

◆ ───◆◆◆─── ◆

Maddie was second guessing herself for just dropping into this hotel looking for a job without an appointment. She could tell the person on the other side of the counter wasn't much older than she was and that made her feel a little better. "Hello, can I help you?"

"Yes, I was hoping to speak to someone about putting in an application for the summer. I know it's early for that, but I'm a teacher, and due to the snow, I have the day off."

"Aah, okay, you will need to talk to the manager. His name is Carlton. I'm not sure if he is in his office right now, but I can check."

"Thank you." *What was I thinking? I'm not dressed for an interview, not to mention I don't even have my résumé with me. How stupid of me. They will think I am totally unprepared...which I am.*

"Hello, I'm Carlton Edwards," the man introduced himself as he extended his hand. Carlton was a tall, slim man in his late twenties with strawberry blond hair and a slight mustache that he had been working on since high school.

"Mr. Edwards, hello, I'm Maddie Abbott. I'm a teacher here in the Nashville area, and even though it is a bit early, I'm looking for a summer job and was wondering if I could put in an application?"

"You're right it is a bit early to start thinking about summer help, but sure we can take your application... and call me Carlton."

27

"I was unexpectedly in the area and saw your hotel and made the decision to stop in."

The manager gave a soft smile. "Never hurts to ask."

Carlton and Maddie spoke for another half hour which she took as a good sign. He was very kind and gave her the information she needed about putting in her application.

"Thank you for your time, Carlton. I hope to hear back from you." Maddie left the hotel excited about such a promising opportunity and glad she had stopped in.

On her way home, Maddie couldn't get the conversation with Carlton out of her mind. She was so eager to jump on this job.

Sitting on the couch in sweats and a long sleeve T-shirt in front of the TV eating peanut butter and crackers, it dawned on her that if she got this job her shoestring budget days could be over. She thanked the Lord for the snow day, her lunch with Ethan, and giving her the opportunity to talk to a hotel manager. However, she wasn't naïve. She would continue her search and put in other applications in case this one fell through.

Caroline didn't mind helping on occasion at Dunning Plumbing. Richard had mentioned that Monica the receptionist was going to be out that morning. Usually Katie, Richard's older sister, covered the front desk when the receptionist was absent. But since this was a snow day, Katie needed to stay at home with the kids. Caroline remembered those days and how she would've loved to be home with Joshua instead of working. But as a single parent, that was never an option. She rang Katie to say stay home and enjoy and she would handle the receptionist duties for today.

Dunning Plumbing was a busy little operation. The receptionist's main duties included answering the phone, taking messages, receiving deliveries and keeping up with the plumbers. They had fifteen plumbers on staff, and all were busy all day, Monday through Saturday. Today, Richard was working on getting a large contract on a new condo development in Brentwood. If they got the contract, he may need to hire more workers.

"Dunning Plumbing, this is Caroline, how may I help you?"

"Hello, Caroline this is Monica. Is Brian in his office?"

"Yes, I believe he is available. Hold on just a moment."

"Hello, this is Brian. How may I help you?"

"Hello, Brian, sorry to interrupt your day, but it's important. I hate to do this to you, but I need to take a leave of absence for two weeks, maybe three."

"A leave of absence? Why? What's going on?"

"It's my cat Snickers. She is very ill and can't be left alone. I took her to the vet this morning. She has eaten something or been bitten that is making her very sick. I have to give her medicine three times a day and watch her carefully for two weeks, or she may die."

"Aah, Monica, I'm sorry about your cat, but I've got to have a receptionist. And it's pretty much impossible to hire someone for three weeks. Can you not have a friend or a relative watch your cat while you work?"

"Oh no, I can't find anyone who will take care of Snickers like she needs to be cared for. I have a few friends that are looking for jobs. Maybe I can have one of them fill in for me until Snickers is better."

Rubbing his forehead and then pinching the bridge of his nose, he carefully weighed his words and explained it would not be worth getting someone trained for such a short amount of time. "Monica, I'm sorry, but I can't grant you a leave of absence over your pet," he explained as gently as he could. "If it were your child, husband or parent, then I would be more than happy to do that for you and help where I could. But you are leaving me without a receptionist for three weeks for a pet. I want you to take today and seriously think about this. You do what you have to do, but I have to have a receptionist that I can count on. Okay?"

"Well, like I said I can't leave her home alone, but I will give this more thought. I'll also call a few friends to see if one of them can take care of Snickers for me while I work, and I'll call you back by the end of the day."

"Alright, bye, Monica."

"Bye."

As Brian hung up the phone, Richard walked in. "These papers need your signature."

"You're not gonna believe this one. Monica just called and wanted a three week leave of absence because her cat is sick," he said with a sarcastic tone.

"Are you serious?"

"Totally. I can't put up with this any longer. I mean, she is a sweet girl, but she calls out too often, comes in late and leaves early. And now she wants a leave of absence because her cat is sick, and she's only worked here about six months. People just don't have respect for their employers anymore, or know how to work at a job." Richard could tell Brian was overall irritated with Monica and especially this situation.

"Looks like we are once again looking for a receptionist. Should I go ahead and place an ad in *The Tennessean*?"

"No, I'll give her the benefit of the doubt. She said she may have a friend who can watch her cat. Let's wait and see what she says tomorrow. Do you think Caroline can fill in until we get someone?"

"I'll ask her. Maybe between her and Katie they can keep it covered," Richard responded on his way out the door.

Friday could not come fast enough for Maddie. She was tired from the workweek and anxious to hear back from Carlton. Patience was never her strong suit. It had been four days since she'd spoken with him about a position. She scolded herself for thinking they would call her this soon for a summer job. Her search had just begun, but so far, the hotel was the only possibility that sounded promising.

Fridays at four o'clock meant school was done for the next two days. By three-thirty, all the kids were gone except those who stayed for aftercare. Today wasn't her day to work in aftercare, which meant she could complete her duties quickly, and the weekend could begin.

Maddie worried on Fridays that Mrs. Daniels would appear and give her another stack of papers to grade or a bulletin board to decorate right before she left, which had happened before. Maddie walked with purpose and looked around cautiously as she headed for the door. "See you Monday Maddie," Amy yelled out from midway down the hallway, causing Maddie to almost jump out of her skin.

"See ya."

As the door closed behind her, she caught herself smiling over her victory as she walked to her car. Just then, her phone rang.

"Yo, Maddie, glad I caught you. Can you meet me at the restaurant instead of me coming and picking you up?" Ethan said exasperated on her cell.

Evening traffic was always an issue, but on Fridays it was much worse. Everyone wanted to get home as soon as possible to start the weekend, making rush hour traffic even more tense.

"I…I guess. Is there a problem?" she asked sinking into the driver's seat of her car.

"Not really. It's just taking me longer to leave work than normal, and I didn't want you to have to wait on me."

"Sure, are we still on for six?"

"Yes, you're a doll. See ya then." Ethan closed his phone, surfed the web and played a few games before shutting down his computer for the day. It was too early to drive to the restaurant, but he had run out of things to do while he waited.

Parking in the back of the restaurant and glancing at his watch, he was sure he had at least forty-five minutes before she would arrive. Pushing the lock button on the car door, he laid his head back on the headrest to catch a short nap. Usually he didn't like waiting for someone, but today he didn't mind. It had been a busy day, and now he could relax for a few minutes while not having to drive anywhere.

Maddie was hoping to unwind for a moment before showering and getting ready for her date, but now she would have to speed things up a bit to get there on time. Meeting instead of being picked up meant two trips downtown in one week. Luckily her little old car was easy on the tank.

Ethan awoke suddenly to the sound of a car pulling in beside him. He had slept longer than expected and was now running a bit late. He quickly looked in the visor mirror checking his hair and teeth to prepare to meet Maddie.

She sat at the table waiting for Ethan for fifteen minutes. They should have gotten there at about the same time, but she guessed he had gotten caught in traffic.

"Sorry I'm late. I didn't think I would ever get out of there," he explained before giving her a quick kiss. "There were some receipts that didn't add up, so I had to stay until it all balanced out."

Quickly picking up a menu, he asked, "Have you been waiting long?"

"About fifteen minutes."

"How 'bout a large sausage and pepperoni with extra cheese? I'm starving."

"Make that a thin crust, and it will be fine," she responded.

Ethan went to the counter and ordered, then motioned for Maddie to come over.

"I have a problem," he said fumbling his pockets. "I can't find my wallet. I must have left it at work. Do you have any cash or a credit card?"

"Uh, I think I have some cash." Maddie really didn't have the money to spare. She only had twenty-four dollars, and fortunately that covered the bill. She reluctantly paid the girl behind the register and looked at the remaining change with remorse.

"I'll pay you back when I pick up my wallet. How was your day?" Ethan asked as they sat down at the table with their soft drinks.

"Not bad. I got a lot done before I left today, so I am totally free for the whole weekend." Ethan smiled at her causing her to forget all about him not picking her up, being late and not having his wallet.

"That's great, so am I. I love the feeling of having no responsibilities for a couple of days," he said, cupping his hand over hers on the table. "So what will you do with yourself?"

"I'm planning to clean out my closet, then lay around and watch TV. What about you?"

"Oh, I don't know, just hanging out I guess. Something will come up. It usually does. I was hoping we could do something tomorrow evening." She smiled at him.

Within twenty minutes, their steaming hot pizza showed up at their table. Just the sight of it made Maddie even hungrier. She gently bowed her head and quietly asked the Lord's blessing for the food. She always did that, and it always embarrassed him. Ethan cautiously scanned the room to see if anyone was watching.

When Maddie was starving, she ate less food than when she was barely hungry. Her friends always laughed at her for this idiosyncrasy. She ate her two pieces and tried not to scrutinize Ethan as he devoured over half the pie.

As Ethan walked Maddie to her car on the other side of the building, he took her hand. "Want to go back to my apartment and watch a movie?" she asked.

"Sure, I'll follow you."

There were times Ethan just didn't get the hint that he needed to leave, and this was one of them. It was one-thirty in the morning, and she could barely hold her eyes open. When the show finished, she took advantage. "Okay, I can't watch anymore. I can barely stay awake."

"Okay, sleepyhead, see you tomorrow." He gave her a kiss that lasted a bit longer than the hello kiss at the pizza place, then left.

Maddie's eyes slowly opened. Her bed was warm and comfortable, so she scrunched down farther into the bed and hugged her pillow. Her mind eventually began to wake up as she lounged a little longer. Once she realized she didn't have to get up, she could no longer sleep. Refusing to rise, she rolled over and continued to lay there until her stomach started growling.

On the couch in her comfy pajamas with cereal bowl in hand, she settled into her morning while watching a DVD. Her cell phone rang with her first mouthful. It was Carlton Edwards.

"Hello," she said, her voice slightly muffled.

"Maddie, good morning. I hope I haven't called too early."

Spitting her food out back into the bowl, she quickly answered, "No, not at all."

"Good, would it be possible for you to come in for an interview? We recently had a position to become available."

"Yes, when were you thinking?"

"I know you're tied up with your regular job during the week, so could you possibly come in this afternoon around one?"

"Sure, one will work for me."

"Great, I'll see you at one."

Maddie ended the call and went straight to her bedroom forgetting all about her cereal and the DVD.

With a fresh motivation, as she headed to her bedroom she almost rammed into Meagan, whose focus was also elsewhere. "Where are you headed to in such a hurry?" Maddie asked.

"I have to work today, and I overslept. Thank goodness it's Saturday, and it won't matter as much, but I was supposed to be there forty-five minutes ago."

"Chalk up another positive for working in a school and having weekends off," she said, making a check mark in the air.

"What about you? You seem to be in a hurry yourself," Meagan inquired before she reached the door. Maddie quickly explained about her phone call from Carlton.

"Good luck on the interview. See ya later."

"Thanks."

Eating cereal in the living room while watching DVDs until noon was one of her favorite things to do on Saturday mornings, but today would be different. Standing in front of her closet with hands on her hips looking at her clothes, she sighed, "No doubt, this will be the hardest part."

As she drove towards Nashville, her nervousness started to kick in. Her little trick to overcome that was to go over her list of chores for the day. Being alone in her car, she did this aloud. "Okay, I need to do the laundry and clean my bedroom. Oh my room…I'm glad no one goes in there but me." She and Meagan weren't great housekeepers, and both certainly enjoyed not being told to clean anything. By the time she found the turn for the parking lot, Maddie was a little more at ease.

"May I help you?" A woman with Emma on the nametag of her dark blue blazer politely asked from behind the counter.

Maddie introduced herself. "Hi, I'm Maddie Abbott. I'm here for an interview with Carlton Edwards."

"Wait just a minute please." Emma left Maddie standing there as she disappeared through a doorway behind the counter. "Carlton, there's someone out here saying she has an interview with you."

"Alright, tell her I'll be right out."

Emma left his office giving him a moment for a little personal inspection.

"Maddie, I'm glad you could come in on such short notice. Come on in my office where we can talk," he said, guiding her into the small and slightly cluttered room.

The interview seemed normal with questions about her goals, availability and qualifications until the comments became a bit too personal making her a little uneasy. She convinced herself she was being silly.

"Working nights and weekends will cut into your social life. Will that be a problem for your boyfriend?"

Seeing the look on her face, "I noticed on your application you're single. It's hard to believe someone as lovely as you not having a boyfriend," he added with a warm smile.

Responding with a nervous half smile, Maddie quickly turned the conversation back to the interview.

"Over the phone you said a position had become available since we talked on Monday, but my responsibilities at my current job don't end until the end of May."

"Yes, a position is available. We had someone to leave us this week, and we like to keep a full staff at all times. This position requires working behind the counter handling customer check in and out along with catering to their needs. Also you would help our guests with restaurant suggestions and inform them of any entertainment that's happening in the city, things like that. Right now, the hours would only be one or two nights a week and some weekend shift."

Carlton continued talking, but she had already decided to pass on the offer because it would interfere with her weekends and require her to work on Sundays. She really liked her lazy Sunday afternoons, and not to mention, it's the day of rest. Then he surprised her with an hourly pay rate which was almost twice what she made as a teacher's aide. After hearing that, she missed his next words, but she quickly picked back up as he explained about the music business clientele. "So, if you take this job, can we count on you not to get all starry-eyed and bother the guests?"

"Oh, certainly! That won't be a problem, I assure you."

Carlton excused himself to handle a small matter at the front desk giving Maddie a moment to think. Things were happening too fast. She needed this job, but now that it was being offered, she found herself hesitating. It all sounded good except for the hours. *Nights and weekends, of course nights and weekends, what other time is left for me to work...Besides, the man said, "Some, not all,"* she reasoned with herself.

"So Maddie, does this sound like a job you would enjoy?" Carlton asked after returning.

"Yes, it does, but I need to make sure you understand my schedule at North Side Academy. I certainly don't want there to be any confusion."

"We'll schedule your hours here to work around hours at your other job. We have other employees working here as their second job."

Within the next few minutes, Maddie was filling out the necessary paperwork to start her first shift on Tuesday evening. She was excited and scared at the same time. On her way home, she thanked the Lord for the new job. She had set out to find a summer job and had come back with a second job instead, one that started right away. She got a funny feeling in the pit of her stomach that didn't agree with her. Then she remembered the pay and how much it would add to her small account, and the feeling subsided. She kept telling herself she would make it work for as long as she could.

Three

Ethan and his friends had another late night playing poker. Only this time he was in the hole for fifty dollars when he threw in his pocketknife to cover his bet and lost the hand. Not accustomed to losing, he spent the rest of the night working on a plan to get some extra cash until payday. It didn't take him too long to come up with the idea of selling a few items online. Mentally going through his belongings, he came up with an old mp3 player than he hadn't used in ages, several video games, and some DVD's he no longer cared about. He had to get his pocketknife back immediately. The idea of someone else owning the knife his grandfather gave him was not sitting well. He had to get some cash quick before the new owner became attached to it.

A knock on the door distracted him briefly. "It's open," he responded.

"Hey, any plans today?" Trevor asked.

"Some. I'm in need of some extra cash, so I'm going to try and sell off some of this stuff online," he explained looking toward the stack on the floor.

"Dude, you're selling your complete collection of Star Trek?" Staring with his mouth gaping open, "How much are you asking?"

Ethan told Trevor how much he was asking. His eyes widened. "Dude, you will never sell them for that price. Why would someone buy your used collection when they can go online and buy the same collection brand new for less?" Trevor then made Ethan a good offer for the set, but he stuck to his price.

Ethan could be quite cunning when it came to money. He liked to buy low and sell high, but Trevor was a business man as well. He understood the value of things that interested him, and Ethan was out of the ball park on this one.

"Trevor, you don't have any idea what you're talking about."

"Well, when they don't sell, come see me, 'cause I would like to buy them…and help you out as well, but I will not pay that ridiculous price."

Letting the matter drop, Ethan gave Trevor a hard look and continued his posting.

"Want to play video games?"

"Sure, soon as I get this posted."

The two guys played video games for the next two hours. At the end of the last game, Trevor mentioned his empty stomach. "Let's go grab some food. I'm starving." With only a few bucks in his wallet, Ethan agreed, and the two left in search of burgers.

Tired from her work day, Meagan walked in and found Maddie on the couch in her jammies eating popcorn.

"I hate working Saturdays. There's only one good thing about working Saturdays and that is the boss has lunch brought in," Meagan explained as she took her shoes off and plopped in the chair next to the couch. "Of course the *boss* wasn't there. He was enjoying his Saturday while the rest of us worked."

"What was for lunch?"

"Pizza."

The way Meagan was talking she assumed lunch was a big fancy spread, not a pizza.

"I was about to starve too. It didn't get delivered until one-thirty," she grumbled, her frustration obvious.

Meagan headed to the fridge for something to eat, it was seven o'clock and she hadn't eaten any supper. Looking back to the table, then the stove, she had no clue what Maddie had eaten.

"Maddie, have you eaten or is that popcorn your supper?"

"Yes, I had a bowl of Campbell's soup."

"You and Ethan didn't go out?"

"No, he called this afternoon and said he had business to tend to, so I've had most of the day all to myself. And guess what? I got a part-time job," she cheered.

"Great." Maddie shared all of the details as Meagan looked for something to call a meal.

Looking in the fridge again and studying its contents, Meagan found few options. *I don't want soup. I guess a hot dog and chips will have to do.* She took her food in the living room so she could watch TV with Maddie, but before she could take her first bite, her phone rang.

"Yes. Oh, I would love to, but I just got home. I had to work today, and I'm beat. Call me the next time y'all do something, okay? Thanks, bye."

Tossing her phone on the side table, she began telling Maddie about her conversation with one of her friends.

"I can't believe that! When I have nothing to do, none of my friends have anything going on. Then I work all day, and on such a beautiful day might I add, then I get a call to go out with friends. That stinks."

"Maybe next time."

"Yeah, there probably won't be a next time any time soon. I'm telling you, Maddie, you and I need to get out and do some socializing. Life must have more to it than working. I mean we do go out, but we don't hang out with friends and meet new people, preferably guys. I want to meet some new people, Maddie.

"I go out thank you. I'm dating someone remember."

Meagan gave Maddie a strange look, but kept silent.

Caroline could not believe she was hearing that sound. She must be dreaming because there was no way it was Monday morning already. It was Friday evening just a few short hours ago, and now the alarm clock was disturbing her.

Katie and Caroline had figured out a work schedule since Monica left Dunning Plumbing a few weeks ago. Brian and Richard weren't sad to see her go due to her spotty work attendance, but now they were short a receptionist, which was an absolutely necessary person in their world. Katie always jumped in when needed and was grateful when Caroline offered to help also.

The two women split the hours and responsibilities except for payroll. Katie had been responsible for payroll for so long she wouldn't know how to let someone else do it. She never could understand why the receptionist job was so hard to keep filled. It wasn't hard work, and the pay was good. Sitting behind a desk all day can be tiring, but that was the nature of the position. Caroline didn't need the work, but it helped her husband and gave Katie time at home with the kids. And seeing Richard through the day was a bonus she couldn't turn down.

The smell of coffee made its way to Caroline's nose as soon as she stepped out of her bedroom. She followed the aroma until she found her husband sitting at the kitchen table enjoying a cup himself.

"Awww you made coffee. Thank you."

"You're welcome. I move a little faster on Monday mornings than you do," Richard teased.

"I think a turtle moves faster than I do on Monday mornings." He chuckled at her comment.

"We need to get a move on. I need to get to the office a little early today. Brian has a meeting, and before he goes I need to talk to him."

"Richard, why didn't you tell me this last night? Now I have to hustle to get ready." After one sip, she roughly put her cup down and left the room.

Shortly after Richard and Caroline arrived at the office, he went to the break room for a cup of coffee and noticed a dozen doughnuts sitting on the counter near the coffee pot. Not just any doughnuts, but his favorite, strawberry jelly filled. He stopped abruptly. Looking around he called out for Brian, but there was no response.

"Caroline, have you seen Brian?"

"No."

"Who bought doughnuts?"

"I don't know, but I'm glad they did."

"Who all is here?"

"A few of the guys, why?"

"Just wondering that's all." He turned and walked away.

Richard went to check Brian's office just in case he had slipped in without being noticed. Finding it empty, he took his cell phone out and tapped Brian's number on the screen.

"Yo, I know I'm running a bit late, but I'm parking as we speak," Brian said, not giving Richard a chance to say anything.

"Great, come straight to your office. I need to talk to you."

"Alright." Brian would find out soon enough what had his brother in such a state so early in the day, but a cup of coffee would have to come first.

Setting the coffee pot down, he saw the box and couldn't resist. "Mmm doughnuts, don't mind if I do."

Richard turned to see his brother coming through the office door eating one of the mystery doughnuts. Placing his hands on his hips, he said, "Brian, do you know who brought those doughnuts in this morning?"

"No," he answered with his mouth mostly full.

Richard was now annoyed by the doughnut mystery. He remembered not so long ago when one of their female employees had a serious crush on him and often brought in his favorite doughnuts. She knew just how he liked his coffee and had a cup sitting on his desk most mornings when he arrived. She resigned two weeks before he and Caroline married, and the coffee and doughnut scene suddenly stopped. This memory made him uneasy as he watched Brian take his final bites.

"Why does it matter who brought in a box of doughnuts?"

"It doesn't. Here are some contracts that need your signature before lunch," he pointed out laying them on Brian's desk. "Oh and I need to see a list of employees we've recently hired," he explained as he turned to walk out of the office.

"Why?"

"I just do. Is there a problem?" He growled.

"No, just wondering."

Sitting down rather hard, Richard was determined to not let the mystery doughnuts weird him out. After all, nothing terrifying happened. It was simply awkward, extremely awkward. He would clear his head and get on with his day.

———◦———◦———◦———

The morning was busy. As soon as Caroline hung up the phone it would ring again. All of the plumbers were out on calls except one. In the office, Brian was looking frantically for some documents for a meeting he was nearly running late for already. Richard was still waiting on his signature on contracts that had conveniently become misplaced as well. The meeting was nearby at a contractor's office just a few blocks away. He could make the meeting if traffic wasn't heavy. As he scavenged through papers, Brian could hear his father's voice echoing in his head about how he kept his office in such a mess, but there was no time for guilt. He had to find those documents.

"Brian, you need to leave now, or you'll be late for your meeting. I'll look for the documents and if I find them, I'll have someone bring them to you," Richard offered much to his brother's relief.

"What if you don't find them?"

"Then you will have some smooth talkin' to do, little brother."

"Oh, have you signed the contracts I left for you?"

"Aah, no, they are on my desk…somewhere."

"Brian!" Richard started digging where he had laid the papers and finally found them under a couple of folders and a used napkin. "Sign, right now!" he demanded holding out a pen.

Brian turned and with a purposeful stride walked out of his office as Richard continued to shuffle through mounds of papers on his desk. Caroline saw the commotion and began scanning the computer for the documents also. When Richard ran the business, things like this never happened. He kept everything organized and orderly. Now with Brian back at the helm, documents went missing, contracts were in whatever stack he laid them down on and it drove Richard bonkers. It didn't sit well with their father either.

Brian kept looking at his watch wondering if Richard would find and deliver the documents in time. He was planning a way to buy some time with this major client until he arrived. If he blew this deal over misplaced documents, his father would have plenty to say about it. Not to mention Richard would never let him forget it.

"Is this it?" Caroline asked standing in front of the filing cabinet. With high hopes, Richard quickly walked toward her. She handed the stapled papers to her husband and explained, "They were laying under a stack of papers here on the cabinet."

"Yes! This is it, thank you! Send Brian a text telling him I'm on my way." Giving her a quick kiss, he hurried out the door with fingers crossed that traffic wouldn't be an issue.

Brian was beginning to sweat when his phone vibrated. Seeing the text from Caroline, he breathed a sigh of relief. He excused himself and walked to the receptionist's desk where Richard waited with documents in hand. "Oh thanks, man. I was starting to sweat. I had one idea to bluff my way through, and that was it."

"Don't thank me. Thank Caroline. She found them in a stack of papers on top of your filling cabinet. Brian, you really need to be more organized."

"Yeah, I know." He quickly returned to his meeting as if he had the documents the whole time.

Richard walked in and saw his father sitting in his usual chair near the receptionist's desk. "Hey Dad, I didn't know you were coming in today?"

"Yeah, got here early this morning. Talked to the fellas. I needed to get out of the house today. Your mother is having some women over. Trust me, Son, whenever there is a group of ladies gathering at your house, it's best to either stay in the garage or just leave. No offense, Caroline." Richard and Caroline laughed out loud at Todd not wanting to be near a room full of women.

After lunch, Brian walked in with a six pack of Dr. Pepper and set it on Caroline's desk. "For you, my dearest sister-in law," he said wearing a big grin. "Thanks for finding those documents. I could have sworn I had them in my briefcase."

"You're welcome. You need to take a full day and do nothing but get that office organized," she encouraged in a half serious tone with the chaotic hunt still fresh in her mind. Brian was definitely someone who couldn't work in a clutter free office. But in situations like today, it did bite him on the backside.

Once again before she could leave for the day, Maddie was faced with a messy classroom and decorations to hang up. Fortunately, she had some peanut butter and crackers in her lunch bag to snack on before tackling the messy room.

"Are you going to the game?" Amy asked poking her head in Maddie's room.

"Yes, if I get this classroom back in order and the bulletin board decorated in time."

"I'm working the door so I'll see you when you get there."

Tonight's game was a home game, North Side versus Pleasant View. Her plan was to stay at the school until almost game time, which saved on gas and her budget. This shifted her thoughts to her new part-time job. She was relieved to know next month she would have a few extra dollars.

She had invited Ethan to join her at the game, and he said he would try. Tonight she was relieved of door duty as well as tending to the concessions stand, so she could watch the entire game seated in the bleachers. She was definitely looking forward to it, but that also meant eating at the concessions stand. She was unsure how Ethan was going to react to that. The burgers were actually decent with the chips, but the popcorn was usually too salty.

As she lined up the chairs in the classroom, she focused a little longer on Ethan. She noticed more often he ran late for their dates and hoped this evening he would arrive on time.

The girls varsity game ended in a loss for the home team, and now the varsity boys were on the court taking practice shots, and students and parents were milling about finding their seats, talking to friends and getting their refreshments. Maddie was hungry. She had been thinking about their cheeseburgers all afternoon. But since she didn't want to be rude, she would wait and eat with Ethan. She found their seats and waited patiently.

Fifteen minutes into the boys' varsity game, Maddie had almost forgotten about Ethan until he showed up. North Side was up by two points. Maddie loved games where the score was so close it kept you on the edge of your seat. And tonight's game had been like that from the tip-off.

"Oh great you made it."

"I would have been here sooner, but you know how evening traffic is. Who's winning?

"We are."

"Who's we?" She shot him a look that made him feel a bit embarrassed.

The energy was high, and the crowd was loud. Maddie was enjoying every moment of it. He had never seen her like this. He enjoyed watching her watch the game. At halftime the score was tied, and there was a mad rush to the concession stand.

"Let's go get in line at the concession stand. I'm starving, how about you?"

"Aah, yeah I guess so." Ethan responded.

"One of us should stay here or we may lose our seats." Maddie explained.

"Okay, you go and I'll stay. Just get me a soft drink and popcorn." She stood and turned to look at him a few seconds.

"What?" he responded.

"Nothing." Something suddenly clicked in Maddie: a pattern with Ethan. Lately, on their dates, she ended up paying for their meals.

"Hi, Maddie, what can I get for you?" James asked.

James Adcock, one of North Sides newer and single faculty members, had become more friendly with Maddie. He hung out with her and the other single faculty from time to time, but he seemed to gravitate toward her more than the others. She didn't mind. He was friendly and a lot of fun to have in the group, and there was no romantic attraction from either of them.

"Oh hi, James, I see it's your night to work concessions," she said, chuckling. "I'll have popcorn, a bag of potato chips, and two Pepsis, please." Maddie could smell the burgers cooking making her mouth water, but she didn't have enough money to buy both of them food.

"Comin' right up." He brought her order quickly. "Hey, some of us are going out after the game, want to go?"

"I would love to, but I have someone with me. I'll check and see if they want to come along. If that's okay?"

"Sure, the more the merrier."

"I'll let you know after the game."

Carrying their food, Maddie saw Ethan from across the gym. He puzzled her at times. She really liked being with him, and despite being handsome and most of the time fun to be with, he made her want to scream at times. For reasons unknown, she chose now to consider their relationship. How deep were her feelings for him? How deep were his feelings for her? After returning to her seat, she sat there eating her chips and occasionally glanced over at him. She truly did not have an answer.

By the end of the day, Caroline's legs ached from sitting behind the desk. She was looking forward to a quiet drive home and the weekend. She was happy to help Katie and the family, but Caroline was hoping her days as a receptionist were short lived. Abruptly recalling the issue with the doughnuts, she started to ask Richard about it, but after a big yawn, she dismissed it.

Instead of driving straight home, Richard turned the opposite direction. "Sweetie, where are we going?"

"It's been a busy day for all of us. I was thinking we would stop in at 417 Union and eat supper." It was one of Richard's favorite places to eat. He, Brian and his father ate there often.

He wouldn't get any complaints from Caroline since it meant an easier evening for her.

"Hello, my name is Rhonda, and I'll be your waitress. What can I get you two to drink?"

"Two sweet teas, please."

"Alright, take your time looking at the menus, and I'll be right back."

Looking at the menu, Richard couldn't make up his mind. "What are you getting?"

"The fried chicken," she responded happily. "Having trouble deciding?"

"Yeah, everything here is so good. But…I think I'm going to have the country pork chops."

"Here you go, two sweet teas. Have you made up your mind what you would like?" Rhonda asked.

Richard gave the waitress their order as they sat in the small, unique restaurant in downtown Nashville. They leisurely sipped their teas allowing the day's frustrations to fall away.

This was Caroline's first visit to 417 Union, but she knew it was popular. "I wonder if that bar has been here all through the years," she said gazing at the rugged structure extending along the side wall, then at the table they were sitting at. "I mean look at these tables, if these tables could talk…"

Grinning at his wife, he quickly responded, "If these tables could talk, I would run out the door." Caroline chuckled a little, softly slapping at his arm.

The buzzer went off signaling the end of the game. North Side won by two points, but up until the last shot, it could have been either side's game. The championship game for this team was definitely within their reach.

Ethan followed Maddie to the gym entrance where she spoke to a guy he didn't know. He couldn't hear everything they were saying due to the noise, but as he leaned closer, he heard Maddie apologize and say maybe next time. Driving to Maddie's apartment with the noise of the game still in his head, he couldn't help but think about how much he had learned about her this evening. He had no idea how much she enjoyed watching a basketball game. Most women he knew didn't care one way or another about sports. *She seems to have a lot of friends, male friends.* He wasn't sure how he felt about that.

Sitting in her apartment, the game was still on Ethan's mind. "You really like basketball, don't you?" he asked while Maddie poured him a glass of Pepsi.

"Yes, I do. I used to watch a lot of games with Daddy when I was growing up. He explained the rules to me and how to play the game. Now, don't ask me to actually play because I can't… I am a watcher not a player," she joked as if there was a story behind that comment.

"I'm making myself a sandwich, want one?"

"Sure, what kind?"

"Grilled cheese."

"That sounds good."

After the first bite of his sandwich, he quickly took another. He was sure it was the best grilled cheese he had ever eaten. The cheese was thick, and the bread buttery. Ethan smiled at her and for the first time since they had been dating, he noticed how lovely her eyes were. He continued looking at her. She was a small framed girl, but not a tiny person. Her dark brown hair just touched her shoulders and cut to compliment her round face. She was beautiful. He wondered why it took him so long to really notice her. Was it because he saw some guy talking to her at the game, or was he developing serious feelings for her?

———————✦———————✦✦✦———————✦———————

Katie sat down at her desk and clocked in. It was her Saturday to work. She and her dad were always the first ones in the office when Todd still ran the business. She cherished their alone time. Often, they would get caught up on what was happening in their lives or just enjoy a cup of coffee together before the phone started ringing and other employees came in. Todd didn't tolerate tardiness from anyone and taught his children that being late was rude and wasted other people's time. Somewhere between her teens and her college graduation that little golden rule stuck, and now she was teaching her children that same principle.

"Good morning, Katie."

"Good morning, Rich...Hey, what are you doing here today?"

"I have some paperwork that needs my attention. I plan to be out of here by noon," he said, filling his coffee mug with the hot liquid he loved so. Just the aroma alone would make his mouth water. Mindlessly opening the doughnut box, he noticed it was filled with his favorites again. "Seriously! Katie, did you bring these doughnuts in this morning?"

"No, I..."

"Who keeps bringing in these doughnuts? I mean, I love doughnuts. And we used to have them a lot then...we didn't anymore. Now here we go again. It has to be someone who gets here before I do, and I want to know who it is."

Katie stared at her brother and had no idea what in the world was wrong with him. *All this fuss over a doughnut?* Before she could speak, their father walked in the room, poured himself another cup of coffee and grabbed a doughnut.

"Have a doughnut, Son. These are my favorite: strawberry jelly filled. For some reason, I've been wanting doughnuts lately so I figured I would bring in a few for everybody. Go ahead, help yourself," Todd said walking toward Katie's desk while taking a bite out of one.

"Dad. Are you the one who has been buying the doughnuts?"

"Yes, who did you think it was, the doughnut fairy?" he teased.

"Funny, Dad. Why didn't you tell me? Not knowing was driving me nuts. It reminded me of Sydney."

"Sydney! Why did it remind you of her?"

"Remember how she used to bring my favorite doughnuts in and have my coffee ready for me when I got to my office? I mean, how did the woman know how I liked my coffee? She would do little things like that for me and ….it was weird. I think she had a thing for me."

Todd let out a chuckle. "Sure she did. But she was bringing the doughnuts for me," he grinned.

"Did she make you coffee just the way you like it?"

"Yes, she did."

Katie was reveling in this weird conversation between her father and brother. It was so amusing that it was hard for her to keep a straight face while listening, and she couldn't wait to tell her mother.

Four

Maddie walked in the door of her apartment and dropped her purse on the floor and her keys on the table. Her feet ached so badly she didn't think she could take another step. Her first shift at the hotel wasn't bad, just tiring. There were many things to learn which wouldn't be a problem, but the most important one was to wear comfortable shoes. It never occurred to her that she would be on her feet most of her shift. She wanted to look professional which in her mind meant high heels. Big mistake. Now all she wanted was a hot shower and crawl into bed.

She struggled to get up after yesterday, but she did roll out of bed on time. Her feet were sore from the torture she'd put them through less than twenty-four hours ago, but she managed to walk to the kitchen without hobbling.

"So, tell me how your first night at the hotel went," Meagan inquired while making her breakfast.

"Fine, and tiring. The work isn't hard. It's just a lot to remember right now. The only mistake I made was wearing high heels." Getting a box of cereal out of the cupboard she continued. "I'm not sure about the manager though. I'll need to keep my eye on him."

Meagan looked at Maddie unsure by what she meant by that, but Maddie's cell rang and she didn't get the chance to ask.

⸻ ⸱⸳◦⸳⸱ ⸻

Maddie and Ethan had only seen each other once in the past two weeks, and he was getting a little annoyed about it. She had been too busy to notice how much time had passed. But tonight he was coming for a quiet dinner at her apartment where they could be alone. Her two jobs kept her constantly on the go, and so far she was handling it pretty well.

Maddie made baked spaghetti for dinner, and as she pulled it out of the oven, there was a knock at the door indicating Ethan's arrival.

"Hello, Ethan, come on in. Maddie's in the kitchen. See you later, Maddie," Meagan yelled over her shoulder walking out as he walked in. She wasn't exactly excited about Ethan dating her roommate; there was something about him that just didn't sit right with her. Ethan was relieved to see her leave. She didn't necessarily hide her feelings about him, but it didn't bother him at all. This allowed him to have Maddie all to himself for the whole evening. Walking toward the kitchen he paused to notice the romantic candlelit dinner sitting on the table. Yes, he was glad Meagan left.

Meagan and a few friends went bowling at a family bowling center near her apartment. The place was really busy as usual, but that added to the fun. The one thing Meagan didn't like about bowling was the shoes. She couldn't understand why anyone would design shoes so hideous. And adding to her distaste, she refused to think about how many people had worn the pair on her feet.

In the meantime, Ryan and Nathan along with a small group of guys were just getting their game started in the lane beside them. As Meagan and the others were settling in with their gear, she noticed one of the neighboring players looking their way.

With the music blaring and the pins crashing, people needed to talk louder to be heard which wasn't an issue for anyone, but the pizza they ordered was. After two bites, she opted to simply leave it on the plate. *It's not worth the calories.*

The guys beside them were fun to watch not just because they knew what they were doing, but they were obviously having a good time. For unexplained reasons, Meagan kept glancing in their direction and caught one of them looking her way as well. Now she needed to focus on her game so not to embarrass herself in front of a group of guys, especially the one who had caught her eye.

Ryan kept sneaking looks at Meagan all evening, especially when it was her turn to bowl. She wasn't necessarily a big powerful girl, but she threw the ball with some force getting several strikes along with a few spares. Her uniquely colored light brown hair was stunning, and he blamed that for the two gutter balls he threw. Before finishing their games, Ryan eventually spoke to her which resulted in introductions.

Meagan quietly unlocked the door around midnight and stepped lightly into the dimly lit front room. The girls always kept a light on after going to bed. Maddie heard her arrival, but just rolled over. She really wanted to get up and talk to her, but needed to be up early to deal with little kindergarteners and Mrs. Daniels tomorrow. She burrowed further under the covers and tried to keep her mind quiet so sleep would come.

Maddie had been working at the hotel for a little over a month, and all was going well. After learning the ropes, she was more comfortable with her duties. Her body was getting used to working the extra hours, but getting out of bed the next day continued to be a challenge. Sitting at the lunch table, Maddie pulled out her cell phone and saw she had a message. "Hi, Maddie, this is Carlton. Give me a call when you have a moment, please."

"Maddie, glad you called, I was getting worried. Listen, Shelly can't come in this evening, can you cover for her?"

"No, I have aftercare today until six-thirty, sorry." This was really beginning to aggravate her. When she put in her application, she made it clear to Carlton her available days and times. In the short time six weeks she had worked there, this was the fourth time someone called during school hours asking her to cover for them.

"If I can get someone to cover the first half of her shift, can you cover the rest?" She didn't want to work this evening since she worked last night. She was looking forward to a calm evening at home. Ethan was planning on stopping by, and she had to deal with papers and folders as well.

"I'm sorry, Carlton. I really can't. I have work to do for tomorrow. If I could I would, but I just can't."

"Okay, I'll try someone else." She could hear the disappointment in his voice, which she tried to avoid all of the time, but there was nothing she could do to prevent it.

Looking at her watch Maddie was relieved to see that it was six-fifteen on the dot. It had been one of those days that caused a teacher to ask themselves why they come to such a place each day and subject themselves to such torture. Today consisted of rowdy children, a moody Mrs. Daniels, and two little boys fighting resulting in one bloody nose. And the grand finale was the frantic one who threw up in the hallway on their way to the bathroom. All that Maddie really wanted was to call it a day and head home to a warm bath and a hot cup of tea, but the pile of papers wasn't getting any smaller, and her laundry had been neglected too long. After that, maybe she could check off the day as done. She enjoyed the hotel, but working two jobs was beginning to wear on her. She hoped when summer arrived that it would be easier, but she was unsure she could keep up the pace until then.

The hot water soothed Maddie's tired body. The trials of the day began to melt away as she lay in the lavender scented tub with bubbles nestled up to her neck. As the relaxing atmosphere calmed her, memories of her school days came trickling in like water from a faucet that was not turned all the way off. She could see the influential faces of those who had educated her in her mind and how they had made teaching look so easy. For any teacher in any grade level no matter what decade, trouble in the classroom was the norm, but days like this one, topped off with an inadequate paycheck, would make any person want to throw in the towel. But then she quickly shifted to her other job and how much she had enjoyed it so far. And then a momentary grief came upon her, and for the first time ever, she second-guessed her career choice. *Lord, I wanted to be a teacher for as long as I can remember.* Not knowing where these feelings were coming from, it saddened Maddie to consider she may have wasted so much time in becoming something that not only made her unhappy, but also couldn't pay the bills.

The half hour soak was just what the doctor ordered along with a hot meal. She shrugged off the doubts that had rattled her and got out of the tub to move on with her evening. When she finished grading papers, she could then set aside being a teacher until morning.

Sitting at the kitchen table in her sleep shirt and sock feet, she was relieved that Ethan had called to cancel their date which allowed her to finish her work. She quietly blew out a sigh as she placed the last paper in its folder. There wasn't too much evening remaining, but she would make the best of what she had left. The couch provided immediate comfort. Clicking the remote she brought the TV to life, settled down easily with a cozy but light blanket and began to surf for something to watch.

"Umm, hello?" Maddie answered, sounding a bit drowsy.

"Hey, I'm about three minutes from your apartment. Want to watch a movie?"

"Aah Ethan? What time is it?"

"It's about nine forty-five. I'm about to pull onto your street."

"Ethan, I'm sorry it's getting late. I'm afraid I wouldn't be very good company. I fell asleep on the couch watching TV... I've had a rough day. Besides, weren't you doing something with one of your friends you haven't seen in a long time?"

"He left. Come on. I'll fix you a snack, and we can get comfy on the couch."

"No, really, Ethan, I can't. Tomorrow is a work day, and I have to get up early...and so do you."

Ethan could tell she was serious and was a bit put out. "Fine. I'll see you this weekend. Bye."

"Please don't be mad. I've had a tough day, and I don't need you getting mad at me just because I'm tired. It's too late to start watching a movie. I really need to go to bed."

"I'm not mad. I was just hoping to see you, that's all. I'm disappointed, but not mad."

"Then why did you cancel our date?"

"I told you I had an out of town friend stop by that I hadn't seen in about three years."

"Ethan, I'm sorry."

"Yeah, me too. I'll see you this weekend."

Ethan drove home. He desperately wanted to see that girl with the lovely eyes, the one who got so excited about a basketball game. Instead, she was tired and sleepy. He would be forced to go back to his apartment and spend the rest of the evening with the guys.

Tossing, turning and not wanting to look at the clock, Maddie found herself wide awake and a bit upset. When she walked into the kitchen for a drink of water, she discovered Meagan on the couch watching TV.

"Why aren't you in bed? It's after two."

"Couldn't sleep. Why are you up?"

"Same reason, plus I needed a drink of water."

Maddie plopped down in the chair next to the sofa and began watching too.

"I didn't know you liked old black and white movies."

"I don't, but there isn't anything better on."

Without reason, Maddie started sharing what had happened with Ethan earlier and how he reacted. Meagan had kept her feelings about their relationship to herself and questioned if this was the right time to express her opinion.

"Can I be honest with you? I mean really honest?"

"Sure."

"You are a very sweet, loving and giving person, and I'm afraid you're going to get hurt in this relationship. I don't think Ethan treats you very well."

"Thank you, but Ethan isn't going to hurt me. He may not be the best boyfriend a girl could have, but he's pretty harmless."

Meagan held back most of what she wanted to say. She couldn't understand what Maddie saw in him. Just about everything they did together was done his way or on his terms, and she treated him far better than he treated her. The hard truth was Meagan didn't trust Ethan as far as she could throw him.

Morning came way too early for both girls. Neither had slept much that night, and as usual, Meagan was running late. Being late often made a person get a move on, but Maddie had trouble doing that. Her eyes stung and her legs felt heavy. *A hot shower…I need a hot shower.*

Driving in the morning traffic Maddie listened to a local radio station and yawned which triggered a dozen yawns to follow. She was tired from the lack of sleep, which she thanked Ethan for, and begged the Lord to allow her to have a better day than the one she had yesterday. She repented of wishing Ethan a sleepless night as she had suffered.

Finishing up her second cup of coffee from the teachers' lounge, the wall clock regrettably revealed it was time to head to her classroom. She didn't drink coffee every morning, but today the caffeine was welcomed and much needed. When she walked in, all of the children were scurrying around, and Mrs. Daniels was instructing everyone to put their things away and be seated. Yawning, she walked to the office with the attendance sheet and lunch information as she normally did hoping the caffeine would kick in soon. Amy was leaving the office as she was about to enter.

"Hey, Maddie.

"Hi, Amy."

"Hey, have you seen that cute guy again, you know...from the game?"

"No...and I don't ever want to." Maddie would rather forget that whole incident, and maybe she could if Amy would let her. This was the second time she had been asked that question which reminded her of that embarrassing evening.

"If you had to have your drink spilled all over you, at least you had a cute guy doing it. See ya later. Gotta get my class started."

Amy sped up toward her class, not giving any consideration to the effect her words had on Maddie. She had prayed for a better day and mentioning that night at the game did not fit that description.

"Come on in and sit down. I just need a minute to finish getting ready." Maddie said to Ethan. "We had to wait on one of the parents to come and pick their child up. They said they got stuck in traffic, but who knows. I don't mean to be critical or talk badly about others, but sometimes parents are dishonest about that. They say they were stuck in traffic when really they stopped to get gas or run in the grocery."

Ethan sat in the living room waiting for Maddie to change her clothes. Looking around the room, he saw her open purse sitting on the coffee table. Tomorrow night the guys were having their normal poker night, and he needed a few bucks to get in on the game. He could hear the water running in the bathroom. Looking around and seeing no one, Ethan was in and out of Maddie's purse within seconds.

"Okay, I'm ready."

"Great, let's go. Do you want to eat before or after the movie?"

"If we have time before, I'm starving."

Five

The local schools were on spring break. Schools were taking different weeks of the month to enjoy the commercial for summer. Caroline's son Joshua planned to be home later that day to spend his spring break with her and Richard. She loved it when he was home because she missed him when he wasn't. That detail she kept to herself, she didn't want to bother him with her empty nest sorrows. This was his second year at the University of Tennessee Knoxville, and thankfully, however, he did make time to come home once a month. A few of Caroline's friends didn't see their college kids but maybe twice a semester and she didn't know how they endured it.

"Do you know what Joshua's plans are for the week?" Richard asked before taking a bite of biscuit and gravy.

"No, not really, but I'm sure he will want to sleep in and see his friends."

"Most of his friends are at college with him," Richard pointed out, chuckling. Smiling at her husband from across the table, she looked forward to being with her two favorite men for a whole week.

"I'm so glad that Joshua's spring break isn't the same week as Ashley and Jake's, or your dad would have to play receptionist at the office."

"Ha-ha yeah, he could do it, but we both know after a while he would find someone else to answer the phone." After another bite he continued, "I can't believe it's taking this long to find a new receptionist."

"Neither can I."

Maddie couldn't help but be energized about the day. In ten hours her spring break would begin. She didn't have money to go anywhere exciting, but she did have plans. She couldn't wait to stay up late, sleep in as long as she wanted, and go out with friends. The second job allowed her a few extra dollars to play on, and she was excited to have more fun without worrying so much about her funds. School, teaching and children would be put on pause for nine whole days. Her phone ringing brought her back to reality. She picked it from her lap and answered it.

"Hello, Maddie, this is Carlton. I was wondering if you could come in tomorrow at noon instead of two? Sharon has to take her son to the dentist."

Holding back disappointment, she responded, "Sure, I can come in early."

"Great, it looks like you and I will be spending tomorrow together, or most of it anyway. Thanks for being a team player."

"You're welcome, Carlton. See you tomorrow."

Maddie wasn't thrilled about spending most of her Saturday working, but the extra hours meant extra pay. Turning up the radio and singing along, she felt sure that it was going to be a great day.

Four o'clock couldn't come fast enough for Maddie. Her work day would be done, and the fun could begin. She and Meagan were meeting some friends at Pizza Perfect around six. She had invited Ethan to come along, and he agreed.

Walking into the restaurant, the smell of oregano hit them full in the face. Their mouths now watering for the delicious pies, it reminded Meagan of how long it had been since she had eaten lunch. Peering down at her watch, she didn't know if she could wait for their friends to arrive or not. Sitting at one of the longer tables, Maddie checked her phone for missed messages. *Ethan should be getting here soon.*

Looking toward the door, Maddie recognized the person coming in. "Hey there's James," as Maddie waved to get his attention.

"Hey, I didn't see you at school today. I thought maybe you started your spring break early."

Maddie laughed at his comment. "Oh, James, this is Meagan, my best friend and roommate. Meagan, James Adcock, he teaches at North Side." They exchanged smiles and pleasantries, then Maddie invited him to join them for pizza.

"Sure, if you say it's okay."

Waving her hand, "It's okay."

It wasn't long until everyone had arrived with the exception of Ethan. James was relieved to see someone else from school and instantly felt more comfortable. After twenty minutes Maddie suggested they go ahead and order. They both opened their purses to pay when Maddie spotted a major problem. "Meagan, I hate to do this, but can you loan me a few bucks? I could have sworn I had forty dollars in my wallet, but all I have is a ten," she explained, bewildered.

"Sure. No problem. That happens to me often."

As Meagan paid for their meal, she told Maddie to keep her ten in case they went somewhere else afterwards. Maddie stood there puzzled and wondered what had happened to her money. "I know I had forty dollars in my wallet on Monday, and I haven't spent any cash since last week."

"Like I said, it happens to me a lot. Don't worry about it."

For now she would dismiss it, but when she got home she would look for the missing cash. She worked too hard for too little to just forget about it.

A night out with friends was a great start to spring break. Both girls were energized by it. When the pizza arrived, all eyes followed the hands that held the pans. Maddie could not wait to get her mouth around that cheesy deliciousness. There was something about that first bite of pizza that was so satisfying. Ethan didn't show up until after the food had arrived at the table. It surprised him to see how many were joining them. Not one to feel out of place in any group, he held his own in the conversation, but didn't seem to care for Maddie's co-worker James. He remembered James from the ballgame and how he and Maddie had talked briefly, but he still didn't know about what. As far as Ethan was concerned, James talked to Maddie a little too much. He was a bit surprised at this new emotion he was experiencing, and in all honesty, he didn't like it.

Everyone was having a good time, and everyone was included in the various conversations. When they got a bit loud, they quickly noticed and toned it down. Long after the pizza had been devoured, someone suggested ice cream. They agreed the place to go was Mike's on Broadway. As everyone was getting up from the table, Ethan touched Maddie on the arm and spoke close to her ear.

"Hey, how about we go for a drive, or back to your place and watch some TV."

"Aah, I wanted to go to Mike's. Don't you want to go?"

"Not really. I was hoping for some alone time with you. We can stop at Kroger and pick up a half gallon and eat it by ourselves," he offered with a grin.

"I'm sorry you don't want to go, but I drove my car. And Meagan rode with me, and to be honest, I really would like to go. Please come with us."

"Alright," he said without much conviction, but his facial expression showed something very different. He walked her to her car then sought out his own passing a friend of his on the way.

"Yo, Ethan, what's up man? I haven't seen you in a while." The two guys continued to talk in the parking lot for several minutes.

The group was en route to Mike's Ice Cream and Coffee Bar. As Maddie settled into a parking space, her phone rang.

"I've decide not to go for ice cream. I'm heading on home. It's been a long day."

"Are you sure? I really wanted you to join us."

"I know. You go ahead and have fun. I'll talk to you tomorrow."

"Alright. Bye, Ethan."

From the conversation, Meagan could tell that Ethan wasn't coming for ice cream which made her secretly a little happy.

Mike's was one of the best ice cream shops downtown. The small seating area was easily overlooked by the quality and enormous selection to choose from. Out of habit, Maddie slid her hands into her jacket pocket. And to her surprise she pulled out some folded bills, the same amount that was missing from her wallet.

"How...when did I..."

"Meagan, look. Here's the money I was missing. I must have put it in my jacket pocket at some time or another." Handing her some cash to repay her for the pizza, they both chuckled. "Now let's get some ice cream."

As Maddie turned around with her cup of chocolate ice cream, she accidently brushed up against someone. "Excuse me. I'm sorry," she apologized quickly without really seeing the person.

Barely glancing that direction, the man replied, "No problem."

Taking a seat at the counter, he elbowed his buddy who was already seated. "Hey man, look over there. You know who that is, don't you?" as he softly laughed. "Wanna go over and say hello?"

"Are you kidding? I'd probably dump her ice cream in her lap." After a few silent moments, Nathan was ready to leave. "Come on let's get out of here."

"Why? I'm not finished with my ice cream."

"Hello, Ryan...right?" Meagan inquired.

"Yes, hi, Meagan. You here with friends?"

"Yeah, just having a little ice cream. Been bowling lately?"

"No, not since the other week. I've been thinking of joining a league, but not sure I want to be that involved." She teased.

"You would be good on a league." Awkwardness stealing her ability for conversation, she turned and noticed her group had found a spot to sit. "I guess I ought to get back to my friends. It was good seeing you."

"Yeah, good seeing you too." Ryan watched her walk to the other side of the room.

When she sat down at the small table with her friends, it suddenly dawned on her that he remembered her name.

"Dude, you ought to get her number and give her a call. I think she likes you."

"Maybe."

"Come on. Let's get out of here."

"What's your hurry?"

Nathan really wanted to leave. Not because he was running, but because he didn't want to meet her eyes and have her remember the embarrassment he caused.

"I was just kidding. She's with friends and probably won't even recognize you."

Sighing, "Just hurry up and finish, okay?"

Sitting across from James and Meagan, Maddie never noticed as she ate her ice cream that he and Ryan were sitting directly across from them. But Meagan, on the other hand, most certainly did and kept glancing in their direction.

It appeared as if Ryan was correct. Maddie hadn't recognized him, but he sure did recognize her. Of all the places in downtown Nashville, she had to walk into the same one he was in. The memory of her standing there with Pepsi all over her blouse was still vivid. No, he would not look her way again; he would let Ryan finish eating then leave with his dignity.

Ryan finally finished, and the two got up to walk toward the door. As they did, Maddie and all of her group did the same. The workers behind the counter said good night assuming that everyone was together.

Ryan was already out the door when he sensed something wasn't right. He didn't have his keys. Nathan stopped when he noticed his friend go back inside. As he turned to follow him, someone collided right into his chest.

"Oh I'm so sor..." There they stood extremely close, his arms holding her steady.

"Are you alright?" Nathan sincerely asked.

"Yes, I'm fine I...."

Maddie and Nathan's eyes locked on one another; both seemed to be unable to look away.

Quickly, Nathan apologized and let her go. At that moment, Ryan walked up just as Nathan turned and continued on his way.

After the ice cream, a few weren't quite ready to call it a night. Too much fun was still being had. So Meagan invited the rest to their apartment to play games and eat popcorn. Amy, James and one of Meagan's coworkers were playing a rowdy round of Uno when Maddie's phone suddenly sprang to life. Looking at the screen, she saw Ethan's name and face. Not wanting to interrupt the game, she let it ring to voicemail.

"Wow, what a game," James said as he took the empty popcorn bowl to the kitchen sink. "Thanks for the invite, ladies, but I gotta go." James' exit triggered the others to leave as well since it was getting late. Saying goodnight to her guests she suddenly remembered Ethan. Picking up her phone she immediately returned his call.

"Hi, I see you called."

"Yeah, is it too late to stop by?"

"Ethan, it's after midnight."

"I know. You're not in bed are you?"

"No, but I will be soon. I thought you were going home after we left Pizza Perfect."

"I went by Trevor's and hung out awhile." His words stung a little. "I have hardly seen you today, Maddie."

"You had all evening to see me, but you chose to leave and go hang out with Trevor." Ethan could hear the irritation in her voice.

"So I can't come over?"

"No, I'm going to bed. I have to work tomorrow."

He was a little hurt he couldn't see Maddie, and clueless of his bad decision to hang out with his friend over her. He had no other place to go but home.

He was a little hurt he couldn't see Maddie, and clueless of

Sunday morning it was all Maddie could do to keep her eyes open. Her seven hour shift at the hotel yesterday turned into a ten hour day. Working overtime and getting to bed late on Friday night had caught up with her. When her alarm went off, she rolled over thinking she hit the snooze button, but turned it off instead causing her to miss Sunday School. When she did wake up enough to read the clock on the bed side table, she shot into motion. "Oh noooo!" She had forty minutes to make the morning service.

Walking in the auditorium, Maddie took a seat next to Meagan. "Why didn't you wake me?"

Laughing a little, Meagan answered, "I did, twice. After that I figured you were either extremely tired or sick, so I left you alone."

As the pianist began playing, their conversation quickly came to an end. Maddie had made it to church on time, but her body needed a few more hours of serious sleep.

Ethan sat at his desk gazing solemnly at the balance in his bank account knowing he had to do something. He was now in debt to a poker friend for a hundred and fifty dollars, an amount his account would not cover. For Ethan, this wasn't the first time he had been down this road and basically shrugged it off since he usually found a way out of it. Just a few weeks ago, his pocketknife was held as collateral for a loan, which didn't sit well with him. But he did get his knife back after several weeks of scrapping to find some extra cash. The only consequence was that he had to pay an extra twenty dollars. Now here he was again, just with a different person. His solution to sell some of his personal items really wasn't very lucrative as Trevor had predicted. So he would need to figure something out, but he wasn't too worried.

Arriving at their apartment, Maddie and Meagan saw Ethan sitting in the parking lot. He got out carrying a couple of Sonic bags with burgers and fries.

"Hey, ladies, I bought lunch," Ethan said holding them up with a sheepish grin on his face.

"Aww thanks, Ethan. That was so sweet of you." Maddie kissed his cheek, and they walked to the door. Feeling like a third wheel, Meagan started devising an exit strategy for herself, which didn't take too long.

While sitting on the couch with his arms wrapped around Maddie, Ethan's cell phone rang. With this, Maddie got up to go to the bathroom to give him privacy.

The phone call excited Ethan. There was a poker game later on that evening, and he was desperate to get in on it. After buying lunch for the three of them, he had little cash. He immediately thought of a plan. He needed to pay the other guy whose patience would soon wear thin. Ethan noticed Maddie's purse sitting on the coffee table. Staring at it, he tapped in Trevor's number.

"Dude, I got a problem and wonder if you could help me out." Ethan then explained further about the money he owed and how he had tried to get the extra cash but failed.

"Trev, man, could you loan me a few bucks until payday... Just enough to get in the game? I really need to pay this guy. You know me. I can get one-fifty in a poker game in my sleep."

"Really? I recall you recently losing your pocketknife."

"That guy got lucky. That's all."

"How much?"

"Seventy-five. I'll pay you back at the end of the week when I get paid. I promise."

Trevor and Ethan had been best friends for many years. He knew what kind of guy he was, and yet remained friends. He was fully aware of how well he played poker and that he would probably win the money back like he had said. It went against his better judgment, but Trevor agreed to loan him the money anyway. He certainly didn't want to lose a friendship over seventy-five dollars.

Thinking about Ethan losing his knife a few weeks ago, he was curious. "I gotta ask. Why did you put something as valuable as your pocketknife on the table?"

Ignoring Trevor's question, Ethan responded, "Thanks, Trev, man I owe you one. And I'll pay you back too. You'll see."

When Maddie returned, right away she noticed Ethan's mood had changed. After his phone call he seemed happier.

"That must have been good news."

"I'm just happy to be with my sweetheart," he said, wrapping his arms around her again.

⸺⸺◆⸺⸺

Ethan wanted to spend as much time as possible with Maddie during her spring break. She had two full days off, and he wanted her to spend it with him. For Monday night, he planned dinner at the park right after work. He imagined them sitting on a blanket on the grass without anyone near enough to hear their conversation, Ethan could then have her all to himself for a change. He didn't like sharing her with Meagan or her friends from work. He preferred it to be just the two of them.

With the meal finished, both were relaxed and in a good mood. Ethan took her hand. "Maddie, don't you think it's time for this relationship to go to the next level?" She gave him a curious look.

"What do you mean by the next level?"

"We have been seeing each other for a few months now, and it seems we should be more serious in our relationship... you know." He said moving even closer to her.

"Ethan, I like the level we are on. I mean, I don't think we should rush into anything. I'm happy with things just the way they are. Why mess it up?"

Unfortunately that wasn't the response Ethan was hoping to get.

Ethan paid Trevor back the money owed as promised, but he ignored his friend's advice about gambling. Ethan loved the chance to win and win big. Why Trevor didn't understand that, he didn't know. The games were friendly, and he never lost major money. His grandfather's pocketknife was the highest stake he had lost, and he vowed he wouldn't let that happened again.

Knowing Ethan was on his lunch break, Maddie called. "Ethan, hi. I hate to call you at work, but I need to let you know I can't make our date this evening... I'm working. Someone called in, and I have to cover for them."

"Seriously?" he moaned.

"Yeah, I'm sorry."

"Maddie, you were supposed to work two maybe three evenings a week, and just about every week someone calls in for you to cover their shift, and you do. It's getting old, Maddie."

"You're right. I guess I do need to say something. I'm really sorry, Ethan."

Rushing to get to the hotel, Maddie forgot to bring her supper. Sharon had called out again, and LeAnne was leaving at seven which left her working the rest of her shift with Carlton, again. "Hey, LeAnne, could I get you to do me a small favor, please? I left in such a hurry I forgot my supper. Would you run up to Sonic or Subway and get something for me?"

"Sure, what do you want?" She followed Maddie to the back to get her wallet. "Funny how you always end up working with Carlton, isn't it?"

"Do I? I hadn't really noticed."

"Carlton has a thing for you. He wasn't scheduled to come in this evening. I know this because I saw the schedule, and he wasn't on today. He called Burt and switched nights. You watch and notice how often you two work the same shift." She stood there in shock with her mouth hanging open thinking LeAnne had to be joking.

Maddie didn't put too much stock in what her co-worker was telling her. Over the many times she had worked with Carlton he never was out of line. They talked, laughed and joked around a lot but nothing out of the norm. Then it dawned on her. *Except for the times he puts his arm around me and teases me about my boyfriend being jealous and asks what Ethan would do if he saw us like that.* If anyone saw the look on her face at that moment, they would ask if she were alright.

Climbing into bed at one a.m. with her tired legs, she was mentally spent. The hotel was completely booked with a convention. She barely had time to eat the food LeAnne brought back for her. Walking back to a side desk she took bites between guests coming into the lobby. Fast food eaten quickly made for a lousy meal. Driving home she couldn't decide which she wanted most, to eat something or go to bed. The comfort of her bed won.

It was Monday morning, and spring break was over. Only eight o'clock in the morning and Mrs. Daniels was already in a sour mood. When it came to Mrs. Daniels, Maddie had developed a thick skin, and most of the time she didn't take it personally. But today was not the case. *What was this woman's problem?* She did everything she asked and more. Maddie was always polite and gave her no reason to criticize her work performance. It appeared she went out of her way to find fault with Maddie no matter how small.

Mrs. Reeves asked Maddie to stop in her office before she left for the day. Maddie was hoping it was good news about a teaching position that had come open, preferably Mrs. Daniels' class.

"Come on in, Maddie, have a seat. I have a question for you. Is everything going ok in the classroom?"

"Yes," she answered uncertainly. "Why do you ask?"

"Well, Mrs. Daniels has been complaining that you don't seem too happy in your work." Maddie was speechless.

"I...I don't know what made her say that. I honestly have no idea why she has a problem with me."

"It's not a problem with you. It's just that she thinks you may not be happy working here." Suddenly, something stirred in Maddie.

"If that were truly the case, why did she not bring this to me instead of going behind my back and taking it to you?" She said a bit abruptly.

"I don't know, but I will tell you this. She and I will have a talk also after you and I get things cleared."

Mrs. Reeves was aware of Maddie's second job. Most school teachers needed the second income to survive. She was simply glad that Maddie hadn't given up teaching before she had really gotten started.

"May I speak freely?"

"Yes, please do."

"Mrs. Daniels is not the easiest person to work with. I never know from day to day what mood she will be in. I had gotten where I could just ignore it, but I don't think I can ignore this. Perhaps Mrs. Daniels is the one who isn't happy with her job."

Mrs. Reeves heard everything Maddie was saying, and what she wasn't. Mrs. Daniels had worked at North Side for several years, and sensing there was more going on, she listened carefully.

"This is not a reprimand of any kind. Please don't take it that way. I just wanted to get your side of this issue before I went back and talked to her."

"Now tell me, how are you doing holding down two jobs?" Seeing another surprised look on Maddie's face, she couldn't help but smile. "Yes, I know all about your other job. Goodness, Maddie, half the teachers here hold second jobs. When I was a teacher I held two, and it about killed me, but I had no other choice." Mrs. Reeves then walked out from behind the desk and leaned against the front of it to be closer to Maddie. "My job isn't just dealing with the students. I'm here for you teachers as well. And I want you to feel free to come to me if you have a problem of any kind, and that also means if Mrs. Daniels is giving you a rough time. I will not allow one of our senior staff to run over our younger teachers, especially those that are just getting started. Understand?"

"Yes, ma'am."

After their meeting, Maddie felt more at ease. It was as if she had had a free session with a counselor. The problem with Mrs. Daniels still remained, but she wasn't as upset about it as she initially was. She assured Mrs. Reeves she would talk to Mrs. Daniels about this matter, but not alone. They would do so in her office, and hopefully this would be the end of it.

Six

Two more weeks until North Side would break for the summer, and not a day too soon as far as Maddie was concerned. Despite their meeting in front of Mrs. Reeves to clear the air, Mrs. Daniels had made the last few weeks unpleasant. She was tempted on the last day of school after all the children were gone to tell this woman everything she had been keeping inside.

As a young girl, Maddie was taught the golden rule. She knew that vengeance belonged to the Lord. She had turned the other cheek and tried treating Mrs. Daniels the way she would want to be treated. She had dealt with her complaints and criticism as long as she could. This woman has stolen the joy of her job and invaded her life with her negative attitude. Yes, it was time Maddie stood up for herself and put Mrs. Daniels in her place. She would not scream or shout, but firmly tell her of the hurt she had caused.

Four o'clock finally arrived, and Maddie hustled out of the school building to her car. If she hurried to her apartment, she could get in a twenty minute nap before leaving for her other job. The couch was so comfy as her tired frame nearly melted into the cushions. She set an alarm on her phone just in case she overslept, but Meagan came in before it was needed.

"Oh great, you haven't left yet. Seems like I hardly see you anymore."

"What are you doing home so early?"

"The boss gave us the rest of the afternoon off. Ha-ha and, girlfriend, he didn't need to tell me twice. I was out of that office within five minutes. But I'm glad I caught you. I have something to tell you."

"You talk while I change." Getting off the couch and walking toward her room Meagan continued to talk as she followed.

"A couple of months ago, I went bowling with some friends, and while we were there I sort of met this guy. Then, I ran into him at Mike's a few weeks ago when a bunch of us went out. Well, today I was having lunch at Wendy's, and guess who walked in? He and his friend sat at the table beside me, and we started talking. And to make a long story short, I have a date with him this Friday night."

"That's wonderful, Meagan, what's his name?" she asked slipping her shoes on.

"Ryan, and I can't wait until Friday!"

"I am so happy for you." Looking for her hairbrush, she continued, "Maybe we can double sometime. I want to hear more, but unfortunately I gotta run. Promise you'll tell me everything later?"

Within ten seconds Maddie was walking out the door.

Meagan stood in the now empty room looking at the closed door Maddie just exited from, a little out of breath. "I...I think I just ran a sprint."

— ◦ ◦ —

Clocking in right on time, Maddie started her routine at the hotel. Carlton started his as well looking for reasons to be close to his favorite staff member. She learned that LeAnne was right. Carlton had changed the schedule so he could work with her on multiple occasions, and lately he had been buying dinner for the two of them while at work, even though she would tell him she brought her own. It was becoming uncomfortable.

Maddie was on the phone with a customer when she heard her stomach growl. It had been over six hours since she had eaten. If anyone walked by, they were sure to hear the odd noise. Ethan would be stopping by on her dinner break in half an hour with burgers and fries. She could hardly wait.

"Maddie, I've ordered a pizza. It should be here in about twenty minutes. When you get your break, come to the back," Carlton requested

"Aah, I'm sorry, Carlton. I'm having my break with Ethan. He's bringing my dinner. You should have checked with me before you ordered. I'm…sorry."

Carlton held his composure, but inside he didn't like what he heard. "No problem. Just offering that's all." Not meaning to hear any of the conversation, LeAnne didn't make eye contact with either of them.

At seven on the dot, Maddie clocked out and joined Ethan in his car in the parking lot. In a white paper bag was a Wendy's burger and fries waiting for her. They ate and enjoyed their short time together. "Thirty minutes for lunch or dinner break should be against the law. I mean, you barely have time to eat. I bet bosses and CEO's don't take thirty minute lunch breaks," she complained. It really wasn't like her to complain like that, and Ethan looked at her with questioning eyes.

"Are you okay? How about I bring you a frosty after work?"

"Thanks, that's sweet of you, but I have to say no thank you. That will be entirely too late to eat anything, especially dessert," she declined with disappointment. "Thanks for bringing me my dinner. I really do appreciate it." She said giving him a kiss. "I've got to go back in now. Talk to you tomorrow?"

"Sure, I'll call you." She gave him another quick kiss, and then walked back inside not knowing Carlton had been watching them almost the entire time.

Maddie was busy the rest of the night with reservations, assisting guests as they came in and out, and giving dinner recommendations. Carlton had stayed in the office mostly, so she hardly saw him the rest of the evening. He typically found projects that allowed him to be near her, and they would joke back and forth and chat about nothing in particular, but not tonight. Something was off with him, and the other staff noticed it as well. He was cold toward her and snapped at her when he spoke. This continued, and after a week of his attitude, she could no longer endure it.

"Carlton, got a second?"

"Sure, what do you need?"

"I need to know if you are upset with me."

"Why would I be upset with you, Maddie?"

"I don't know. You tell me. For the past week, you've been cold toward me and when you speak to me it isn't very civil. And that's not like you. What have I done to upset you?"

"Maddie, please go back to the front desk. The hotel is full of guests."

I don't know what it is that I keep doing to tick people off lately. She was being hard on herself, and she couldn't keep her mind off of it for the rest of her shift. Ten minutes before her time to leave, it dawned on her what it was. *He's mad at me for having my dinner break with Ethan the other day and not him.*

When her shift ended, she sought him out. "Carlton, are you upset with me because I had dinner with Ethan after you ordered us pizza last week?" Carlton looked at her with disinterest.

"Maddie, I'm not upset with you. Your shift is over. Now go home."

"Ethan and I planned to spend my dinner break together that morning. I'm sorry if I hurt your feelings. It was never my intent."

"Good night, Maddie."

Carlton was not even going to discuss it. He sat there pouting as she left his office.

It was finally Friday, the last day of school. It had been a tough week. Between Mrs. Daniels' mood swings and Carlton giving her the cold shoulder along with less hours, Maddie was about to lose it. The children she helped with were more mature than these two adults.

"Mrs. Daniels, I need to speak with you before I leave today. Is that possible?"

"Alright, but you will need to be brief. I have a lot to do before I can leave today."

"It won't take long. I assure you," Maddie responded kindly.

Maddie had devised a way to get everything off her chest with Mrs. Daniels. She had rehearsed her speech in the car on the way to work this morning, and now she was ready. She also prayed and asked the Lord to allow this to be resolved so she could be done with this uncomfortable and stressful situation.

Before leaving, each student gave Maddie a big hug and told her how much they loved and would miss her over the summer.

She also received endearing gifts of affection, colored pictures and candy. One little boy gave her a handful of flowers, which were actually dandelions and grass, but Maddie doted over them as if they were a dozen red roses.

"Oh, thank you, William. That is so sweet of you." She bent down and gave him a hug causing the little boy's face to light up with delight. "I have the perfect vase at home to put these in. I'm going to miss you over the summer, but I know you will have lots of fun." He then began telling her about his plans for the summer that included doing special things with his grandpa.

Finally, the last student was safely on their way home which meant she no longer had kindergarten students to look after, and her heart saddened with this thought.

Praying silently Maddie walked back to the classroom to confront Mrs. Daniels, and with each step she became more nervous. She left the door open unintentionally so anyone walking by could hear their conversation. When she walked in, she found Mrs. Daniels sitting at her desk mulling over some papers. As she began to speak, she could feel her body beginning to slightly shake. She took a deep breath and demanded her nerves to settle.

"Mrs. Daniels, I have something to say to you."

Feeling her body tremble, Maddie persevered and let everything fall off her chest. She told Mrs. Daniels how she had taken all of the joy out of her job. "What have I done to cause you to dislike me so?" She continued in detail to Mrs. Daniels how she had disrespected her in front of the class and had attempted to discredit her by going behind her back to Mrs. Reeves. After she finished, Maddie braced herself for the hard blow from this cold, hard woman. She was ready for anything.

Mrs. Daniels sat there looking slightly shocked. She couldn't believe Maddie was speaking to her like this. "Wait just a minute, young lady," she snapped back quickly with a little too much volume.

Walking by in the hallway, Mrs. Reeves heard voices coming from Mrs. Daniels' classroom, so she stepped inside and closed the door. Maddie hadn't noticed her, but Mrs. Daniels had and knew she needed to get the situation under control quickly.

Maddie immediately cut her off. "Yes, I am a young lady, but you've treated me like a disobedient child that needs to be told every move to make and then scolded me for the way I did it."

"Ladies, it's important to get to the bottom of this, but let's make sure we do it in a Christian manner."

Maddie quickly whipped around unsure of exactly what Mrs. Reeves had overheard, and actually didn't care. She was glad she was standing there. This way she would be aware of the entire ugly mess firsthand instead of Mrs. Daniels going behind her back again with only one side of the story.

The undeniable truth had been revealed, and Mrs. Daniels couldn't argue her way out. She stumbled over her words as she spoke. Maddie sensed she was reaching for anything and everything to say, but there wasn't one plausible reason for treating her that way. Feeling like she had finally won the battle, Maddie suddenly noticed her eyes.

Oh no, don't you dare cry on me, woman! This is your doing, not mine.

"Mrs. Daniels, has Maddie done something to cause you to dislike her or to treat her unprofessionally?"

After a half hour discussion, the truth finally came out and Mrs. Daniels revealed the reason for her resentment. She felt the children loved and cared for Maddie more than they did her, their teacher. Neither Mrs. Reeves nor Maddie ever considered Mrs. Daniels to be a jealous person. That acknowledgment caught them both completely off guard. The previous school year rapidly flashed through her mind like a movie on fast forward. Throughout the year, the children were constantly hugging Maddie, giving her pictures they had colored just for her, and telling her about their pets and best friends. Mrs. Daniels on the other hand rarely received such attention or affectionate rewards. Maddie couldn't help but feel sorry for her.

Without warning, Mrs. Daniels jumped up from behind the desk and gave Maddie a hug apologizing for her behavior. Shocked, it took a second for Maddie's brain to catch up to what was happening, but then she graciously accepted and let her anger subside.

. During the entire drive home, the conversation between her and Mrs. Daniels replayed in her mind. It wasn't supposed to be this way. By now she was supposed to be teaching her own class and fully enjoying it, not quarreling over who gets the most attention from the students. Emotionally drained, she pulled into her parking space and sat there a few seconds before opening the door.

"Must of have been some last day of school party. You looked whooped," Meagan pointed out, chuckling as she tossed her purse on the coffee table and saw Maddie lying on the couch.

"Meagan, I've made a decision. I'm done with being a teacher's aide."

"You had it out with Mrs. Daniels, didn't you?"

"Yes, we got it all cleared up. It was all jealousy...not how I did my job, not my attitude, just jealousy. She was jealous over the way the kids showed love and attention toward me and not her. I'm telling ya, Meagan, I'm done."

Saturday morning, Maddie slept until eleven. Sleeping that late was unusual for her unless she was ill or unable to sleep through the night. Last night found her mind restless with worry about her job situation. Like puzzle pieces being assembled, she looked at this problem from all angles, and it seemed that her only real options were to keep things as they were or to quit both jobs and start over.

Both jobs were stressful, so it really wouldn't matter which one she quit. *Lord, I don't understand. I can't seem to get this job situation worked out. I have to have something that pays enough for me to live on. I really don't want to go back and live with my parents. Nothing seems to be working out.* The idea of facing another school year as a teacher's aide made her stomach churn, and working for someone who pouts when they don't get their way frustrated her. Before falling asleep, she finally concluded that she had the entire summer to figure out what kind of job she liked and that paid decently. The fact that there were people everywhere looking for that same job failed to give any comfort.

Tossing and turning, she was reminded in her heart: **I LOVE YOU, MY CHILD. I WILL NEVER LEAVE YOU NOR FORSAKE YOU.**

Looking at her phone, she had missed two calls from Ethan which didn't really bother her. She wasn't in the mood to deal with him today either. He too was difficult to be around at times. Just seeing his profile picture and phone number made her tired. Suddenly she remembered their conversation about taking their relationship to the next level. She was unsure of what level they were on now, and she didn't want to think about it and certainly didn't want to talk to him in her current mood.

Maddie kindly greeted Sharon and a few other employees as she walked in to start her day, but that lightness quickly faded when she saw that Carlton was on the schedule for today as well. Since the pizza episode when his feelings were hurt, she had been indirectly avoiding him by simply keeping to her work duties so they didn't speak often. She considered him a friend after they started working together, but now it was awkward whenever they interacted.

Walking out of the small office toward the front desk, Carlton nearly ran into Maddie. For a brief moment they stood face to face. She immediately felt uncomfortable. "Ooh, excuse me, I'm sorry," Maddie automatically responded.

"No problem. How are you, Maddie?" Carlton asked looking right into her eyes.

"I'm fine thanks, and you?"

"I'm good. Seems like I haven't talked to you in a long time."

"You've....kind of been avoiding me."

"I'm not avoiding you. What makes you think that?"

So, you're going to turn this around and let it be about me, a misunderstanding on my part. Ha-ha, no you don't. "Yes, I believe you have." The front desk phone began to ring which allowed her conveniently to leave him standing there to go do her job.

Most times she was indifferent when the phone rang, but not this time. She was absolutely delighted the phone was ringing right at that moment. She didn't want to talk to Carlton, not about work, not about anything. He had pouted for two weeks, and she was done with trying to appease him. But since she opened her big mouth and said what she did, there would be no getting around it.

Still disheartened about her job situation, but better rested, Maddie and Meagan walked into their Sunday School classroom and sat down in their usual seats. Meagan was still floating from her date with her new guy. Maddie had yet to meet him, but from what she had heard, he sounded wonderful.

Caroline Dunning had been teaching the single ladies' Sunday School class for the past month. She appeared to be enjoying it, but she still had some nervous jitters each time she stepped behind the podium. These ladies were fun and easy to be around, and they seemed to respond positively to Caroline as well. They were becoming more comfortable around her, and they usually learned something new each week.

"Good morning, ladies. How was your weekend?" Caroline asked as she plopped her stuff down in a nearby chair. She always engaged the ladies in some conversation before starting the class. This not only helped her get to know the girls better, but gave her a chance to catch her breath before starting the lesson. After a few minutes of casual chatter and taking prayer requests, Caroline was just about to begin the lesson when she remembered to make an announcement. "Oh my, I almost forgot. Do any of you know of anyone needing a job? Dunning Plumbing desperately needs a full-time receptionist. If you do, please let me know." Caroline and Katie were tired of filling that position and had decided to take matters into their own hands.

As Caroline spoke about Jesus and his ministry while He walked on this earth, all Maddie could think about was the receptionist position. *Lord, is this You giving me the opportunity for a new job?*

After the service, Meagan and Maddie ate lunch with a few other young singles from their church at O'Charley's in

Rivergate. The conversation centered around summer plans and Meagan's new boyfriend.

"So when am I going to get to meet this guy?" Maddie asked.

"I don't know. With your work schedule it's hard to plan anything."

"I know. I'm sorry."

"So tell me, what's your game plan? You said you were done being a teacher's aide. Are you going to try and get more hours at the hotel?"

"Oh goodness no. I can't work with Carlton every day." She surprised even herself with her quick response.

After heading back to their apartment, Meagan spent the rest of the afternoon talking on the phone with Ryan, and Maddie chose to lie on the couch watching her favorite DVD while her mind continued to churn over her job predicament. *I'll talk to Caroline this evening.*

"So you're interested in the receptionist job. That's great. But, Maddie, it's a full-time position, and you already have a full-time job at North Side."

"I know. I was just wondering what the qualifications were, what the job would entail, how much it pays, all that stuff."

"Are you thinking of leaving North Side and teaching?" No one could ever accuse Caroline of being a nosy person, but her concern for Maddie was apparent as she asked the question. Seeing Maddie's facial expression, she led her to a quiet area where they could talk in private. After listening to all of the details around her situation, Caroline gave her the best advice she could.

"I'm sure you have prayed about this, but in case you haven't, you need to. Tell the Lord everything, Maddie, even though He already knows all of it. Tell Him all of your hurts, frustrations and needs. If there is anything I can do to help, just let me know." They hugged, and Caroline continued. "Now, let me tell you about this job."

When Maddie went to bed that night, she prayed and asked the Lord to help her make the right decision. "Dear Heavenly Father, you know I've always wanted to be a school teacher, but it doesn't seem to be working out. These last few months have been a mess. I've been treated poorly, Lord, and overlooked again for the teaching position I was promised. I seem to bring out the worst in my co-workers Mrs. Daniels and now Carlton. What am I to do? Father, I'm tired of dealing with it all, and I really could use a good night's sleep for a change. Dear Father, if you don't want me to take the receptionist job, will you please allow me to not be a good fit for that, and keep them from offering it to me. For it is in Your Son Jesus' precious and holy name that I ask these things. Amen."

Seven

Sitting in Richard's office waiting for Brian to come in, Maddie was surprised by her calmness and by how normal this felt. She had never been a receptionist before, but it seemed like a nice change of pace and a challenge she was more than ready for.

"Maddie Abbott, this is my brother Brian. He and I run things around here. I'm sure Caroline filled you in on what goes on here, and what your duties will be if you choose to take this position." Richard, already knowing Maddie, would hire her on the spot, but Brian had never met her and he would go through the standard interviewing process.

"Yes, she did. I didn't hear anything that scared me."

Chuckling, "Great. If we offered you this position, when would be the earliest you could start?"

"As soon as you need me. School is out for the summer, so I don't have to be available to them right now. But I do have a part-time job that I'm ending as soon as I find something else. My hours there are mostly weekends and some evenings. When I have a new position, I will give both employers a two week notice.

"Sounds like you have things under control. I think Brian has a few questions for you, so I'll leave you two to do that."

She was sure she would be nervous talking with Brian since she didn't know him at all like she did Richard and Caroline, but surprisingly she wasn't. It was more like chatting with an old friend. He asked the typical interview questions about her education, skills and reasons for leaving her current job. After a short time, Richard came back in. Listening to them banter amused her, and caused her to miss her own brother.

"Richard, you and Caroline know Miss Abbott. And from what I have heard today, if she wants the job, she's got it. She can start first thing in the morning as far as I'm concerned."

"Well, what about it, Maddie? Do you want this job?"

"Yes sir, I do," she smiled. An unexpected peacefulness washed over her. Being offered the position wasn't in her plan, much less accepting it all in the same day.

"Great, welcome aboard. If you have the time today, Brian will get you started with your paperwork. And there are a few other formalities we need to go through, then Caroline will show you around. If not, we can schedule that for another day this week."

"No, I have the time."

"Good. Don't be afraid to ask any questions that you may have."

"Oh, Maddie, you don't have any pets, do you?" Brian asked.

"No sir, why?"

"Oh, just asking."

After everyone left his office, Brian took a deep breath and slowly exhaled. He was relieved to have this position filled. Hopefully it would be a permanent fit. After he thought about it, he smiled thinking about which Dunning would be more relieved

On her way home, Maddie thanked the Lord for answering her prayer and giving her a new job. She mentally made a list of things she needed to do today, and the first thing was to type up her resignation letter and give it to Carlton this evening. She would stop by and give Mrs. Reeves hers after Lunch. Hearing her cell phone buzz, she glanced and saw Ethan's face pop up on the screen. She let it ring through to voicemail and would return his call later to tell him the good news when she got home.

Mrs. Reeves saw this day coming. Maddie Abbott wasn't someone to put on hold for too long. She seriously wondered how the girl was making ends meet. The new job sounded wonderful, and Mrs. Reeves was truly happy for her although she would miss her. Wishing her all the best, she revealed to Maddie she hated to have someone who was so skilled with the students slip through her hands. "Maybe it isn't the Lord's will for you to teach here at North Side, but, believe me, our loss is your new employer's gain."

Maddie thanked her for her kindness and for being an excellent role model. And on her way out of the school for the last time, she thanked the Lord for having placed Mrs. Reeves into her life these past few years.

Maddie's parents were very pleased as well as relieved when she shared her news. They worried about her living on her own with such little income. Ethan was happy for her too, mostly because she would be quitting her job at the hotel. He didn't like her being around Carlton. Secretly, he wanted to see Carlton's reaction when she handed him her resignation. He wished he could stand beside Maddie with his arm wrapped tightly around her waist with a sneering grin that pierced though Carlton's losing heart. The two had never exchanged any cross words, but there was a mutual dislike between them that didn't need to be voiced.

Like ships in the night, Meagan was coming home just as Maddie was walking out. A brief conversation covering the basics usually occurred and then they parted. This was the new normal as of the past several months. She was thrilled her friend had a new job which meant things were looking up for her, but she was even more excited that she would have her roommate back.

"Dinner for one again. What will it be?" Meagan spoke to no one. She pulled out a Lean Cuisine frozen dinner. "Oh yes, five cheese rigatoni with iced tea of course." She didn't mind being alone, but would rather not eat alone. Sitting in the living room with her microwaved meal in hand and tea sitting on the coffee table, she ate while Pat and Vanna challenged her mind with letters and the big wheel.

Seeing the envelope lying on his desk, Carlton immediately recognized the handwriting. Quite sure of himself, he assumed Maddie had poured her heart out to him on paper which pleased him considerably. Closing the door to his office for privacy, he couldn't wait to open it.

His excitement soon turned to disappointment. Carlton instead found a typed sheet that seemed way too formal. After only reading through the second sentence, a dreadful feeling sunk into the pit of his stomach. "What?" As he read further down the page, each word assured him she was definitely not pouring her heart out to him; she had resigned instead. With the words still echoing in his mind, he smacked his leg with the letter in disbelief. He couldn't accept that Maddie had given her two week notice.

During her next shift, Maddie moved through her tasks normally making sure she left no room for Carlton to be critical of her work. She was almost home free until Carlton walked up to her fifteen minutes before her shift ended and asked her what was going on.

"Excuse me."

"What's your resignation all about? You want a raise? Is that it? Not getting enough hours?" he demanded.

"No, Carlton, I do not want a raise, nor do I want more hours. I am quitting. Two weeks from today will be my last shift. I'm leaving." He stood in front of her staring at her stone-faced before he continued to speak.

"Why?"

"I explained it all in my resignation letter. Did you not read it?" she responded ignoring her irritation.

"Yes, I read it. So what. You got another job. You can still work here a couple nights a week. I don't see the problem. I'm sure you need the money."

Unsure if he meant for his words to be insulting or not, she let them go keeping her composure. *He would have no idea if I needed the money or not, we never spoke of personal issues and most certainly not of my financial situation.*

Carlton despised losing, and he was on the wrong end of the stick when it came to Maddie. He tried getting close to her, with the hope of dating her, but Ethan was an obstacle. Most of the pretty girls that had worked with Carlton he had either dated or tried to date. He truly believed that he needed more time with this one.

"With my new job I won't need a second income. There is no need for me to stay."

"You're still mad at me, aren't you?" he said with a little too much confidence. "You're mad because I never asked you out."

"What?!"

"Maddie, dating co-workers is never a good thing, especially when you are the supervisor. But now that you'll be working somewhere else, there is no reason we can't."

"First of all, I never wanted to go out with you. I thought we were friends. And second, *you're* the one that got mad. Going out with you never ever entered my mind. I'm seeing someone, and you know that." Suddenly a light switched on in Maddie's head. "Aha, I was right. That's why you got mad at me...Ethan. You got upset that night because Ethan showed up here, and we ate out in his car on my dinner break all the while you had plans for us to eat together in the break room." Clarity rushed over her like a refreshing breeze.

"Believe what you want. You know...it...it doesn't matter. When you need a job again, you'll be back here, and maybe, just maybe I'll hire you back," Carlton said storming off.

Realizing it was five minutes past the end of her shift; she clocked out quickly and left. On her way home, she could only think about the way he had talked to her and how he had tried to turn the tables making it her fault. "How am I going to deal with him for the next two weeks?" she spoke out loud to herself. Then she quickly realized she wouldn't have to deal with him every day for two weeks, just six more days. "Unless...unless I can give my hours away to Sharon or LeAnne" As she laid out her plan, she became less angry.

It was a beautiful morning, and Maddie chose to not allow Carlton to invade her mind. She still had a few days to work at the hotel and trusted he wouldn't be there. The night before she and Carlton exchanged words, and it still bothered her. She had prayed about the matter and now worked to fill her mind with positive, joyful thoughts. She shifted her focus on her driving and then flipped on the radio. "Yes," she decided. She would cast Carlton out of her mind and look forward to a new day and a new job.

As she walked in the door at Dunning Plumbing, an older man thoughtfully greeted her and offered her a doughnut.

"Hello, young lady, my name is Todd Dunning. I started this company many years ago. How about a doughnut? They're fresh from Krispy Kreme."

"Thank you." She giggled. "I love doughnuts, especially the Boston cream filled. I'm Maddie Abbott, the new receptionist," she introduced herself before taking a bite of her doughnut. Todd had been told that a new receptionist had been hired, and he couldn't resist greeting her with doughnuts. "Mmm...that is soooo good. Of course, now I need a cup of coffee."

"Please, allow me. Let me guess, sugar and lots of cream?"

"Yeees," she giggled again. Maddie found Todd Dunning to be very delightful.

Brian came around the corner and started to introduce Maddie to his father, but quickly discovered it unnecessary. She excused herself and walked over to the desk to start her day.

"Thanks for the doughnut, Mr. Dunning."

"You are most welcome." It was obvious to Brian that these two had hit it off immediately.

Caroline arrived at the office to begin showing Maddie the ropes and the general layout of how the business operates. She was a quick study so her assistance wouldn't be needed very long.

"Each Thursday we make our bank deposits. Why Thursdays? I have no idea, but that's when we do it. I'm sure you know how to make a deposit, but there are a few additional things we do when making it for the company."

The process wasn't difficult. It was simply inputting the same information in different places, and to Maddie that seemed redundant. She figured there was a good reason for it, but at the moment she didn't have a clue.

"Brian or Richard used to make the deposits. Then it got to where they wouldn't get to the bank on a regular schedule, and things piled up, which made it hard for Katie to keep the books straight not to mention paying bills. So Katie began making the deposits, and from there it became the receptionist's responsibility."

"Each week Brian will count the money, fill out the deposit slip, and have it ready for you to drop off at the bank on your lunch hour. So, let's log in and get started." Maddie listened attentively and made a few notes on things that she didn't want to forget.

"Of course you don't deposit the credit card slips. The companies that process the cards take care of all that. The credit card amount will be separate from the checks and cash, then added later to make sure it all balances. But Katie does that." Caroline continued explaining their process stopping periodically to make sure Maddie was still following. "There is a place to record credit card transactions and another one for cash, and checks are like cash. And we keep every deposit receipt just like you do for you own personal deposits. There is always some cash here in the office, but Brian and Richard deal with that, so you don't need to worry with that. There may be times they take cash out of the bag, and if they do, they will let you know so everything will balance out. If it doesn't balance, we have to go back over this until we find the error."

Caroline assured her it would get easier and faster each week eventually taking only about thirty minutes. As she continued with the details, it sounded simple and effortless, but today it was a little bit overwhelming for Maddie, but she looked at it as a new challenge.

"At most places, the receptionist doesn't have the responsibility of making deposits, but here you do. To be honest, I didn't mind doing it because I got to be out and away from the office," she grinned. "It makes for a longer lunch hour."

The day finally arrived: her last day to work at the hotel, and the last day to deal with Carlton and his attitude. Her plan was to offer any of her shifts to anyone who wanted them, but she ended up only giving two away. The final days were blessed with not having to work alongside him, but today, unfortunately wasn't the case. She groaned under her breath when she saw his name had been added to the day's work schedule. *Lord, I asked...I begged for You to not allow the two of us to work the same shifts again, but his name has been added to today's schedule.* Mumbling to herself, she headed to the front desk. "Five hours, Maddie. Just five more hours until all of this will be over forever." To say the evening was busy would be an understatement. The hotel was booked solid with three separate large groups, one being a wedding party. Crazed women running around dealing with a wedding says enough about how the night went.

Phones ringing nonstop, reservations being taken, directions given along with the never ending question of 'where's the best place to eat around here?', Maddie didn't hardly have time to go to the bathroom much less take her dinner break. Hungry or not, she wasn't about to ask Carlton to cover for her while she ate. Instead, she snuck a few bites here and there when she had the opportunity. All the while, Carlton was just as busy running back and forth from the office to the front desk. She silently thanked the Lord for the busy shift and his civility.

Eleven p.m. on the dot, Maddie clocked out for the last time. Her back ached, as did her feet, but her heart was feeling light and relieved. On her way home, she spoke out loud to the Lord and thanked Him for getting her through these past two weeks. "No more working nights and weekends; no more calls to come in on my day off; and no more Carlton." She was so happy to be rid of this situation. She was happy to put the entire experience with Carlton and the hotel behind her, like closing a book never to be read again.

Exhausted and achy she crawled into bed and would have been asleep in record time had it not been for her cell phone.

"Hi, Ethan. Sorry I couldn't take your call earlier. The hotel was so busy...everybody in the world is staying there this week," she embellished. He had been away visiting his parents and had called twice already, and she didn't have the time to talk to him. Even as tired as she was, she couldn't put him off any longer.

"How's it goin'?"

"Well, I got home about ten minutes ago, and I've just crawled into bed. It's been one long hard day."

"I would come by, but I've just arrived home myself, and I'm beat."

"How was your trip to see your parents?"

"Fine. Nothing exciting going on, you know how it is when you go back home to see the folks. But we had a good time, and I saw a few friends I hadn't seen since the last time I was there. Funny, they always want me to come see them whenever I'm home, but they never even consider coming to see me. I'll let you go so you can go to bed, and I'll call you tomorrow."

"Okay, good night, Ethan."

"Alright, deal me in." Ethan said to the big man shuffling the cards after he ended his call and sat back down at the table.

There had been a poker game going at a friend's house since seven that evening. At this stage Ethan was doing fairly well, but that wasn't good enough for him. Trevor played about three or four hands then was done. When gambling, he had a firm rule: betting money went in his left pocket and winnings in his right. Money never came out of the right pocket, and when the left was empty, it was time to quit.

Tonight instead of going home, Trevor hung out at the table and carefully watched the hands being played. He noticed that Ethan was on a down swing compared to earlier rounds. Stephen, the guy with the intense poker face, was using it to his advantage. No one could read him. On the last hand, everyone had folded except Ethan. The hour was late, and the two were staring each other down trying to read each other's bluff. At the last call, Ethan fell short, and Stephen won, again. Trevor then spoke where only Ethan could hear him. "Dude, it's late. Just call it a night before you lose any more money."

Ethan didn't like getting out of a game except on his own terms. He had a hundred dollars left, and he was determined to walk away with the pile of cash sitting in front of Stephen.

"Trev, I'm fine. I've got plenty of cash to play with."

The tone of Ethan's voice told him he was wasting his time. Ethan would not listen.

"Maybe you should listen to your friend and go on home," Stephen said, trying to provoke him.

"You should be more worried about this next hand than my friend," Ethan responded.

They played another hand, and Ethan was sure he had won when suddenly Stephen threw down a straight flush.

When Ethan got up to stretch his legs and get himself a cold drink, Trevor walked over to him. "Seriously Ethan, will you listen to me? You need to quit."

"Trevor, you worry too much. Have some adventure. Get back in the game. I can win this. I know I can."

Eyeing his friend, Trevor could tell he wasn't concerned for a second. He was enjoying himself; Ethan loved the thrill of a poker game. "Whatever, I'm going home."

Trevor couldn't sit and watch his friend lose his last dollar, again. Nor could he bear seeing him carelessly toss sentimental items that couldn't be replaced into the center of poker table when his cash ran out. He had witnessed this with the pocketknife his grandfather had given him years ago. And he didn't want to be available for Ethan to ask for a loan.

Meeting tonight at O'Charley's for dinner, Meagan would finally get to introduce her best friend to her new boyfriend. She had been waiting to do this for a while now, but with Maddie's crazy work schedule, it was pretty much impossible. She invited Ethan out of obligation, but wasn't looking forward to him coming along. To be honest, she didn't want to sit across the table from him. She didn't want to force herself to make conversation with him, and then watch him stick Maddie with the check, as he most often did, giving some lame excuse why. What she saw in that guy was a complete mystery to Meagan.

They had only been waiting in the foyer for a couple of minutes when Maddie arrived. Both stood up as Meagan excitedly introduced her dear friend to Ryan. Right off the bat, Ryan remembered Maddie from the ballgame and Mike's Ice Cream & Coffee Bar. He held his composure and didn't mention their meeting prior to that moment hoping she wouldn't remember it either.

After the introductions, they shook hands and said warm hellos with smiles on their faces. Their name was then called shortly after so they were led to their table and given menus. Out of politeness Meagan asked if Ethan would be joining them.

"No, he isn't available this evening, and that's ok." After giving the waitress their drink order, the conversation continued and Ryan asked who Ethan was. Mattie explained that she and Ethan had been seeing each other for several months, and that it was nothing serious. Ryan also asked how long the girls had been friends, which opened up the door for lots of fun memories.

"I think that's great. I have a good buddy, and we hang out a lot, but we're not roommates. I live in a tiny apartment that's too small for one person, much less a roommate." Both girls chuckled at his banter. As the conversation continued, Maddie found out that Ryan worked for Dunning Plumbing.

"Oh really? I've just started there as the receptionist."

"I heard we had gotten a new one, but I'm out on jobs most of the day. So, how do you like it?"

"So far, I love it. It's going to take some time to get it all down to a routine, but I'll do it."

Before any more could be said the waitress arrived with their tea and water.

Maddie's earlier spoken words about Ethan echoed in her head. Their relationship really wasn't serious, and she truly didn't know why she was still dating him. But there were times he made her feel good about herself. Maybe that was the extent of it; maybe that was all there was or would ever be to their relationship.

Watching them Maddie could tell Ryan and Meagan got along very well. She laughed often, and he appeared to be very attentive to her. When they held hands, the sparkle in Meagan's eye couldn't be missed. She was happy for her friend, but a persistent sadness that she couldn't explain filled her heart.

After returning home from the restaurant, Ryan stayed for a while. Not wanting to intrude, Maddie said her goodnights then headed to her room to give them privacy like Meagan had done for her and Ethan on several occasions.

"Your friend is nice. I can see why you two are close."

"Yes, I just wish she would dump that jerk Ethan...I'm afraid he's going to hurt her."

"She said they weren't serious."

"Hey, what about your friend? Do you think he would like to meet her?"

Ryan's eyes widened with slight panic at her suggestion. He wanted to avoid keeping a secret from her, but also didn't want to betray his best friend and tell Meagan these two had already met.

Noticing the deer-in-the-headlights look on his face, Meagan asked, "Is that not a good idea?

"No, no, I don't...that's not a..."

"Great! We should arrange a way for the two of them to meet," Meagan said eagerly without really hearing Ryan's response. The wheels were already turning in her head.

"Oh no," Ryan chuckled waving both hands. "Setting your best friend up on a blind date goes against the guy code." Meagan grinned at him and gave him a gentle kiss. The discussion was then forgotten.

Once in her room, Maddie tried to call Ethan. It went straight to voicemail. Sighing, Maddie considered their relationship. They were dating, but it was certainly not a normal kind of dating. Their dates were mostly at odd times, like Saturday during the day versus the evening or on Thursday night instead of the weekend like most couples. They spent most of their time at her apartment which led her to another thought. For the first time, Maddie became conscious of how many times she had paid the bill when they were out, and not been paid back like he claimed he would. She had chalked it up to his finances, but now it didn't sit right. *Wasn't that what dating is mostly about? Going out on the weekends and the guy paying for your meal or the movie?* Every time she invited him to church, he just said 'thanks, but no thanks.' She had gotten to the point where she just stopped asking him. That heavy sadness from earlier flooded in once again, only a bit stronger now, and the reason was staring her right in the face: Ethan.

Ethan didn't treat her the special way she desired, and he didn't look at her like Ryan looked at Meagan. Her thoughts surprised her. The notion of them no longer dating really didn't stir up any sad feelings. She actually felt numb about it. Pulling back the covers with Ethan on her mind, she picked up her cell phone and tried calling him again. Maybe if she heard his voice right now she would feel better about their relationship. Still no answer.

Slipping under the sheet on this summer night, she settled in with her pillow just right, and laid there staring at the ceiling as if the solution were written up there in bold print waiting for her to notice it. Eventually she could feel herself drifting off to sleep. She loved that feeling of falling into a welcomed slumber, but it was rudely interrupted by the sudden ringing from her phone. The sound nearly caused her to jump out of bed.

"Hello."

"Maddie, did I wake you?"

"Aah, no, I was almost…aah, no I'm awake."

"Oh, my little Maddie can't keep late hours," he chuckled.

They chatted briefly about nothing in particular, and then Maddie asked him about his evening.

"It was boring. A cousin from back home was in town and wanted me to show him around Nashville. Believe me, you would have been bored as well because…to be honest, my cousin is a bore. And I didn't want to put you through that. Besides, he hits on every pretty woman he sees, and he would not have been able to resist such a beautiful face as yours." Maddie was unsure how to respond. Did he really feel that way toward her? If so, why was she just now hearing it?

"So when does your…cousin leave?"

"His plane takes off tomorrow morning. I hate getting up early on a Sunday, but gotta get him to the airport." A few silent moments passed before Ethan spoke again. "Sorry I couldn't come over this evening, but with my cousin here. You understand, don't you?"

For the first time Ethan felt a twinge in his stomach for not being totally honest with her, but it was easy for him. He convinced himself it really wasn't much of a lie. *My cousin was in town, and I did show him around Nashville. Maybe I should have left out the part about his departure. I had to lie to her. No girl wants to hear her boyfriend would rather spend his Friday night sitting at a poker table with a bunch of guys than spending it with her. She would never understand my love for the game.*

"I understand, no problem," she said without feeling.

After their call ended, Maddie settled back down under the sheet and tried to go to sleep, but she kept thinking about Ryan and Meagan's relationship. She didn't want to compare it with her and Ethan, but couldn't keep from it.

"So, I'll see you tomorrow?"

"Yes, you can come by and hang out here if you don't mind," Meagan replied.

"I'd be happy to hang out with you anywhere, anytime." Ryan gently brought Meagan close to himself and gave her a soft kiss. Neither wanted the date to come to an end.

Ryan met Nathan and a couple other guys at Steak 'n Shake after he left Meagan's. They had just finished eating when he came in and sat down.

"Hey guys."

"Hey! Out with Meagan again?" Nathan teased.

"Yes, I was."

The waitress came to the table and asked Ryan if he wanted anything.

"Just a Sprite please."

"You know, Nate, she has a roommate," he half-way teased.

"Ha-haaa, thanks, but no thanks. I don't think I need any help finding a date."

"Suit yourself."

Trevor stopped by Ethan's on Saturday afternoon. After knocking a few times with no answer, he looked around and saw Ethan's car and figured he may be in the shower. Waiting a few minutes, he took out his phone and called.

Trevor could barely understand the muffled words.

"Ethan, dude, I'm outside your apartment. I knocked and knocked, but I guess you didn't hear me."

"Aaah, yeah, hold on I'll be right there."

When the door opened, Trevor's mouth dropped open and his eyes grew larger.

"What happened to you?"

"Nothing...it's nothing."

Something had happened, and it was serious. Ethan's face was bruised, his mouth had a cut, and his right eye was red and swollen.

Trevor quickly put two and two together. "Poker night get out of hand? Was it Stephen? I told you that guy was bad news."

"No, it wasn't Stephen...it was his thug buddy. I have a week to get the money to him, or he's gonna come back."

"I knew those guys were trouble. How much do you owe him?"

"Five hundred."

"Five Hundred! Ethan, man, I told you to stop while you were ahead."

"My luck changed and I won…up until the last two hands." He laughed and then winced with pain.

"Yeah, right. That was four hundred dollars," he remembered. "Ethan, man, if you would have walked away then, you would be four hundred dollars richer, and your face wouldn't be busted."

Trevor put one hand on the top of his head and the other on his hip trying to take it all in. His friend blew two thousand dollars in a poker game, and owed money he didn't have.

Ethan looked rough. He laid on the couch running his fingers through his hair, then looked toward his friend. Trevor knew that look and headed him off. "Dude I don't have it. I bailed you out last time, and even got your pocketknife back. And by the way, you still owe me a hundred and twenty bucks." Staring in amazement at his friend, "What's your boss going to say when he sees you? No one wants their bank teller to have a face that looks like that."

Despite himself, Trevor took pity on his not-so-bright friend, again, and got him an ice bag for his face, aspirin for the pain and something to eat. He assured him they would put their heads together and figure something out. Of course, asking Ethan's parents for the money wasn't an option. After two hours, they weren't any closer to a solution when Trevor came up with the idea of pawning off anything of value.

Ethan had already gone that route before and come up empty. He did have his rent money set aside, but he promised himself long ago to never borrow from the rent funds. There was only one other option. He hated having to do it, but he had no other choice.

Eight

The summer was slipping by too quickly, and the children would be back in school in no time. Maddie loved her new job, and going to work was once again a joy. She questioned why she was not saddened by not returning to the classroom, but she enjoyed being around the people at Dunning Plumbing. She liked having her own desk, not to mention a computer for her own use. She had a special fondness for Todd Dunning and looked forward to seeing him each day. Although, there were days he didn't come in; when he didn't she missed him. He was such a delight to her. He had wisdom, insight, and he told some of the most hilarious stories. This job suited her, and she could see herself working here for many years to come.

When in the office, Todd usually could be found sitting near the receptionist's desk, drinking his coffee and reading the newspaper. Maddie was in the midst of updating the schedules. Several of the plumbers had either called or walked up to her desk asking her about their schedules for that afternoon and the next day. A voice suddenly steered her focus away. She quickly glanced in its direction, and saw someone talking to Todd and couldn't stop herself from taking a second glance, almost causing a crick in her neck.

"Here ya go, Mr. Dunning. She's ready to go."

"Great. Thanks for getting it done so quickly. I sure do appreciate that. I don't like being without my truck."

"I know what you mean. You should be good for a while with new tires, new brakes, and I replaced that valve that we talked about. It was pretty much shot."

"I figured it was getting bad. Just send me the bill."

"Sure thing, Mr. Dunning." As the young man turned to leave, he noticed the receptionist staring, and without meaning to, he stopped.

"Nate, this is our new receptionist, Maddie. Maddie this is my mechanic Nathan Baxter, best mechanic in the area. If your car ever breaks down, just give it to Nate. He'll fix it…and won't overcharge you like those big shot fancy mechanics do."

The two just looked at each other; both stunned to see the other. "Aah, hello." Maddie managed to utter.

"Hi, I didn't know you worked here."

"I just started a few weeks ago."

He just nodded his head, "They're good people to work for."

Todd sensed these two had met before and was finding it all very interesting.

Turning, "Mr. Dunning, if your truck gives you any problems, just let me know. Oh and tell Coop I'll talk at him later."

"Sure thing, Nate. Come back and see us anytime."

Maddie tried to go back to her work, but her mind refused. The whole incident poured in on her like a waterfall. *I cannot believe this! He's Mr. Dunning's mechanic. Oh this is great. He probably works on all the Dunning cars and will be in here all the time. I knew this job was too good to be true.*

"So, you two know each other?"

"Aah, no, not really, we…ran into each other a few times. That's all." *Talk about an understatement.*

Grinning, Todd snapped his paper and went back to reading.

———————•◦•———————

Nathan couldn't stop thinking about the new receptionist at Dunning Plumbing. *Oh this is just great. Of all the girls in the area to be the new receptionist it had to be her.* He had finally gotten past the incident at the ballgame and briefly seeing her at Mike's Ice Cream Shop, but now here she pops up again. For two people who never wanted to see each other ever again, they sure did see each other often.

Determined to put her out of his mind, Nathan dove right into his work which was never lacking. Cars were lined up needing the brakes replaced and the transmissions worked on. He didn't have time to think about her. Time flew by. A few hours had turned into the entire day, and now it was almost quitting time. He was looking forward to going home, kicking his boots off, and eating a pizza in front of the TV. Tired from the day, he headed toward his truck as he dialed Papa John's to place his order.

Walking through the living room with pizza box in hand, he passed Ethan in the hallway and noticed his face. He didn't say anything because it wasn't any of his business and they were not close friends by any measure. But he couldn't help but think the guy looked like he had face planted on the pavement at high speed.

———————•◦•———————

Maddie arrived at her apartment irritable which annoyed her. For the life of her, she couldn't figure out why she let that man affect her so. She thought about him the entire day and was unable to stop. She didn't want to think about Nathan Baxter; she should be thinking about Ethan. If a police officer asked her to describe Nathan, she could provide details to the point where they would be able to pick him up within ten minutes. But at this moment she couldn't even remember the color of Ethan's eyes.

Meagan came running through the door and into the bathroom like she was being chased. Happy to see her roommate she would be a great distraction for getting him out of her mind.

"No date with Ryan tonight?"

"No, we agreed that we wouldn't be one of those couples who saw each other every day at the beginning of their relationship, because it's just too much too fast."

"True. Hey, want to eat while we watch TV?"

"Sure, put in a DVD."

A good friend, food, and a mindless movie were just what Maddie needed to take her mind off Nathan. She felt herself calm down and eventually relaxing.

At three a.m. Maddie woke up for no reason. No loud sound, no storm, no ringing cell phone. Her eyes just opened as if programmed to do so.

After tossing and turning for a couple of hours, she finally admitted defeat. Sleep wasn't returning, so at five-fifteen she got out of bed and began her day. Trying to be as quiet as possible, Maddie cooked a big breakfast for her and Meagan: pancakes, sausage and a fresh pitcher of tea.

Yawning, "Wow, what time did you get up?" Meagan asked.

"I've been awake since three, but got up a little after five. Pancakes?"

"Yeah, sure. So, something on your mind?"

"Why do you ask that? Just because a person wakes up in the wee hours of the night doesn't mean something is on their mind. It simply means they can't sleep, or they're done sleeping. But for some reason, people just jump to the conclusion that something is bothering them and keeping them awake."

Meagan raised her eyebrows at Maddie's defensive answer. "I never said something was bothering you. You did. I asked if something was on your mind."

"Don't pull that lawyer stuff on me this morning. It's too early."

Meagan just ate her pancakes and sausage, happy for the meal.

Ethan and Maddie had a lunch date at twelve-thirty and she was looking forward to it. More than a week had passed since they last saw each other, and she had some questions that needed answers.

After waiting ten minutes for Ethan to show, she could wait no longer. She ordered her food, and about midway through her meal, he finally walked in.

"What, you didn't wait for me?"

"Ethan, you're late, and I only have an hour for lunch and that includes getting to and from. And you have even less," she pointed out after swallowing a bite of her burger.

"I was just teasing… I'll hurry and get my order."

"How's your day going?" he asked setting his tray down.

"Fine, but I have a lot of work to get done today. As soon as I leave here, I need to stop at the bank and make the deposit." She was irritated at him for being late.

"You do the deposits for Dunning?"

"Yes, along with several other duties. Why?"

Shrugging his shoulders, "I don't know, just didn't know you did that, that's all. Say, how about I come over tonight and we watch a movie. I'll bring the pizza: you provide the Pepsi."

"Tonight?"

"Yes, tonight. Do you have plans?"

"No, I rarely have plans on Thursday evening…and speaking of which we need to talk, Ethan. I haven't seen you in over a week. What's up?"

"Well, I was away visiting my folks, you know that. And since I've been back, I've been swamped at work. We talk almost every day."

"I know, but…"

"But what?" Looking at her watch, Maddie let the subject drop. She needed to get going. "I'll call you or see you later. I really need to be going."

Ethan stood, held her hands, and gave her a quick kiss on the cheek. Not bothering to watch her leave, he returned to his meal and was soon interrupted by his phone ringing. Glancing at the caller ID, he answered quickly. "Ethan." While chewing his food, he listened intently. "I'm in the process of liquefying your investments. You'll get your money as soon as all the paper work is done."

"That better be by the end of the week, or I'm going to have a major problem."

"Now, you understand this is the last of your stocks, right?"

"Yes, I understand, but I plan on purchasing more soon. I'm just having a cash flow problem right now."

"Alright, I'll be talking to you soon."

Ending the call, Ethan ate the remainder of his lunch thankful Maddie hadn't noticed the fading bruise on his eye.

Free from having to be at Dunning, Caroline happily returned to being at home as a housewife and mother. These days her duties as a mother were less since her son was now in college, but the role always remained regardless. She was available for the business at any moment, but her family and household was her priority and always kept her busy. At the end of the day, she often asked herself where the time had gone and scurried to get supper on the table before Richard arrived home.

Following his nose from the garage to the kitchen, he couldn't wait to sit down for one of Caroline's home cooked meals.

"Something smells wonderful," he said before giving her a quick kiss hello.

"It's the chicken. Go wash up, and I'll get the table set."

Richard appreciated her efforts in the kitchen, and looked forward to sharing every meal together. He preferred her company to any other, and the two could talk for hours about anything. When he recalled how close he came to losing her forever, sorrow overwhelmed him. His immediate response was to put a stop to that memory, like abruptly pulling the brake on a speeding locomotive and slamming it to a halt.

"How was your day?" she asked while piling food onto his plate.

"Fine. We signed the contracts for the Brentwood building project. That's going to be a beautiful area for condos. I can see that property being very profitable and in demand. If I were single, I would be looking into one of those."

"Is Joshua not eating with us tonight?"

"No, he and a group of friends are going to a movie then eating afterwards."

"How is Maddie working out?"

"She's terrific. I'm so glad we finally have a receptionist that enjoys that job. No slam to you or my sister, but Maddie really seems to like it, and she and Dad get along great. It's like they're old friends."

"I'm glad. I thought she'd be a good match for that office even though her heart was set on being a school teacher."

"Yes, but I think after receiving a decent pay for the past couple of months, she might have given all that up. It's sad that one of the most important jobs on earth pays so little."

"Oh, I almost forgot to tell you. Melissa and I are planning to go the flea market this Saturday; we'll be gone most of the day."

"Anytime you and Melissa go anywhere you're gone most of the day," he teased.

Richard was right. When Caroline and Melissa were together, they usually lost track of the time which wasn't an issue with him. They had been friends since childhood, just like he and his best friend, Adam.

"Hey Coop, what's up?" Nathan said cradling his phone with his neck.

"Nothin' much. You busy tonight?"

"No, not really. Just finishing putting the brakes in a Ford. I should be done in about an hour."

"Want to grab a bite?"

"You and Meagan not going out tonight?"

"No, she's working late."

"Okay, we can do that. Like I said should take about an hour."

"I'll meet you at your place and we can drive together."

"Okay."

They ate at Steak 'n Shake which was one of their favorite places to eat. Reasonably priced, good food and their shakes were impossible to pass up no matter how much they had eaten. The waitress was so familiar with their order that she really didn't need to ask, but she did just the same.

Ryan needed to talk to Nathan about something that was on his mind, but stumbled with finding the right words. If anyone would have asked him about fixing up his friend on a blind date before now, he would've laughed in their face. Matchmaking was not a guy thing, and he would have no part of it...except he believed Meagan's intuition about these two people.

"Nate, man, I gotta ask you something. I wouldn't ask this if I didn't think it was a good idea, so just hear me out."

"Uh oh."

"Nate, Meagan has this friend..."

"Oh no. No, don't even finish that sentence."

"Seriously, I would never set you or anyone up, you know that, but I really think you would like this girl, and..."

"No."

"You're not even going to hear me out?"

"No."

"Okay, I won't mention it again."

"I'd appreciate it if you didn't."

They dropped the subject as if it were a ball of hot lava and finished their shakes. They shifted their conversation to cars, sports and the filling of the ketchup bottles that sat on the tables, but conveniently avoided the topic of fixing up Nathan with anyone.

It was late when Ryan drove Nathan up to his house. As they pulled in the driveway, they saw two rough looking men beating up a helpless guy. Ryan slammed the brakes and cut the motor taking his keys in his hand. At the same time, Nathan jumped out of the truck and ran towards the guy who was balled up on the ground.

"HEY!!!" The two men doing the beating quickly ran off like cowards to their car when Nathan and Ryan sprinted towards them. Ryan got a good look at the car and license plate and quickly tried his best to remember all of the details.

"Hey, man, you okay? Can you get up?" As the slow moving man turned towards him, Nathan's mouth dropped open.

"Ethan? Come on, Coop, let's gets him up and in the house."

Ryan and Nathan each took a shoulder and gently guided him inside their house and onto the couch.

"We need to call the police," Nathan said.

"Yeah, and I got a good look at the car and plates."

"No...No police."

Looking at Ethan's bloody face and beaten body, Nathan remembered his bruised appearance a few weeks ago and suddenly realized something. "You know who did this?"

"Doesn't matter, they're gone. I'll be alright," he groaned.

Nathan had limited interaction with Ethan. They just shared a house, and that was it. He gave his roommate a bag of ice for his face, but didn't know what to do about his stomach. "I don't know what we should do here. Maybe we should call an ambulance."

"No."

"Man, you may have some broken ribs or internal bleeding. Those guys were giving you some hard punches."

"No police, and no ambulance. I just need to lay here with this ice bag, and I'll be fine. Thanks for helping though...really I mean that."

"Sure, no problem."

Nathan draped a blanket over Ethan and left the room. When the other housemates came in and asked what happened, he explained what they knew. They all agreed that it was probably one of his poker friends he owed money to. One of the guys had a sister who was a nurse, so he called her and asked what they should do. Without taking him to the emergency room, she had limited advice options, but she walked them through the signs for a concussion which Ethan fortunately didn't appear to have. While he was sleeping, Ryan took pictures of him for evidence of the beating in case Ethan wanted to press charges, or if he died. He also wrote down what he remembered about the two men and the vehicle. He advised each one that was there that night to do the same.

It was a long night. Ryan eventually left around two, and one of the other housemates said he would stay up and keep an eye on Ethan making sure he continued to breathe. Nathan was still so shocked that something like that happened in his front yard. Everyone was aware of Ethan's friends coming to the house to play poker, but they didn't know it had gotten that rough.

The next morning, one of the guys poured Ethan a cup of hot coffee and cooked them some biscuits and sausage in the microwave. He attempted to eat, but his sore and swollen mouth prevented that right away. But the hot coffee was heaven sent; it soothed his tender injuries all the way down. Hearing his phone, he grabbed it struggling to answer. Nathan walked in and couldn't decide whether Ethan looked worse this morning or last night.

"Next time, your friends won't be able to help you. You still owe me three hundred dollars, and that two hundred was just the down payment. So here's what I'm going to do. You have seven days to come up with my money, or two things will happen that you may not find pleasant. One I'm going to take that beautiful red, shiny car you drive, and two I'm going have my guys work you over way worse than that little scuff from last night. Seven days, Price." Then the phone went silent. Ethan could only let out a sigh. He was in so over his head that he physically felt dizzy.

"How much do you owe this time?" Chuck, the other housemate asked. He and Ethan had played poker often, and he was surprised how drastically his luck had changed. He had seen Ethan end most nights with a pocket full of cash. "Man, all I have is twenty-three dollars, but it's yours. I know that won't pay these guys off, but it's a start. Anyone else want to contribute?"

Ethan looked shamefully at Nathan. "Look, man, I hate what happened to you, and I'm so glad me and Coop were there to scare those thugs off. But you have a problem, a gambling problem, and I can't give my hard-earned money to bail you out. If you were out of work and down on your luck, honestly, I'd be happy to help, but this is an addiction that's been going on for a while. And giving you money won't be helping you. I say call the police, get some protection until you get your paycheck and then pay them off, and never gamble again."

"They said I have seven days. I won't get paid for another two weeks."

"Go to your boss and get an advance on your paycheck. You gotta do something. Sell your car. You can sell a car like that easily," Nathan gently suggested.

Nathan left for work feeling like a heel. He was taught to help others when possible, but this was a self-inflicted problem and giving him money would only support the addiction, and he couldn't do that.

On his way, Ryan called to ask how things went after he left last night. Nathan filled him in on all the unpleasant details.

"I can't blame you for that, Nate. Why give your hard-earned money to someone so they can go gamble?"

"I think it might be a good time to look for another place to live. I don't like thugs knowing where I live. Got any suggestions?"

"No, but I'll ask around."

In the meantime, as Ethan sat at the kitchen table, he considered asking his boss for a payday advance, but only if that were his last choice. And he refused to sell his car, but he had another idea brewing in his battered brain: Maddie.

Ethan called Maddie to make plans to meet for lunch at Wendy's as they did often. As much as he hated the idea, he would ask her for the money.

Before he ended their call, he quickly added, "Oh and don't be alarmed when you see me. I was in a car accident yesterday after work, and I got pretty banged up, but I'm okay."

"Oh my, what happened? Are you sure you're alright?" He couldn't miss the concern in her voice.

"Yes, I'm fine, just sore and bruised up. My friend was driving, and this car pulled out in front of us. He walked away without a scratch. Go figure."

"Well, thank the Lord you and your friend are okay."

It was one of those days where every task took twice as long without any real reason - she hated days like that. The phone rang almost nonstop, and she had to resolve some unexpected issues that a few of the workers brought to her attention. So, this time it was Maddie's turn to be running late. She called Ethan and explained to him she couldn't make lunch until after one, which he was fine with.

After arriving at Wendy's a little after one, Maddie was in a tizzy from the day. Typically she ordered a cheeseburger with pickle, tomato, lettuce, and mayo, medium fries and a large Tea, but today she had to stop and think.

When she sat at the table, she took a deep breath letting it out slowly then bowed her head and thanked the Lord for her meal. When she looked up, Ethan was walking toward her. She was completely taken aback at his appearance, but didn't say anything.

"You not eating? Here, sit, and let me order for you."

"Thank you, I seem to be a bit scary looking today," he joked, but it wasn't funny.

Maddie ordered Ethan's food and sat it down in front of him. He put his napkin in his lap and slowly began to eat. *Apparently too banged up to say thank you.*

Maddie didn't know what to say. She was glad when he spoke.

"So, how is your day going?"

"Fine. Just busy that's all."

She wanted desperately to ask questions, but she refrained. "Ethan, why don't you come over this evening? I'll cook us a good meal, and we can relax and watch some TV. Does that sound good? I mean, if you feel up to it."

"Sure, why not. I'll come by around five-thirty."

Ethan couldn't bring himself to ask her for money like he planned, especially that much. When she worked at the school, having that kind of cash was out of the question. But now that she was working at Dunning, it was possible.

They both went back to work after lunch. Maddie was even more swamped than she was that morning. Brian came in and laid the money bag down on her desk apologizing for being late with it. He too had been overwhelmed with work.

"If you don't think you can get to the bank before closing, just lock it up in the safe and deposit it tomorrow."

"Yes, sir, I should have time."

Brian's hectic day caused him to be late getting the bank deposit to Maddie. As she finished some typing, she started processing the deposit. Looking at the clock as she finished up, she knew it would be close but if she left now, she could make it. Closing everything up, she poked her head in Richard's office and told him she was on her way to the bank and would see him tomorrow.

The heavy traffic aggravated her. Traffic should not be this heavy for at least another thirty minutes or so, but any number of reasons could be the blame. Finally pulling into the bank parking lot, she knew she would have to hustle.

Quickly walking to the door and pulling the handle, she soon discovered she was three minutes too late.

"Ohhh! Three minutes!!! I missed it by three stinking minutes!" She cried.

Now taking her time, Maddie stopped at Kroger to buy dinner for her and Ethan. She knew he didn't feel well and wanted to do something to help.

When Maddie thought she had Ethan figured out, he would do something to prove her wrong. Tonight he was surprisingly on time. Relieved, Meagan was out with Ryan, so they had the apartment to themselves. Meagan and Ethan in the same room made her uneasy. It was like waiting for the other shoe to drop. They obviously didn't care for one another, and either could say or do the wrong thing at any given moment.

"That was a fine meal, Maddie, thank you. It was just what the doctor ordered," he complimented smiling at her.

After dinner they went to the living room to get comfortable on the couch and turned on the TV. Ethan looked like he could break at any moment. She was afraid to touch him, so she didn't cuddle as close to him as she normally did. She gingerly scooted closer to him without actually touching him.

After such a busy day, sitting still and the flicker of the TV relaxed Maddie immediately. Her eyelids heavy, she moved several times to keep herself awake. When Ethan went to the bathroom, she was awake, but when he returned he found her curled at the end of the couch asleep.

"Maddie... Maaaadieeee." She was sound asleep. Taking a throw blanket from the back of the couch to put over her, something on the coffee table caught his eye. A money bag with the name Dunning Plumbing in black block letters sat conveniently on the table next to her car keys. It had been there all evening. Why had he not seen it until this moment?

"Maddie?" Still no movement.

With the TV still on as Maddie slept, Ethan slowly and quietly unzipped the bag and thumbed through the bills. *There has to be a couple of thousand dollars cash in here*! Looking back at his sleeping girlfriend, then back to the bag, he quickly took out four hundred dollars and quietly returned the bag to where she had placed it earlier. After putting the money in his pocket, he sat back down on the couch and watched the rest of the program. As the credits rolled across the screen, he called her name again touching her arm this time. She woke up with a confused look on her face.

He chuckled. "It's time for me to go and for you to go to bed. You've been asleep for the past half hour."

"Oh I'm sorry."

"Don't be. It's alright." She walked him to the door, and he gave her a long kiss good night and went home.

Nine

Karen Dunning was stunned by what her husband was saying to her. He wanted to invite people over to fellowship, as he called it. They hadn't done anything like that in years.

"Okay, dear, if you want to do this, you will sit right here and help me make the guest list." Again shocking her to no end, he pulled out a piece of folded paper and handed it to her.

"There, if you want to add some names, that will be fine."

"Todd Dunning, what are you up to?"

"Nothing. Just wanted to have a few friends over that's all."

"Do you have the menu planned as well?"

"No, sweetheart, I'll leave that up to you. I don't know anything about putting a menu together."

Staring at her husband from across the table, she held back her grin with effort. After all these years, he still surprised her from time to time, and this was definitely one of those times. *Now to figure out what he is up to.* She didn't want to discourage him, but she had to explain that there wasn't enough time to pull this little social event off. Invitations needed to be mailed to give people enough time to respond as well as planning the many details. He assured her he would take care of the invites. The whole thing was a little humorous at first, but now it was beginning to frustrate her because he hadn't thought it all through.

Todd was on the ball. "Forget mailing invitations that will take too long. I'll just personally invite them myself." Grabbing the phone, he began tapping in numbers, starting with his son's. By the time he finished, he had invited twenty people who had all agreed to come to their house next Saturday evening for a little socializing. While he was calling everyone, Karen planned the menu around some of her southern favorites and headed to the grocery.

⸺⸺◈⸺⸺

The typical morning scene at Dunning Plumbing appeared as it did most days: Todd sitting in his usual spot reading *The Tennessean* and drinking his coffee while Maddie sat busy at her desk as people came in and out.

"You're still coming Saturday night, aren't you?" he asked making sure she had not changed her mind.

"Yessir, wouldn't miss it."

"You can bring some friends if you want. I know you have a roommate. She can come too."

"Thank you! I'll ask her this evening."

"Richard, call me as soon as you get this message." Brian spoke into his phone. Walking to the receptionist's desk, he asked, "Dad, have you seen Richard?"

"No, son, I haven't. Not since this morning."

"Oh, he had an appointment to go to. He said he would be back around two," Maddie quickly added.

"Thank you, Maddie."

An employee walked through the office causing Todd to look over his paper.

"Hey, Coop, you coming stag to the party Saturday, or do you have a date?" He teased. He liked Ryan a lot and always enjoyed poking fun whenever he could.

Coop? Ryan is Coop? Remembering Nathan telling Todd to say hi to Coop the day he brought Todd's truck in, she began to put the two together. She had met Ryan, but didn't know they called him Coop, and now she remembered seeing him with Nathan at the ballgame.

"I have a date...a beautiful date."

Todd chuckled, and he continued.

Meanwhile, Brian and Richard finally connected. "I'll be in the office in about an hour. We'll talk then. Have you discussed this with Dad?"

"Not yet. I'll wait until you get here."

Friday about an hour before Maddie's quitting time, Brian asked her to come to his office. After she entered, he offered her the chair opposite his desk. A few minutes later Richard walked in and sat in the seat next to her.

"Maddie, you have done a wonderful job for us, and we all appreciate it. We regret you didn't come to us much sooner. We all are very happy with you and your work. You are self-sufficient. We never have to ask you twice to do anything, and you seem to be happy here. You're just perfect for this job."

Maddie sat and listened to the compliments knowing there was a 'but' coming at some point of the conversation.

"Do you like working here? Is everything going well for you?"

"Yes, sir. I love working here, and I enjoy this job. Really, I do."

"Forgive me for getting a little personal here, but I assure you it's necessary. Are things okay financially for you?"

"Well, I'm doing okay…way better than I was when I started," she chuckled. "I'm saving up to buy a car, and if I stay on target, I can do that in about five or six months," she said happily.

Conversations like this one were especially difficult for Brian. He would rather take a hard punch in the nose at this moment versus having this discussion with her. Richard was visibly uncomfortable as well. All things business were always shared with Todd, whom they had spoken to only a moment ago, before they confronted Maddie. He advised them to handle this matter with kid gloves.

"Maddie, as you know each week, myself or Richard count the money and fill out the deposit slip. When you do the drop off, the bank teller looks at it, counts what's in the bag and makes the transaction. When there is a discrepancy, they contact us either by letter or e-mail telling us of the error in the deposit. Then we have to figure out where the mistake came from.

"This morning, I received such an e-mail from our bank telling us that there is a four hundred dollar error in our deposit. I have looked this office over to find the discrepancy. I have gone over it in my head thinking maybe I wrote it down wrong." He paused hating what he was about to say and hoping she would not misunderstand. "Maddie, I want to say right now, and I want you to believe me, no one is accusing you of anything. But while you had the money bag, was it out of your sight at any time? Like, maybe you laid it down somewhere and turned your back for a brief moment, or maybe you left it unlocked in your car, anything like that?"

Maddie's face spoke volumes. She was being questioned about stealing money from the company. They were being nice about it, but to her she was being accused of stealing, and was going to lose her job and possibly be arrested.

"No, sir. I left here on Thursday to make the deposit as usual, but due to the traffic I got there a few minutes too late, and they had already closed. I stopped at the store, but I hid the bag under the seat, and I was sure to lock the car. After that, I went home and took the bag inside with me. I went to the bank this morning, which was the reason for me being late... Honest."

"Alright, we believe you." Rubbing his chin, he continued, "Before you left the office with it, where was the bag sitting?"

"I put it in the filing cabinet."

"Did you lock it?"

Taking a moment to search her mind, "I can't remember."

"Did anyone see you put it there?"

"I don't think so."

"Alright, well now we have to figure out what happened to four hundred dollars. I don't want you to be upset by this, but go home and think, retrace your steps from the time I laid the money bag on your desk until you gave it to the bank teller. Will you do that?"

"Yes, sir, I'll let you know if I remember anything different from what I have told you."

Driving home, she tried not to cry, but the tears flowed beyond her control. Sobbing while having a conversation with the Lord caused those in the car next to her at a stoplight to stare. "Lord, I need you to clear this up for me. Please! I have no idea what happened to that money!"

Wiping her tears, ideas flooded her from all directions as she tried to figure out this mystery. *Maybe Brian miscounted. Or dropped it putting it in the bag. Or someone went in his office and took it before he gave it to me. Maybe it was the teller. That's it. It had to be her. She certainly had easy access to it. That's probably it. The bank teller probably wouldn't even be questioned.*

When Meagan walked in the door, she could tell Maddie was extremely upset.

"Oh, Meagan, I'm so glad you're home." She began to cry. "I'm in trouble, and I need your help. Someone stole money out of the deposit bag while I had it. Now the Dunnings think I stole it! Meagan, you gotta help me. They think I'm a thief! What am I gonna do?" Looking helplessly to her friend, "I'll be arrested and lose my job."

"What? Whoa, slow down. You're talking too fast. Now sit down, take a breath and slowly tell me what happened," she said as she guided her to a kitchen chair. Meagan could feel Maddie's body shaking.

Maddie told the story from beginning to end leaving nothing out while her roommate listened intently. If it wasn't her roommate in question, she would enjoy this interesting mystery. But it was Maddie, one of the sweetest and most honest people she had ever known.

"Okay, now…you know you didn't take the money, and I know you didn't take the money, and anyone who knows you will say the same," she reassured trying to help her think more clearly. "Did they come right out and accuse you of stealing it? Did they tell you they were going to fire you and have you arrested?"

"No, they were very nice about it and said they believed me, but I know that's what they're thinking. I mean, what else could they think? Brian counted the money and gave it to me, and when I deposited it, it wasn't all there." Putting her face in her hands, "I didn't steal the money, Meagan. Honest I didn't."

"Of course you didn't. Just calm down and we'll figure it out…together. Here let me get you something cold to drink, and we'll put our heads together and work this whole mess out."

This situation seriously concerned Meagan. There had to be an answer here; money didn't just get up and walk away. There had to be a third party involved somewhere, and she was going to try her best to find out who it was.

Maddie was now calmer knowing that her friend not only believed her but was going to help her find out what happened to the money. The entire evening was emotionally exhausting, and after lying in bed for hours, sleep evaded her. She kept replaying the scene in Brian's office over and over until she threw the covers back and got out of bed. Fixing herself a cup of hot chamomile tea, she sat at the table and mindlessly looked through a magazine.

Caroline could not believe her father-in-law was throwing a party, and for no particular reason. It was so out of character for him. As she continued to ponder and shake her head, she looked through her closet for something to wear. Joshua was home for the weekend. When she invited him to the event, he agreed to go but only if he could leave when he wanted.

"Richard, what are you wearing?"

"Wearing where?" he asked from his easy chair while he and Joshua watched a ballgame.

"To your parents. The party is today."

"Oh, yeah, I'm just wearing what I have on."

"Aah, honey…"

"What? It's just my parents. I don't have to wear a suit and tie to my parent's house."

"No, but how about wearing jeans without holes and a better shirt."

Letting out a sigh, Richard got up and changed into a casual button-up shirt, nice jeans and cowboy boots. Caroline was pleased.

———— ◦—◉—◦ ————

Meagan was nearly ready for the party, but she was distracted by Maddie's situation. She lay awake late into the night trying to piece it together and always leading to the same conclusion. There had to be someone, other than Maddie, who had access to the money bag.

The knock on the apartment door brought her back into reality. She was expecting her date at any moment. "Ryan?"

"Yeah, it's me."

She quickly let him in then went back to scurrying around to finish getting ready. "I'm a little early. You don't have to rush."

When Meagan was distracted by something heavy on her mind, she tended to run behind schedule.

"You seem a bit out of sorts. You okay?"

Her look indicated it was something serious. She told him the details and made him promise to not speak to anyone about it but her. His mouth dropped open a little as he sat down heavily. Meagan continued to fill him in on their suspicions on what could have happened.

"I don't know Maddie like you do, but it sounds pretty obvious what happened. But if you believe she didn't do it then, maybe she didn't."

Giving Ryan a stern look, she insisted, "She didn't do it."

"Okay. I'll do anything I can to help. Where is she anyway? Is she going to the party?"

"She's in her room. And no, I don't think she is."

Maddie wasn't in the mood for a party and had changed her mind four times about going. Ethan would be here any minute, and she still needed to change her clothes. She had made the decision not to go, but changed her mind because she thought it might make her look guilty.

As they drove to the Dunnings' house, Ethan noticed her mood. "Maddie, you seem a little sad or something. Are you okay?"

She shared the whole story. "Ethan, if I don't find out what happened to that money, I could lose my job, or...or worse."

"Worse? What do you mean?"

"All the evidence points to me. They could bring me up on charges, make me pay it back. I don't have that kind of money."

"Maddie, you worry too much. You're not going to lose your job or be brought up on charges," he assured her calmly.

"Ethan, this is serious. You make it sound like I lost the stapler or broke the pencil sharpener."

"You said the Dunnings were Christian people."

"They are."

"I didn't think you Christians did that kind of thing. Don't worry. It will all work out. The money will show up. You'll see," he reassured her again holding her hand close to his chest as he drove. "Now let's just go to this party, forget all about the missing money and have a good time. Trust me. It's going to be okay."

Maddie wanted to do just that, but this was too serious. As they continued their trip to the Dunnings', she again silently prayed that the Lord would work this all out and clear her name. Suddenly, she remembered hearing a sermon or a Sunday School lesson about unbelief and worry, but right now she was unable to recall any scripture about it.

⸻ ❖ ⸻

Katie and Russ arrived early to offer Karen help on last minute details, and Richard, Caroline and Joshua arrived soon after. Todd sat at the kitchen table drinking a glass of iced tea while waiting for their guests, and the guys joined him.

"So, Dad, expecting a lot of people today?"

"Yep, everyone we invited said they would come."

Todd was completely relaxed while Karen buzzed around the house with the finishing touches. She was thrilled when the girls arrived to give her a hand. Their help was welcomed, and their presence calmed her.

"I remember now why we haven't done this in years," Karen said to the girls as she set the napkins on the table. "Way too much stress and work...but it wasn't me who wanted to do this. It was your father. And where is he? Sitting at the kitchen table talking and drinking iced tea as if today were any other Saturday afternoon."

Katie was sure when the guests started arriving her mother would settle down and enjoy herself, but until then she would scurry around double- and triple-checking even though everything was already in place.

The doorbell rang. Brother George Whitehurst and his wife Emily arrived first outside of family. Todd was glad; it gave him and Karen a few minutes to chat with their closest friends.

138

George was the pastor of the Marydale Bible Church, and he and Todd had been best friends since their youth. Both men greatly valued their friendship. Todd explained to Richard not too long ago if he attended the church where his best friend was his pastor and something went awry he would not only lose his pastor, but also his best friend. George joined the other men at the kitchen table, and Emily sat in the living room with the ladies for a short visit. It wasn't long before the doorbell rang again.

Multiple trips to answer the door gave Todd the idea of putting a sign up that said, 'come on in', but Karen stopped him in his tracks. She was afraid he would forget to take it down. She clearly knew her husband well.

"Maddie, glad you could come." Holding back his surprised look, he asked, "Who's this young fella you have with you?"

"Mr. Dunning, this is Ethan Price. Ethan this is Mr. Dunning, my boss's father and the highlight of my days." Giving him a wink she teased, "He feeds my Krispy Kreme Doughnut addiction." Peering at him with questioning eyes, Todd extended his hand, and Ethan shook it.

"Please don't be afraid of this face. I've recently been in a car accident."

"Oh my, hope you weren't seriously hurt. Well come on in. Maddie I think you will know most everyone here," he said consciously ignoring the strange vibe he got from Ethan.

Todd walked them into the living room, introduced them to Karen as he pointed out where the food and cold drinks were located and then politely excused himself.

Katie saw her dad walk into the kitchen alone and put one hand on his hip and the other across his mouth.

"Dad. Daddy, are you alright?"

"Hum, oh yes, yes I'm fine. Just thinking."

"About what?" she asked with concern.

"Oh nothing. No need to be alarmed." The doorbell chimed again. Quickly he left Katie to go and answer it.

As the guests mingled, it appeared everyone was enjoying themselves. Additionally, it turned out to be good medicine for Maddie. Todd and Karen were the most gracious hosts. Todd looked around the room as if he were looking for someone in particular. *She's here. Now where is he?*

"Great party, Dad. Didn't know you could throw such a bash." Brian teased. "The food is delicious, and needless to say I'm going back for seconds."

Hearing the doorbell once more, Todd was glad to see Nathan standing on the other side along with Ryan and Meagan. Delighted to see them, he didn't waste time teasing Ryan. "Well, you did find a date… and a beautiful one at that."

Blushing as he chuckled, "Mr. Dunning, this is Meagan Givens. Meagan, this is Mr. Dunning, the founder of Dunning Plumbing."

"Welcome, please come in." He ushered the three inside guiding them specifically toward Maddie and Ethan, but they were in deep conversation.

Richard and Brian were glad Maddie came. They were afraid she would be too upset about the situation to even make an appearance. However, they both believed the issue would be resolved quickly. Although she seemed to be having a good time, they could tell she wasn't her typical, lighthearted self. Her eyes never quite sparkled as they normally did.

"Okay, I guess now I go to plan B, but I don't have a plan B," Todd mumbled to himself in the kitchen. "If she hadn't brought that other fella, I wouldn't need a plan B. How in the world do women do this?"

"Dad, every time I walk in the kitchen, I find you in here alone acting strange. First, you said you were thinking, and now you are mumbling to yourself. Am I going to have to go get Mom, or are you going to tell me what's up?" Katie insisted with her hands on her hips.

"I assure you nothing is up. It's just been a while since we've had a party, and I want to make sure everything is being taken care of. Now go on out there and enjoy yourself." To fool his daughter, Todd opened one of the kitchen cabinet drawers and pulled out a utensil as if that were the reason for going in there. She just looked at him oddly.

Meagan, Ryan and Nathan were nibbling finger foods and talking to Richard and Caroline when Ryan spotted Maddie from across the room. Staring for a moment, he then nudged his friend. They casually moved towards the food table.

"Hey, Nate, isn't that your housemate with Maddie over there?"

Without being obvious, he casually glanced in the direction where Ryan nodded. "What is he doing here?" They stepped back to Meagan who was still talking to Richard and Caroline and continued to act as if nothing were out of the ordinary.

Caroline excused herself to help Karen bring out more appetizers, and it wasn't long until Richard was called to assist. "Meagan, do you know that guy Maddie is with?" Ryan asked.

"Yes, that's Ethan Price. I told you about him the night I introduced the two of you. She told me she wasn't coming."

"Are you serious? She dates him?" Nathan exclaimed apparently shocked.

"You know him?" Meagan inquired a little surprised.

"Sort of. What do you know about him?"

"Well, he works at a bank, drives a beautiful car, and when he and Maddie go out, he usually sticks her with the check. I think he's a creep, but she likes the guy." Looking between both Ryan and Nathan, she sensed there was more. "Why, what do you guys know?"

"Ethan is one of my housemates. We're not friends or anything, but the guy is trouble."

"Yeah, a few days ago, me and Nate ran a couple of thugs off that were beating the fire out of him over some gambling debts."

"He told Maddie he was in a car accident."

Looking at Ethan from across the room, the wheels in Ryan's mind began to turn as he dipped his chicken wing in sauce.

"Wonder if he got the money to pay those guys?" Ryan asked.

"I don't know, but he's walking around like all is well," Nathan answered with an edge.

Meagan didn't like what she was hearing about Maddie's boyfriend. "Come on, guys. Let's go over and say hello. Maddie is my friend," she said looking back over her shoulder as she walked toward them.

"Maddie, I'm glad you're here. You said you weren't coming."

"I almost didn't. I really wasn't in the mood for a party, but as you can see I changed my mind. I didn't see you guys come in. Have you been here long?"

"No, not long."

Ryan and Nathan stepped reluctantly behind Meagan. They didn't know how to handle this awkward situation. Maddie began to introduce everyone to Ethan, but Nathan cut her off, "We've met before."

"Oh, you have?" she asked looking confused at Ethan. He quickly answered.

"Aah, yes, Nathan and I are housemates with a few other guys, but we barely know each other." Maddie looked at Nathan. Their eyes met briefly then she quickly looked away. *What was it about him that made her need to look away?*

Ethan was on his toes. He covered his bases by changing the topic making sure he didn't give anything away. "The Dunning's have a lovely home. Don't you agree, Maddie?"

Todd happened to see this interaction, and a small grin came across his face just as Karen walked by noticing.

"What?" Todd responded to her unspoken question.

"That's what I want to know...what. Something has you grinning."

"I'm just glad to see our guests enjoying themselves. You have thrown a wonderful party, my dear, and I appreciate all your hard work."

"You're welcome. I didn't do it alone, now did I? You have worked just as hard."

Guests were preparing to leave, and Todd had to make a quick and strategic move, or all of his hard work would be for naught.

"Maddie, how is your car acting? Didn't you have car trouble not too long ago?" Todd asked.

Looking at him oddly, she replied, "Right now it's doing fine."

"Nate here is a great mechanic. I mean, this guy can fix anything with a motor."

"Yeah, I know. You've told me that, and he fixed my car once before."

Nathan attempted to hide his shock. Not only did she remember, but she didn't seem to be furious about it.

"Then you know he is a fine mechanic. I don't trust anyone else with my truck."

"When did he fix your car?" Ethan asked jealousy evident in his tone. Maddie noticed immediately. If only she could rewind the last few seconds, she would. Coming to her rescue, Nathan cut in and answered for her.

"It's been a while. She was broken down one evening, and I just so happened to come along and got her going again."

"You know, Maddie, when you're ready to buy a new car, you should give Nate here a call. He knows a lot of car guys. And I'm sure he'd be glad to go with you to make sure you get the right one. Wouldn't you, Nate?"

"Aah, yes sir, be glad to help." Nathan was now fully aware of what Todd was doing and chose to roll with it, especially since he couldn't stop him. He also caught the look on Ethan's face and feared it would make trouble for Maddie.

"Thank you, that's sweet of you, but I think I can handle it on my own."

On her own. I hope that means without that jerk's help. Nathan had to reel in his thoughts before they became spoken words.

"Hi, Maddie," Joshua chimed in from behind her. "Haven't seen you in a while," he said as he gave her a hug. Joshua knew Maddie from church, they were sort of friends, but not as close as Joshua would like to be.

"Hi, I've been here. It's you that's been missing," she cheerily responded accepting his embrace. "What have you been up to?"

"Going to class mostly. You know how it is when you're a college student."

"Yes I do. Oh, I'm sorry, you remember Meagan? And this is Ryan, Ethan and Nathan."

Joshua said hello, and after a few minutes of casual conversation, politely excused himself.

After the last guest left, the Dunning clan sat around the kitchen table to rest their feet before the women began to clean up. Karen silently noted that this was another reason she hadn't done this in so long.

The car ride back to Maddie's apartment was silent. Ethan was out of sorts after hearing that Nathan had helped her and offered his assistance in finding her a new car. The hug Joshua gave her wasn't sitting well either. He kept repeating to himself, *he's too young for her* as he tried to dismiss it. A few months ago it wouldn't have bothered him in the least, but now it did, and he didn't like it. Not noticing Ethan's mood, Maddie's mind however was focused fully on the missing money and on her future. To her it looked pretty grim.

"Maddie…Maddie, hello."

"Huh, what? Oh, I'm sorry. My mind was a thousand miles away."

"Yes, I can tell. Who are you thinking about?"

"What makes you think I'm thinking about someone?"

"Well, are you?"

"No, I'm thinking about this missing money."

"And I told you to stop thinking about that. It will all work out. They'll find the missing four hundred dollars. Now just let it go. Let's stop here and grab a burger. I'm starvin'."

"How can you be hungry?"

"I didn't eat as much at the party as you did. That's how."

In Ryan's car, the festive mood had been extinguished as if a wet blanket had been dropped on them. Nathan voiced his opinion while Meagan and Ryan mostly listened and agreed. "Please someone explain it to me. How does a guy like that get a girl like Maddie?" Nathan bordered on being angry and had to get it off his chest. "What is it about bad boys that attract good girls? And the story always ends the same way: the good girl ends up being hurt and or her life ruined."

The car primarily remained silent mostly because there were no answers to Nathan's questions. Ryan may have been quiet, but he was working on a theory.

"Later guys, and thanks for the ride."

"You bet."

Pulling away from Nathan's house, Meagan had to say it or she would explode. "I think we both agree that Nathan likes Maddie."

"No, Meagan, we have already discussed this, and we are staying out of it, remember? Besides, who needs our help when they have Todd Dunning?" he chuckled.

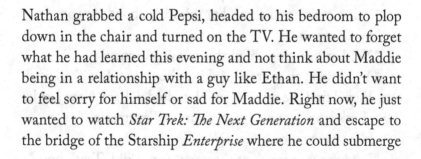

Nathan grabbed a cold Pepsi, headed to his bedroom to plop down in the chair and turned on the TV. He wanted to forget what he had learned this evening and not think about Maddie being in a relationship with a guy like Ethan. He didn't want to feel sorry for himself or sad for Maddie. Right now, he just wanted to watch *Star Trek: The Next Generation* and escape to the bridge of the Starship *Enterprise* where he could submerge himself as Data saved the crew on their mission. So he did just that for the next hour.

If that embarrassing scene at the ballgame hadn't been their first interaction, they might be a couple right now. He kept replaying that scene along with what he learned at the party and became even more frustrated. Another episode started as he was eating a frozen pizza. As he sat there he heard another one of his roommates come home. He suddenly remembered he hadn't seen Ethan's friend Trevor in a while which made him curious.

Nathan tossed and turned for a long time after he went to bed. He didn't understand why he was letting Maddie's situation get to him. He tried to convince himself she didn't mean anything to him, but inside his heart he knew that wasn't the truth. The painful reality was they weren't even friends, just barely acquaintances, but he wanted to be more, much more. He was more hopeful now that she no longer looked at him with angry eyes. *If only she wasn't dating someone like Ethan.* That fact infuriated him. Giving up on sleep, he went to the kitchen to get a snack.

———————— ·◦·✦·◦· ————————

Ethan couldn't believe his ears. It was the first time Trevor ever denied him for a loan.

"Dude, it's not for me. It's for Maddie. She is in a big financial jam, and I want to help her. If she doesn't get four hundred dollars by Monday morning, she will be evicted from her apartment, and she has nowhere to go," he pleaded pacing in the living room.

"Ethan, I'm sorry man, but I don't believe you. I think you have lost at the gambling table again, and you need me to cover for you...again. I can't do it anymore, man," he said as kindly but firmly as he could.

"Dude, we go way back."

"I know. And it hurts me that we've come to this, but the only way I know to help you is to not enable you."

Nathan's body shook with rage as he stood looking in the fridge. He could hear every word of Ethan's phone conversation. He was unsure of how he would react if Ethan walked into the room, but he wasn't moving until he was sure he was gone. He didn't want him to know he had just overheard his entire phone conversation.

At two-twelve in the morning, Maddie's eyes popped open like an alarm was set for that moment. With a clear mind, she jumped out of bed with purposeful steps walked to Meagan's room.

"Meagan, wake up," she called softly gently shaking her. "Wake up. I gotta talk to you....Meagan."

"Ummm...What? What's the matter?"

"I think I know what happened to the money."

Sitting up on her elbows, Meagan blinked her eyes at the bright light trying to focus on the person speaking to her. She struggled for a minute until she woke up a little more.

"Did you hear me? I think I know what happened to the money, and I don't know what to do. I need your help."

Meagan sat up and rubbed her face trying to wake up so that she could see the frantic look on her friend's face.

"It was Ethan. I think he stole the money."

While trying to let that soak in, Meagan's phone rang. "Who is calling me at this hour? Hello."

"Meagan, it's Nathan. I'm sorry to call you at this hour, but I couldn't sleep. So I called Coop to get your number because well, I don't have your number…. Anyway, I think I know what happened to the missing money, but I can't prove it."

"Nathan?"

"Nathan?" Maddie repeated. Staring at her friend, she was confused why Nathan would be calling Meagan at this hour.

Now, Maddie and Nathan were speaking to her at the same time, and she was about to scream. "Whoa, whoa okay. Everybody stop." Taking a second to become fully awake, she came up with a plan. "This is what we are going to do. Nathan, I will put on a pot of coffee, and you get here as soon as you can. Maddie is sitting here telling me the same thing. So come over, and the three of us will talk this thing through."

With wide eyes, Maddie asked her friend how Nathan knew about the missing money? "I'm sorry, but I told him… and Ryan."

"Ryan knows too?" She cried putting her hand on her head.

"No, Maddie, please don't feel bad. The guys can help… and they want to. That is why Nathan is on his way here now."

The smell of coffee coming from the kitchen and a knock on the door at two-forty in the morning wasn't typical for these two. Walking toward the door, Meagan noticed that Maddie had tidied herself up a bit and was wearing her best robe. She had combed her hair and put on a hint of lip gloss. Meagan would file this away to tease her friend later at a more opportune moment, but for now they had a serious matter to deal with.

She ushered Nathan into the kitchen, and the three sat around their tiny table with mugs of coffee and the cookie jar. Nathan couldn't help but notice how good Maddie looked considering it was the middle of the night. Taking a cookie out of the jar, he willed himself to stay focused on the topic at hand.

"Like I said, I think I know what may have happened to the money. I believe it was Ethan."

The two women glanced at each other then back to Nathan without hiding the surprised looks on their faces.

"I know, you and Ethan are seeing each other, and I'm sorry to have to tell you this, but I figured you would want to know. I mean…you should know."

Meagan then explained that Maddie came to the same conclusion half an hour earlier, and then asked him what led him to that conviction.

"I heard him talking on his phone right before I called Coop for your number. He was asking someone for four hundred dollars because Maddie needed it to pay the rent or she would be kicked out of her apartment."

Maddie's face was a mix between torment and relief.

"Okay, Maddie, explain to me why you think it was Ethan?" Meagan asked clearly showing her experience as a Paralegal.

"On our way to the Dunnings, I told Ethan what had happened and how it was my fault because it was my responsibility. Then on our way home I was talking about it again. And he told me to not worry that everything would work out and that the four hundred dollars would show up. But I never told him or anyone the amount that was missing."

"But when would he have had the opportunity?" Meagan asked.

"I invited him over for dinner after work that day. We were watching TV, and I fell asleep on the couch. When he woke me to leave, he said I had been asleep for half an hour."

"That would be an opportunity alright."

"So we believe his motive was the need to pay a gambling debt."

"Whoa, what gambling debt?" Meagan had forgotten Maddie didn't know about Nathan and Ryan chasing off two thugs that were beating him to a pulp over money he owed. "I didn't know he gambled," Maddie said just above a whisper.

"He had motive, opportunity and means, but..." Meagan paused briefly, "can we prove he took it?"

As morning drew near, the evidence against Ethan Price was stacking up. If Meagan were a lawyer, she would say they had a case, but, unfortunately, it wasn't anything they could use in a court of law.

Nathan sipped his coffee then told the girls the details when they found Ethan in the front yard being beaten up and how Ethan wouldn't let them call the police. "Then on Friday, he started acting like his normal self, so I figured he got the money somehow and paid those guys off."

They sat at the table nibbling cookies and drinking coffee as each one focused on putting the puzzle pieces into place.

"Coop and I were shocked to see him at that party. Then when we learned he was telling everyone he was in a car accident, we suspected something was up. I believe while he was here in this apartment he stole the money while you were asleep."

"Are you sure you never told him the amount?" Meagan questioned.

"Positive. I never told anyone. And I don't believe for a moment the Dunnings discussed this with him either." Tears started to swell up in her eyes. "Meagan, he stole that money knowing it would look like I did it. He knows how upset I've been over this and...he's supposed to care about me." It was almost Nathan's undoing as her tears flowed uncontrollably.

At that moment, like a powerful ocean wave crashing, he became aware of his love for her. He wanted to hold her in his arms promising to protect her and make everything better. His heart was overflowing for this woman who was clueless about his feelings for her. All he could do was sit and watch her sob on Meagan's shoulder.

She could hardly endure seeing her friend so hurt. She suspected the guy was a creep from the start, but was unable to open Maddie's eyes about her suspicions. Had she just simply been straightforward from the beginning, then maybe Maddie would have taken a second look and not be hurting now.

Nathan got up from his chair and placed his hands on Maddie's shoulders. "It's not your fault. If he really cared about you, he wouldn't have done this. You need to tell Brian and Richard what we've figured out as well as call the police and turn him in."

"We can't take this to the police. We have no hard evidence. It will be his word against Maddie's. But Nathan's right, you need to tell the Dunnings and at least clear your name," Meagan explained.

Maddie could see the wheels turning in her friend's head. "If we could only get actual proof, the Dunnings' could have him arrested."

"Arrested!"

"Yes, arrested," she said sternly. "Remember he hasn't been concerned about you being accused of stealing, or you possibly losing your job, not to mention damaging your good name."

With each word Meagan spoke, Maddie felt more used.

"Alright then, let's put our heads together and figure out a way to get the proof we need."

They were mentally exhausted from trying to piece this all together, and Maddie was also emotionally spent. They needed to take a break to clear their minds so they could figure out a way to prove their suspicions. Each agreed to not mention any of this to anyone until they had proof, except for Ryan. Looking at his watch, Nathan suggested they try to get some sleep and meet again after the girls returned from church.

Standing up from the table, "I'll call Ryan in the morning... or in a few hours that is, and bring him up to speed on our suspicions." Meagan voiced.

On his way home, Nathan's mind was more at ease, but his heart ached for Maddie. It wasn't fair that she was being dealt this hand; he wanted to protect her, but would she let him?

The back door creaked as Nathan slowly opened it. With careful steps he walked down the hall to his room hearing Ethan's snoring as he passed his bedroom. He promised himself he would confront Ethan later about the hurt he had caused Maddie.

Falling into bed still in his clothes, he gave a big yawn and fell asleep within minutes.

Ten

Miraculously, Maddie made it to church on time. Her feet led the way knowing exactly where to go and when to get there. Her mind, however, was a mess. She lacked sleep and had no appetite. Meagan had kept a watchful eye over her friend for the past thirty-six hours or so, and today she would continue to be just as vigilant.

Yesterday at her in-law's party, Caroline noticed Maddie appeared to be struggling with something, and now sitting in her class, she looked tired and depressed. She was concerned and certainly didn't want to pry, but to Caroline, there was more to teaching a Sunday School class than standing in front of the room and spouting information. She truly cared about them and wanted them to know she was always there if they needed her support. Caroline would look for an appropriate time and place to speak with Maddie.

"Good morning, everyone. It's so good to be in the house of the Lord!" A chorus of Amens echoed across the room. "Brother David, come lead us in praises to our God," Brother Whitehurst eagerly exclaimed.

Brother George Whitehurst loved being in the house of the Lord. Each service was the same, but different. For an older man, he had mounds of energy, and his enthusiasm was infectious to all.

Brother David led the congregation in some traditional hymns which remained steadfast in Biblical truths, but still spoke powerfully to the hearts of God's people. The singing helped everyone to settle and prepare their spirits to be fed by the sermon to follow.

"That was a wonderful song service, don't you agree?" Amens once again rang out across the large auditorium. "You know, folks, if you don't like coming to church, you are not going to like being in Heaven. Because just think for a minute, let your mind go to that heavenly place as best as you can picture it. There is gonna be singing. There is gonna be shoutin'. There is gonna be praising Jesus and worshiping Him like we never have here on this earth. I don't know about you, but I'm ready to go now." Many amens and a few hallelujahs reverberated across the auditorium.

"That isn't my sermon today. That was extra," he teased receiving a jovial response. "The title of today's sermon is: 'What Are You Meditating On?' And if you would please turn in your Bibles to Philippians, the fourth chapter, and hold that spot. I have a few questions I want to ask you, and I want you to answer to yourself. Do you bathe each and every day? Now if you don't in a few days, everyone around you will know, because that is a smell that cannot be described." The congregation laughed out loud at the ridiculousness of the question. "Next question. Do you brush your teeth at least once a day? If not, your teeth will start to eventually fall out." Again there was laughter. "Do you eat at least once a day? If not, it will not take long before you become weak, and if this continues you will become seriously ill. There are some things we need to do every single day, and some of those more than once a day. Last question. Do you read your Bible every day?" The room got quiet, and Maddie was curious where he was going with his line of questioning. "If not, you are spiritually starving yourself. And each day you become spiritually weaker, and you are not growing in the Lord like you should...like you could. I want to encourage each of you to read the Word of God every day, even if it is just for a few minutes."

Maddie did a mental check on the past week and was ashamed that she had not. As a matter of fact, she had not read God's Word since last Sunday while sitting in church. She continued to listen as the pastor spoke and made a mental note to try to do that this week.

"Several years ago, I was going through a rough time, one of the roughest times I had ever been through, and I could not get my mind off of it. Each day I focused on that issue more and more...and each day that problem I was meditating on got bigger and stronger. I would pray and cry out to the Lord and ask for His healing. And one morning as I prayed, I sensed the Lord say to me, 'George, why are you meditating on this and not My Word?' Let's read Philippians 4:8. 'Finally, brethren, whatsoever things are true, whatsoever things are honest, whatsoever things are just, whatsoever things are pure, whatsoever things are lovely, whatsoever things are of good report; if there be any virtue, and if there be any praise, think on these things.' You see, I had gotten myself mentally messed up, so I had to work and work hard at not meditating on my problems, but to meditate daily on the Word of God. Again, I ask, what are you meditating on?"

As the music played softly, Maddie with her head bowed sensed the Lord was speaking to her in her spirit. There was no doubt that she had spent too much time worrying about the missing money. She had played the scene of being fired with a S.W.A.T. team coming to take her away for stealing repeatedly, and each time the scene got longer. She silently prayed and asked for forgiveness for not letting the Lord have this problem and for trying to handle it herself. As she did so, she also asked forgiveness for not taking the time each day to read at least a few verses of the Word of God.

"Thank you for your attention. Since it's the Lord's day, all day long, some of us will be back here tonight, and I hope you'll come and join us." Brother Whitehurst called on one of the deacons to dismiss in prayer, and after the amen, everyone started to leave their seats and mingle toward the door.

Maddie's heavy heart was lighter on the way home from church than it was on the way there. She had such a peace after giving her situation with Ethan and the money over to the Lord. Even though she didn't know how it was going to end and was still a little fearful, she was sure her Lord could handle it. Passing several fast food restaurants, Maddie realized her appetite had returned. "I am sooo hungry."

Meagan looked at her. "I take it you're feeling better?"

"Yes, much. I still need the answer to all of this, but I gave it over to the Lord, and I'm trusting that He will fix it."

"Yeah, I guess we've been meditating in the wrong area these past few days."

When the girls arrived back at their apartment, Ryan sat in the parking lot waiting for Meagan. As she turned off her engine, Nathan pulled in beside her. When he got out of his truck he was carrying two large pizzas and a couple of two-liter soft drinks.

Walking past Nathan, Meagan could smell the delicious aroma, "Pizza! thanks guys."

Sitting at their kitchen table with a pizza slice in hand readied for a bite, Maddie asked "Did you guys just come from church?"

"No," Ryan answered. "I'm a lazy bum. I like to sleep in on Sunday mornings," he joked. She looked toward Nathan, and he added to Ryan's teasing words.

"Yeah, we're both bums."

"I've asked Ryan to come to church with me, but you know there isn't too much you can do with bums." Meagan cheerily joined in with the guys. Maddie didn't mean to put either of them on the spot, she was just asking.

While they were eating, the conversation shifted to the mystery of the missing money. All the evidence obviously pointed to Maddie. But like Meagan said, anyone who knew her knew she would never take what didn't belong to her. They brainstormed for ideas of how to prove it was taken without her knowledge.

"I got it," Ryan said snapping his fingers. "Why don't we have the police run prints on the bag, you know like they do on cop shows?"

"If Ethan doesn't have a criminal record, the police won't have a set of prints to compare them to. We would need to get a set of his prints to compare what is on the bag, and who knows how many prints would be on it," Meagan answered. "But I could ask one of the defense lawyers at work if there is anything we could do to prove our theory."

Everyone liked that idea wholeheartedly, and it was then settled. Meagan would speak with one of her co-workers and see what could be done, legally. Meanwhile, the hardest part for Maddie was going to work and doing her job without falling apart.

———————◦———◦⟨◦⟩◦———◦———————

Maddie slept very little that night. Facing Brian and Richard wasn't going to be easy. Then another thought suddenly occurred to her; she remembered Todd. *Does he know about this?* The pit in her stomach sickened her even more with the possibility that Todd knew. She prayed silently and asked the Lord to not only reveal the truth about this situation, but to help her move through her day and to do her job as normal.

"Good morning, Maddie. It was so good to see you and your friends at the party. I hope you had a good time."

"Thank you, Mr. Dunning. We had a wonderful time." The smile she gave didn't reach her eyes, and he couldn't help but notice the sparkle was gone, as it was on Saturday.

"Maddie, come sit. I want to talk to you, and I want you to listen." Sometimes Todd Dunning couldn't turn off the father in him, no matter who he was speaking to. "I know what's going on, and I want you to know we do not think you stole that money. Now the way I see it, the Lord knows all about it, and we need to let Him handle it. So you, young lady, need to keep your chin up."

"Yes, sir," she said as tears begin to form in her eyes. "Thank you, I was afraid y'all didn't really believe me and..."

"Now now, there's no need to cry. It's going to be alright," he comforted as he put his arm around her.

The clock on the wall read four o'clock, and Maddie was wrapping up the last of her work for the day. The day had gone smoothly for the most part. Both Brian and Richard treated her as usual and talked to her as if nothing had happened, and she tried to do the same.

Just as she was finishing her last task, her phone rang. "Hey, Maddie, so I did some digging at work, and this is what I found out. One of the defense lawyers told me he has a friend who's a police officer. He thinks he can call in a favor and get them to run the prints on the bag. The only problem is we would need Ethan's prints to compare it to."

"Are you serious? They can do that? Would that be enough to prove he stole the money?" Maddie asked hopefully.

"No matter how many prints are on the bag, if his are on there, it's sound evidence that he touched it. That's enough to bring him in for questioning, but not really enough to charge him with anything. He could come up with numerous reasons as to why he touched the bag that don't involve taking out money."

Maddie listened with relief, and Meagan continued to explain they would need to get the money bag from Brian. "Patch me to Brian or Richard, and I'll explain our suspicions and what we plan to do to prove your innocence."

"Thanks, Meagan, I mean it. I really appreciate all you've done to help me, but I think it would be better if I talked to Brian myself."

Maddie walked to Brian's office and tapped lightly on the door. "Can I talk to you for a minute?"

As Maddie explained her suspicions about the missing money, Brian was surprised, but also relieved. He refused to believe that Maddie would steal from anyone, but there was still four hundred dollars unaccounted for.

"I'm happy to do whatever I can." Finding a plastic Walgreen's bag on the floor by his desk, he placed his hand inside and used it as a glove. With the money bag enveloped inside the plastic bag, he handed it over to Maddie. "I hope it works."

She blew out a breath, "So do I."

Driving home from work, Nathan's mind drifted to his living arrangements and how he needed to find a new place as soon as possible. Renting a room at this house was ideal for him at this stage of his life, and it annoyed him that it was Ethan's fault that he needed to move. It wasn't the poker nights or the other guys. It was Ethan's attitude, his involvement with Maddie and what he had done to her. Right now he wanted to avoid any possibility of an altercation between the two of them, and he certainly didn't want to tip their hat about nailing him with the truth.

"Ethan, I wasn't expecting you," Maddie said as she opened the door.

Stepping through the doorway, he quickly scanned the room happy to see Meagan wasn't there. Wearing a satisfied look, he spoke. "I have something for you, and I couldn't wait."

It was odd for him to be there right after work. Maddie had not been home more than ten minutes. He held both of her hands and gave her a kiss. She had to resist not pulling away. She looked at him questioning what he had to give her. At this point, she only wanted the truth from him so she could be rid of him, but she would have to play it cool for a little longer until they got the evidence they needed.

"I want you to take this and give it to your boss," he said placing a wad of bills in her hand.

"Ethan, what is this?"

"It's four hundred dollars. And it's all yours. You can take this to work tomorrow, and this whole thing will be over."

"What? No. I can't accept that. Ethan, if I take that to my boss, that's admitting I took the money, and I didn't take it," she said angrily, putting the money back in his hands. "And you know that."

"Maddie, you don't understand. You can give them this money, and when they find the lost money they can pay you back." She looked at him furiously. "But no need to worry, it's all yours...No strings attached and you don't have to pay me back."

As Maddie took a deep breath, she felt the Lord's peace come over her. She finally had the strength to do what needed to be done.

"Please have a seat." He walked to the couch as she took a nearby chair across from him. Looking at him she wanted to cry but demanded her tears to stay put. She had reached her limit and the time had come. She was tired beyond her years, tired of him, this relationship, and his dishonesty. Before she spoke, she quickly said a prayer in her head and asked the Lord to provide the words she needed at that moment.

"Ethan, where did you get this money?"

She caught him completely off guard. "I earned it. It's from my savings." With half a chuckle, "Where did you think I got it?"

"That's just it. I don't know." She was going to make him confess to what he did. "I do know that when we go out, and rarely on the weekends I might add, most of the time I pay the check. For whatever reason, you don't have the money, and now here you are offering me four hundred dollars…in cash and with no strings attached. It doesn't add up. Where did you get this money? Just be honest with me. No matter what the truth is, just tell me."

"You have lost your mind," he snapped. "I come here to help you out of a jam because you are my girlfriend, and this is how you say thanks? I thought we meant something to each other, but I see now I was wrong."

"I care about you, Ethan, but you don't treat me like someone you have feelings for. I think you are hiding something from me, and if you ever did care for me, you will tell me where you got it. Just tell me the truth." She stared him square in the eye, and he never blinked.

"What could I possibly be hiding from you?"

"You tell me. I think it's strange that someone who never has money suddenly has a lot of it to give away."

Staring back at her, but giving no hint of anything, he growled. "Fine, don't take it then; be stubborn."

That's it. He's not going to admit to stealing the money. He's going to continue to let me be blamed for it. "Ethan, I have thought and prayed long and hard about this, and I feel it would be best if we don't see each other anymore," she said, followed by relief that she got the words out. She prepared herself for a big blow up, but at this moment she didn't care how mad he got. She wanted him out of her apartment and out of her life.

His furious look scared her. "Fine, be that way," as he stepped up right into her face causing her hair to move with his breath. "But, little girl, you remember this: it was me that came to your rescue not Carlton, and not your mechanic. It was me! And you are so stupid. You turned down free money." Before stomping out, he turned and took one more shot at her.

"I don't know what I ever saw in you." The door slammed hard with his exit.

He pulled out of the parking lot and didn't looked back.

Closing the door to her bedroom, Maddie scanned the room and found a few trinkets that Ethan had given her: a t-shirt she slept in, a teddy bear, and a CD of one of her favorite bands. On her bedside table sat a small photo of the two of them she had taken with her phone. Tears began to flow at the sight of it. Wiping at her face, she picked up each item and placed it in a box, then deleted his name from her phone. She wanted no more of Ethan Price or memories of him. For reasons she would never understand, she had allowed him to make a fool of her and hurt her deeply. Come morning, she would throw out the box.

When Meagan came home from her date with Ryan, Maddie told her about Ethan's visit, his offering her four hundred dollars and their breakup.

"Where did he get the money?" Meagan inquired.

"I have no idea."

Richard and Caroline had dinner with his parents, and during the course of their meal, business matters came up. Most of the time business was not discussed at the table, but Todd brought the matter up about the missing funds, and Richard explained the latest development. Caroline and Karen sat listening carefully.

"I know that girl didn't take that money. I've spent a lot of time talking with her, and I believe I've gotten to know her a little better than you boys have."

"Dad, we believe her," Richard cut in.

"I have to agree. I don't think she did either. We're all overlooking something here," Caroline chimed in.

"This whole mess just hangs over us like a gray cloud," Richard continued. As of right now, we are suspecting her boyfriend, Ethan.

"The moment I saw that fella I suspected there was something not right about him. He's got nerve. I'll give him that. Steal from us and then come in my house and eat my food."

"Now, hold on Dad, we have no proof that he took that money any more than we have proof that Maddie didn't."

Todd was getting furious, but Richard was right. They had no proof.

As the discussion between Richard and Todd continued, Karen sat listening intently. She loved a good mystery, and this was a mystery if there ever was one.

"Meagan has some friends in the police department that can run fingerprints on the bag, but still that doesn't prove he took the money."

"True, that would be circumstantial," Karen added. "He could claim he moved the bag from one place to another, or it fell and he picked it up. Or even worse, he could say he saw Maddie take it and implicate her even further. You need to be careful how you approach this."

<hr/>

After Caroline and Richard left, the hour was getting late as Karen and Todd prepared for bed. The conversation at the dinner table still lingered in Karen's mind; she could not let go of it. She had logged enough hours watching mystery movies and detective shows to know there was something missing from the puzzle, and that was…the motive. *Of course anyone who had sticky fingers wouldn't need much of a motive to steal a large amount of cash that just so happened to be in their reach.*

"Todd, I think you and George need to go visit this young man Ethan."

"You mean to face him and tell him we know he stole the money, and we want it back?"

"Oh goodness no, that's not what I mean at all. I mean a church visit. He may not know the Lord. He could be a harvest ripe for the picking."

Once again his wife was right. Even if he was a thief, he needed to hear the gospel.

"And who knows what will come up during your conversation. You may find out his motive for stealing the money…if he indeed stole it. Now don't you misunderstand me, Todd Dunning," she said sternly, "you will be there solely to talk to him about the Lord and invite him to church."

"Well…you're right about that." Todd agreed as he sat on the edge of the bed taking off his wrist watch and glasses. The conversation continued as Karen turned her bedside light off. "Now sweetheart, how are we going to do this? Neither George nor myself know where this fella lives or works."

"No, but Maddie does."

Lord, this woman never ceases to amaze me.

Caroline tossed and turned most of the night. She could not stop thinking about Maddie and how she must be feeling right now. How she had gotten mixed up with that guy was beyond her, and she certainly could not approach her because of the delicacy of the matter. Bringing it up would confirm she was the subject of conversation in her absence, and that could add salt to the wound.

At one-thirty in the morning, Caroline gave up and went to the kitchen to get a drink. Instead of going back to bed, she instead headed to the recliner and television which would be her solace. Episodes of a few of her favorite TV shows were on late night. She was really getting into *Murder She Wrote* when she heard a noise that almost made her jump out of her chair. "Oh Richard, you scared me, honey."

"Sorry, I turned over, and you weren't there. What's the matter can't sleep?"

"No. I can't stop thinking about Maddie, poor girl."

"And Jessica Fletcher and the people of Cabot Cove help?" he teased.

"Yes…they do."

Taking a blanket and her hand, he led her to the couch where he could lay next to her while she watched TV. It was only minutes until he was sound asleep as if in their big comfy bed.

———•◦•◦•———

Todd was sitting at his usual spot at the office drinking coffee, eating a doughnut and reading the paper when Maddie walked in. She looked tired and pale, and her shoulders were slumped. He would be so glad when this mess was solved.

"Hello, Mr. Dunning."

"Hello, Maddie, got some fresh coffee and your favorite doughnut," he greeted in a sing-song tone. Currently his anger at Ethan was under control. How anyone could hurt Maddie was beyond him. Another issue had inadvertently cropped up in the middle of all this: how could he talk to Ethan about the Lord when all he wanted to do was punch him in the face, like that other guy did? He would have to do a whole lot of praying and confessing before he could ever approach him.

The phone rang and Maddie answered. "Yes sir, he's right here. I'll put him on. It's for you, Mr. Dunning. It's Brother Whitehurst," she said, giving him the phone. She walked from her desk and made herself a cup of coffee, but didn't touch the doughnuts. Their conversation was short and to the point. Without telling him why, he told his friend he didn't think he could make this visit. George sensed something was amiss, but didn't pry. He figured if Todd had something he needed to get off his chest, he would seek him out.

"Okay, give me the name and address, and I'll ask one of our deacons to go with me. And you're sure you're okay?"

"Yeah, I just think it may be better if you handled this one alone."

"Alright, Todd, I trust your judgment. I'll try to visit him Thursday after supper."

While sipping her coffee, she received a text from Meagan, which was something the two did from time to time. Meagan was just checking on her friend, making sure she was alright.

Eleven

Nathan talked to Meagan, filling her in about some new evidence they had, and told her he would drop by later that evening when she and Ryan returned from their date.

Sitting and waiting for his order to be brought to the table at one of his favorite restaurants, Nathan could smell food being cooked on the other side of the wall, and it made his mouth water. Looking around the room, the only familiar faces were a few employees. When his meal arrived, he had his fork in hand and was ready to dive into the mashed potatoes when someone spoke, causing him to look up.

"Are you alone?"

He couldn't believe his eyes. "Yes, please have a seat," he answered, standing and pulling out a chair.

In disbelief, she nervously sat down across from him. A few weeks ago, she would have never even come near him, but now that he was right in front of her, she realized this is where she wanted to be.

"Thank you, I don't mind eating alone for lunch, but not my supper," Maddie spoke.

Often he and Ryan would grab a bite after work, or he would take something home and eat in front of the TV. "I know what you mean." He had no clue why he agreed with her just now.

In awkward moments, mindless conversation or total silence were typical results for Nathan. He feared this was going to be one of those times. He was thrilled that she was here sitting and eating with him, but he was unprepared and nervous. "It's been a while since I've eaten here. I love their barbeque." She gave him a small smile.

Their first meeting had been a disaster, and he had tried to erase it from his memory. Now here he sat, nervous that it would be an instant replay.

The waitress brought Maddie's order. She opened her straw and her napkin, then bowed her head and silently thanked the Lord for her meal and His blessings of the day. When she looked up, he was still lost in her smile. His surroundings suddenly fell silent and still as if they were in some sort of sci-fi movie and were the only things moving in real time. They began to eat, and even though he was hungry, he slowed his pace to draw out the meal, and he had already decided he was going to order dessert.

"I want to thank you for your help the other day. You're very kind to take the time out of your busy life to help me." Her sweet smile faded into sadness when she mentioned her situation. At that moment, he wanted to hold her tight and assure her that everything would be fine, but realistically he knew he couldn't promise that. All he could do was assure her that he would be there when she needed a shoulder to lean on. With her unexpected appearance and their pleasant conversation, he almost forgot to tell her the good news.

"Maddie, I have news for you."

Sitting a little taller and looking directly at him, she gave him her undivided attention.

"I found a glass that Ethan had been drinking out of sitting on the kitchen counter, so I took it and placed it in a plastic bag. I was careful not to touch it or smudge the prints. I was going to bring it by your apartment this evening and give it to Meagan, but she and Coop are on their way to a movie."

"That's great!" she nearly screamed. "I think this will prove my innocence to the Dunnings."

"You said they believed you."

"They say they do, but I want to make sure. I guess I need to prove to them beyond a doubt that I am an honest person and don't take things that aren't mine. If I can't prove that, then in the back of my mind I will always think they are questioning my character."

Nathan had never been in her position before, but if he had, he would want to prove his innocence. It was like his father used to tell him, 'If your name is no good, you are no good.' And that is what Maddie was trying to do, clear her good name.

Curiosity overtook him forcing him to ask, "How did you meet up with Ethan anyway? I know it's none of my business, but girls like you should not go out with guys like Ethan."

"What do you mean by girls like me?"

"You know, sweet, a good person, a Christian. I've often asked myself, 'why good girls go out with bad guys,' that's all. I didn't mean anything offensive."

She could feel her face beginning to flush. She was surprised he could think of her in that way after her reaction to their fiasco of a first meeting.

"First of all, I'm not offended, and second, I'm not with Ethan anymore." When those words reached his ears, he could barely hear anything else she said. "I don't know how you can say I'm a good person after the way I treated you at the ballgame. I don't like to think about it, and I'm sure you don't either." Neither one spoke momentarily. She sipped her water. "I'm sorry, Nathan. I should not have reacted like I did, nor treated you like that."

That was certainly a night to forget, and it was time they both did.

"And I am sorry as well."

The conversation continued forward from there. As the clock ticked, they seemed to be more at ease with each other. While he spoke, she allowed her gaze to wander around his face taking in his features. He was very handsome. His brown eyes were so kind and sparkly, and his smile warmed her. She couldn't believe that she had missed all of this until now.

"Do you mind if I ask you a personal question? You can say no, really...it's okay," Maddie inquired.

"Ask away."

"How long is your hair?"

She was referring to his man bun. Most of the time, and always at work, he had it neatly tucked up, but on occasion he wore it straight down. He was accustomed to the looks, especially from women, but her question caught him off guard.

"I would show you, but it would be impolite to do so at the table. So, I'll tell you. It's past my shoulders."

She tried to picture it down. It was a lovely sandy brown color. "Oh, and how long have you and Ryan been friends?" She quickly asked so she wouldn't be caught staring. But it was too late for that, and he handled it well.

"Me and Coop have been buds since middle school. They don't come any better than Coop."

"Why do you call him Coop?" She wasn't intentionally asking rapid fire questions, but she wanted to know all about him.

"I guess because his last name is Cooper. You know how we guys are. We tag a nickname on each other, and sometimes it sticks. But anyway, it was pretty early in middle school. He started calling me Nate, and I started calling him Coop."

Time passed quickly, but neither noticed nor cared. He made her laugh so easily she almost forgot about her troubles. When she and Ethan first started dating they laughed, but not like this. And as the months progressed, the laughter lessened. How did she not see that? How could she be so blind to something so obvious? She never thought herself a fool, but that's the part she had been playing during their whole relationship. The fact that others were aware of it made it worse.

Sensing her thoughts had shifted to her situation, Nathan tried to reassure her. "You know, you're not the first girl to fall for the wrong guy. It happens. But when we are so close to a situation, sometimes we cannot see it for ourselves. Thank goodness for family and good friends who are there to help us."

"Yes, Meagan and Ethan didn't get along. They never said anything mean or ugly to each other, but I could tell. She hinted a few times, but I wouldn't listen, so she held her tongue. I'm glad she's not the 'I told you so' type."

"How about we go over to Steak 'n Shake for a milkshake or something."

"I've never had their milkshakes. I've eaten their burgers and fries many times, but never a shake," she admitted.

"Well, we gotta fix that right now," he said smiling at her.

When Maddie and Nathan walked through the doorway, Meagan was relieved immediately. She had been calling repeatedly and was being routed to her voicemail.

"I've been trying to call you all evening."

"Oh, I didn't hear it ring."

Nathan held up a plastic bag with a glass inside and announced he had the evidence they had been waiting for. "It has Ethan's fingerprints on it." Meagan, Maddie and Ryan looked at the glass as if it were a precious jewel.

"How'd you get it?"

"I was on my way out the door when I saw Ethan standing at the sink chugging this glass of juice. He set it on the counter and left the room. So I snagged it."

With wide eyes, Meagan stared at the bag, she was confident they had him now. They couldn't have him arrested, but this could prove it had to be Ethan that took the money out of the bag like Maddie said. And with him offering her the exact same amount of replacement money, how could anyone think otherwise? But it was getting late, so this evidence would have to wait until morning.

At midnight, Nathan and Ryan left the girls' apartment and headed their separate ways. But Meagan's curiosity was killing her. She needed to ask Maddie a few personal questions now that they were alone.

"How did you and Nathan end up coming here at the same time?"

When Maddie told her about her evening with Nathan, she couldn't contain her excitement and couldn't wait to tell Ryan.

"Did you have a good time?"

"I had the most wonderful time and the best milkshake I have ever tasted," she giggled.

"Well, while you were out having a nice time, I was worried about you."

"I'm sorry. Oh, by the way, thanks for being my friend and not saying 'I told you so.' No one ever wants to hear that, and I appreciate you not saying it."

The next day, Meagan called Dunning Plumbing an hour before closing.

"Maddie, I've got news." she spoke hastily.

Maddie called Richard into Brian's office and explained how her roommate had been helping her clear her name. Maddie's emotions overwhelmed her, so she put Meagan on the speaker phone and allowed her to explain the details. She proceeded like a prosecuting attorney ready to wrap up her case. Maddie sat on the edge of her chair, as if she were the criminal awaiting her sentencing, even though Meagan had already told her the news. Everyone gave her their attention as she spoke with authority. "Chuck Williams, one of the lawyers where I work, took your money bag to a friend that works in the police department lab to see if there were any fingerprints belonging to our suspect. Of course, he found more than one set of prints on the bag as we knew he would. Our friend Nathan, was sly enough to get a glass that Ethan had drank out of and gave it to me to take to Chuck who took it to the lab. The results were very clear that the prints on the glass were the same prints also found on multiple places of the bag. They were found near and at the opening of the bag and a partial print that belonged to him on the zipper. So we can say it is very possible and even probable that Ethan opened and took the four hundred dollars out of the bag while Maddie lay asleep on the couch."

"Yes!" Richard shouted with his fist punching the air. He took Maddie in his arms and gave her a big bear hug. "We knew you were innocent, but you had to prove it, and now you know that we know." Letting her go but keeping one arm around her shoulders, "Meagan, thank you so much for your help, and tell Chuck we say thanks also. Now I want all of us to put this whole ugly mess behind us, and let's get back to normal around here. Oh and one more thing, this is cause for celebration, pizza at my house." Cheers and laughter erupted from everyone in the room, and Maddie let out a breath of relief. The Lord had answered her prayers. He had given her friends, who not only stuck by her, but also helped prove her innocence and clear her good name.

Todd laughed and praised the Lord out loud. Brian was as happy as his brother to have it come to an end, but he didn't like the fact that some thief made off with his company's hard-earned money. But the sparkle in Maddie's eyes had returned. Right now, that's all that mattered.

"But wait a minute, you all are still out four hundred dollars. I say we continue the hunt until we get a confession out him and make him pay the money back. Isn't there anything we can do?" Maddie asked.

"Unfortunately no," Meagan sadly responded. "We cannot prove he took the money out. He could give any excuse for touching the bag, and it's your word against his."

Todd called Karen to share the news and to tell her about the celebration dinner. She too was thrilled, but to her the mystery may have been solved, but not the case. Later when she spoke to Brian, she discovered he had the same thoughts. It wasn't the money itself. It was the fact that they were robbed, and it did not belong to whoever took it. It belonged to them, their company and their employees. The two discussed the facts over and over asking the same questions and finally accepting that they may never know the answers.

Knocking softly on the door, Fred looked to his friend, George. "Too bad you didn't catch this guy at home last week." After a few seconds, he continued. "I think you should do the talking."

"Why is that?"

"Call it a hunch."

"Brother Whitehurst."

"Hello, Nathan, can we come in?"

"Oh yeah, sure, I'm sorry. What brings you two here? Is your car broken down?"

"Oh no, nothing like that. We really came to see Ethan. Is he here?"

"No. Not yet anyway. Why? What's happened?"

"Nothing. Just out on church visitation and wanted to pay him a visit. Oh by the way, this is Fred, one of our deacons. Fred, Nathan Baxter." They shook hands, and Brother George continued. "Nate here is a marvelous mechanic."

"Thanks, I'm glad you think so."

"Is that so? Well, maybe I need to let you look at my Dodge."

"I'd be happy to take a look at it for you." Nathan all of a sudden remembered his manners. "Can I get you guys a cold drink? I think there are some Pepsis in the fridge."

"Sure, that would be nice," George answered.

George and Fred sat at the kitchen table talking to Nathan while he leaned against the kitchen sink. "What seems to be the problem with your Dodge?"

"It keeps overheating."

"Bring it into the shop, and I'll take a look at it."

"Well, Nate we came to see Ethan, but I'm glad we caught you home. We wanted to invite both of you young men to church. I think you know I'm the pastor at the Marydale Bible

Church, and we would love to have you pay us a visit. Who knows you may like us and come back."

"I've been meaning to start going again. I was raised in church. Just kind of got out and haven't gotten back in."

"Do you mind if I ask if you know the Lord?"

"Yes, sir, I was saved when I was a teenager and baptized." There was a brief pause, then Nathan asked, "I think Maddie Abbott goes to Marydale, doesn't she?"

George grinned at him. "Yes, she does."

While they were talking, Ethan walked in the back door that opened into the kitchen. Not expecting to see anyone, he stopped abruptly. And George noticed the change in Nathan's facial expression.

"Oh, excuse me."

"Hi there, are you Ethan?"

"Yes, have we met?"

"Not officially, but I do believe I saw you at a party a few weeks back given by my close friend Todd Dunning."

"Oh yes, now I remember."

"I see your face has healed up quite well."

"Yes, it has," he responded reluctantly.

Ethan needed to get out of the kitchen fast and to his room away from these two old men. He didn't have time nor did he care to talk to either of them.

"This is my friend Fred Lewis. We were talking to Nate here about coming to church. Nate tells us he knows the Lord, but got out of church years ago and has plans to start back I hope this Sunday. You think you can make this Sunday, Nate?"

"Aah..." Then Maddie's face flashed through his mind. "Yes, sir."

"I'm not a church going guy, so don't waste your time." Ethan remarked.

"Why is that?" George asked.

"I really don't see a need in it."

Ethan started to walk away, and George quickly continued to speak. "Being a pastor, I find your honesty to our invitation refreshing, but I would like to know why you don't see the need."

Ethan took a deep breath which showed his lack of interest in continuing this conversation with these two. "People go to church each week, they pray and what good does it do? I mean, look at our world. If God loves us so much, why is there so much meanness and crime, sickness and pain?"

"I think I can answer that question with a question. Why would God love us? What do we do to deserve His love? Have you done anything to deserve God's love this week? I know I haven't. How about you Fred?"

"No, nothin' comes to mind."

"But He loves us anyway. He loves us so much that He sent His only Son to this world to die for us, so that anyone who believes on Him would not perish but have eternal life with Him in heaven."

Ethan remained silent. His mind was divided between what George had just said and trying to come up with an excuse to leave the room. George's motive, however, was to keep him in the room and engaging him.

"Ethan, if you don't want to go to church, well…you don't want to go. But don't get going to church and accepting Christ confused. There are people who attend church every week who do not have Jesus in their hearts. There are people who are truly saved and on their way to heaven that haven't darkened the doorstep of a church in years. The Church is the Lord's house. We go there to worship Him, to learn more about Him and to gather with fellow believers. Now keeping that in mind, let me ask you this, do you believe in God? Do you believe that Jesus is God's Son?"

"Sure, I guess so."

"Okay, do you believe that Jesus died on the cross for you and me because of our sins?"

"Well, I don't know about that."

"Okay, again an honest answer and I appreciate that. I assure you that He did. And He also rose on the third day. He is alive and sitting at the right hand of God at this moment. Ethan, He knows you, knows all about you, and He died for you, son. You don't have to take my word for it. I can show you from the word of God everything I'm telling you is true. Will you let me show you?"

"No, I don't think so," he replied as he turned to leave the room again.

"Here take this. It's my card; it has my name and number on it. If you ever want to talk, just call me, no matter the time. Oh, and one more thing, every human being enters into this world the same way: by birth. There are only two ways out: through death or the rapture, if you're still living when Christ returns to call His children home. Either way, you will have to deal with Jesus, either as your Savior or as your Judge. If you meet Him as your Judge, that will mean while on this earth you rejected Him, and the Bible tells us He will say to you; 'Depart from Me, I never knew you.' And then you will be cast into a place where the flames are never quenched. If you meet Him as your Savior, that means that while on this earth you accepted Him as your Lord and He will welcome you home with open arms. Judge or Savior, it's your choice, son."

Ethan looked away from George without a response and walked out of the room. He wanted to get as far away from these two crazy old men as he could.

Still leaning against the sink, Nathan never said a word; however, he now regretted choosing to stay out of church all this time. And since he told George he would be going this Sunday, he had to go or he would not be a man of his word.

Twelve

Caroline ended her call with Joshua, and with hands on her hips, she began to pace the floor. She had just learned that her son may be put on academic probation and was having a hard time digesting the information. Joshua had worked hard to achieve his grades and had minimal issues getting through high school with the exception of a few classes here and there. He kept up on his homework, set aside time to study for tests and never waited to the last minute to do projects. Like most kids, he needed the occasional reminder that his homework had to be finished before he could hang out with his friends or watch TV. After all of that, she could not stand by and watch him lose it all now. He was no longer in high school. This was college, and he had to step it up.

When she asked the typical question all parents ask at these moments, "How did this happen, Son?" he gave her the typical answer all kids give. "I don't know." After a long talk, she firmly suggested he come home this weekend so they could sit down and work together on finding a solution to the problem. Then she did what she normally did: call Melissa.

"Are you free after work today?"

"Yes, what's up?"

"I need to talk."

"Okay, I'll be home after four like always."

"Great. I'll come by then."

Caroline put meat in the crock pot, prepared a salad, and put it in the fridge so she would have more time with Melissa. She could have called her, but she needed face time with her best friend. Melissa had a way of calming Caroline like no other, and after almost a lifetime of friendship, no topic was exempt between them.

"Caroline, just because his grades have slipped doesn't mean there is something awful going on. Does he have a girlfriend?" After asking, Melissa instantly regretted it.

"No, not that I'm aware of."

"Forget I asked that. I'm sure if he did, he would tell you. It could be he has just lost his focus."

"Yeah, that's probably it."

"I'm sure after you talk with him he will pull it together."

"Oh, he's gonna pull it together alright. He didn't work that hard for a serious scholarship to lose it, and we both know that's what will happen if he doesn't keep his GPA up."

The two talked more about the situation. Melissa asked if it were too much pressure for Joshua, even though they both knew it wasn't. She just wanted Caroline to answer the question for her own sake. She also kindly advised her to not be too hard on him...just yet.

Lying in bed that night, Richard sensed his wife was uptight about something because he heard her sigh a few times.

Clicking on the light, he spoke out, "Okay, what is it?"

"What?"

Richard propped up on his elbow giving her that look he gave when he meant business. "That's what I want to know. You've been lying here sighing for the past hour. So, let's have it, or neither one of us will get any sleep tonight."

Caroline sighed deeply. "Joshua called me this morning with some not good news. He may be put on academic probation. I cannot understand how this could happen. He has always done very well in school," she said in a firm tone. "If that happens, he is likely to lose his scholarship."

"Caroline, this is college. A lot of kids struggle from time to time. If he gets put on probation it may make him work harder." Silence filled the room. "Which classes is he struggling in?"

"I'm not sure, but certainly more than one. I told him to come home next weekend and we would sit down and figure it out."

"Now you see, that was a good step toward fixing the problem." Richard paused before continuing. "At least he has acknowledged this early enough to do something about it, and he still has time to turn it around." Richard was right. There was time to fix this problem, but she had been too concerned to think about that. He gave her a kiss and put his arms around her. "Now if anyone needs to lose any sleep over this, it's Joshua, not you. We'll help him, Caroline, as much as we can, but he is the one who will have to do the work."

"I know."

Nathan walked into the Marydale Bible Church feeling slightly nervous. What if he didn't see Maddie? Then again, what was he going to say when he did? Brother George smiled widely when he saw him come in and then moved toward him.

"Nathan, good morning! It's good to see you!"

"Good morning."

George sensed his nervousness. "Don't worry, son, she will be out here in a few minutes," he teased. "In the meantime we can chat a little. Hey, do you like to fish?"

"Yes, sir, haven't done any in a long while, but yeah, I like fishing."

"Great. Myself, Todd and some other fellas from the church are going fishing next weekend. You're welcome to come along and feel free to bring some of your friends with you."

"Thanks, I'll let you know if I decide to go."

"Alright. Oh, here she comes now."

Maddie was surprised to see Nathan standing near Brother Whitehurst, and feared her face would reveal her feelings if she didn't play it cool.

"Maddie, this young man is waiting patiently for you." Nathan stood quietly thinking, *oh you have no idea*. "I hope you will be kind and let him sit by you so he won't be alone." He said again in a teasing manner.

"I think I can do that."

Right after she and Nathan sat down, Richard came up behind them and said hello. Caroline soon followed and quietly spoke.

"Maddie, I need to speak to you after the service," she said as the music began to play.

"Sure."

It had been several years since Nathan had sat in a church service. It was all so familiar, kind of like going back to your childhood hometown after being a way for a long time.

He knew the songs and how the order of service would go. He didn't think to bring his Bible, but at this moment he honestly didn't know where it was. He was sure that it was in his stuff somewhere. He sensed eyes on him, but he chalked it up to nervousness and ignored it. His mind was mostly on the person sitting beside him, and he could smell a hint of her perfume. It was difficult for him to concentrate on what Brother Whitehurst was saying until he was well into his sermon.

He spoke of how Christian people lived their lives and how important being involved in church was. He then asked if the way they lived their lives pointed anyone to Christ, or did it point them away from Christ. That comment hung around in his head, and unintentionally, he found himself trying to mentally answer the question.

Nathan was a good person, didn't take what wasn't his and was kind and helpful to others. He didn't drink alcohol, do drugs or live a free-for-all lifestyle. He had just gotten out of church. That's all, and now he was being reminded that was not a good choice.

When the final amen was said and the service ended, Maddie turned around to talk to Caroline. Nathan didn't know if he should leave or wait for her. He chose to wait. While he stood off to the side, he and Richard engaged in a conversation of their own.

"Maddie, are you available for tutoring? Please say no if you are not. It really is okay."

"Aah, well it depends on the subject."

Caroline shared the details of Joshua's academic situation with her and that he needed a little help. "Did Joshua agree to this?"

"I haven't said anything to him yet. I was waiting to see what your answer was going to be."

She agreed only if it was alright with Joshua. If so, she would talk to him to get an idea of what the problem was and where to start.

Caroline invited them both to lunch, but since Maddie was put on the spot, Nathan declined.

"I'll talk to you some other time," he said touching her arm as he began to walk away.

She smiled at him saying okay. Caroline could have kicked herself for intruding.

"Oh no, I've caused him to leave. I'm so sorry."

"No, no need. We didn't have any plans. And besides, I didn't even know he was coming today. Really, it's okay."

———◆———◆◆◆———◆———

The following Friday afternoon Joshua drove home to talk about his grades and figure out a recovery solution. He dropped his large bag of laundry right inside the kitchen doorway and tended to his first order of business: opening the fridge and making himself a snack.

Hearing him come in, Caroline made her way to the kitchen. They chatted a few minutes before the plans for the weekend were made and the mentioning of a tutor came up.

"Mom! Please tell me you didn't! Why would you ask her to do that?! I'm not a little kid! Of course, she probably thinks I am now! No! I can fix this by myself!"

Joshua was not only stunned but also a little upset with his mother for talking to Maddie without his consent. Frustrated, Caroline didn't know why her son reacted in this way. Both went their separate ways to cool off.

Richard pulled in the driveway and saw Joshua shooting hoops and decided to join him like he had done on numerous occasions. Grabbing the basketball off a rebound, Richard took a long shot. "How's it goin'?"

"Mom asked Maddie to be my tutor that's how it's going. Richard, can you help a guy out and talk to her?"

"I'm sure she was just trying to help." Taking another shot, he continued. "Doesn't sound too bad to me. I mean, Maddie is your friend, right?"

"Yes."

"What's wrong with friends helping each other out? And a pretty friend at that. Sounds like a no brainer to me." This time the ball bounced off the rim and landed in Joshua's hands.

"I'm ready for some supper. How about you?" he asked walking away. Joshua just stood there holding the ball while Richard's words echoed in his ears.

A week had passed since the blow up between Joshua and his mom, and he honestly knew that a few weeks of tutoring just to get him back on track would do him good. Caroline didn't understand why he was so against Maddie helping him, and being his mother she never would.

Caroline cleared the dishes while he and Maddie sat in the living room going over his schedule, his activities and his class syllabus. Joshua admitted to himself he was embarrassed that Maddie knew about his school trouble, but on the bright side, he was going to get to spend time with her.

"Well, I see a few problems that can be easily fixed already. You have too many extra things going on. You're playing racquetball *and* Ultimate Frisbee," she noted as she read his schedule. *"And* being on a team means practice which takes up two or three hours a couple days a week, right?" He nodded his head. "Then there are the games which take up a big chunk of your time. Looks like you are also in three clubs, which is two clubs too many. The problem here is you don't have the time to study and do the work needed for each class. Here is what I highly suggest." Knowing Joshua was not going to like the suggestion, she bluntly told him, "Cut out two clubs and one sport. Remember, you are there to get a degree in something that you can earn a living at. The sports and clubs are there to help you be a well-rounded person and provide interaction with other students outside of class, not to keep you from studying and passing your classes."

He looked at her with a painful expression. "But I like doing all those things. I've made new friends in each of those."

"I can help you with your studies when you come home for the weekends, but it's not going to do too much good if you don't have the time to do the work. You have to cut some things out. I'm not suggesting you cut out your friends. I'm suggesting you make time to study."

Joshua didn't like what he heard. How could he choose? He and Austin had learned how to play racquetball and loved it. The first two weeks of playing, their knees ached and they both had enough bruises that would have made anyone else quit. The two were having too much fun. They had endured the pain and now were experiencing some of the gain. He would have to make a cut somewhere else, but not racquetball.

When Richard and Caroline came in the room, Maddie continued to talk like they had been there the whole time. "If it's any consolation to you, I was in the same boat my freshman year. For me it was sororities, clubs, going to games and hanging out with my friends. I tried to do it all and was failing everything. I had to do what you need to do...cut some things out *and* got a tutor. When I did that, I had time to do the work, and my grades came up."

Before Joshua left for school Sunday evening, he and Maddie worked out a schedule that allowed him time for one activity and plenty of time for studying. Since he was behind in most of his classes, she agreed to tutor him each weekend until he got back on track.

As Maddie was leaving, Caroline tried to pay her for her time. She refused, but they insisted. Remembering that she was saving up for a new car, Richard kindly suggested she put it into her car fund. She agreed, satisfying everyone.

— ⚜ ⬥ ⚜ —

For the rest of that day and a few times during the week, Brother Whitehurst's comment replayed in Nathan's head. He found it hard to believe his life pointed anyone toward or away from Christ. Right behind that thought was the guilt for choosing to stay out of church. *I'll just start going again.* That was the right answer, but he also knew it wasn't the complete answer. With his head and shoulders under the hood of a 2006 Ford truck, he recognized he needed to do some serious business with the Lord. He needed to confess and to ask forgiveness for getting out of church and staying out for so long. Stopping his work while still under the hood, and with wrench in hand, that is what he did.

— ⚜ ⬥ ⚜ —

The trees in Middle Tennessee were beginning to show the first signs of fall. Maddie loved this time of year. She imagined going to the mountains and just sitting outside on a hotel balcony that overlooked God's beautiful mountains and their many colors while sipping sweet iced tea. Her wallet, unfortunately, would not allow such luxury. Instead, she settled for a wonderful alternative at a nearby park with the single young adults from her church.

Richard and Caroline had been working with the single adults for the past six months. Richard could plan activities and outings easily for the guys, but when it came to the other half; he was at a loss and totally relied on his wife. Today's event was a gathering at Moss-Wright Park for a picnic and a friendly game of co-ed volleyball.

Meagan talked Ryan into attending. He was a bit hesitant, but agreed knowing she would be pleased. Making her happy made him happy. With Nathan possibly coming along, the decision to say yes was easier for him.

Maddie and Joshua worked together all morning and were ready for a break. When he got to a stopping point, they called it done for a few hours and drove to the park. On the way there, they had a chance to talk about topics other than school. Joshua had always been comfortable around Maddie, so chatting with her came easy.

"You know this is kind of weird going to a church activity where my mom and Richard are in charge. It's like being the kid in class whose mother is the teacher."

She laughed out loud. "Joshua that is exactly what it is, silly goose. Besides, your mom and Richard are doing a great job."

Prior to their tutoring sessions, they casually knew each other. After spending a few weekends together over his studies, they had become more like friends. Joshua had invited his best friends Austin and Dillon, and they were meeting him there. He had looked at the computer screen and text books long enough and was eager to be outside for a few hours.

"Joshua, after the picnic we can get in a few more hours of work," she gently suggested.

"Yeah, I know," he sighed.

Richard and Caroline arrived early to get things set up. Both were worried it wouldn't be a good turnout, Richard more so than Caroline. By start time, only two people had shown up, but within twenty minutes, a total of nineteen had arrived ready to eat and play volleyball.

"Dude, I was about to leave. What took you so long getting here?" Austin asked.

"I'm having to study all weekend and was a little late leaving the house. I'm just glad I got to take a break and come to this thing," Joshua explained.

Austin was Joshua's roommate at the University of Tennessee Knoxville and the two hung out a lot. Dillon attended Tennessee Tech in Cookeville and happened to be in town for the weekend.

"Break? Dude, how much homework do you have?"

"A lot," he grumbled.

Joshua explained how he had overloaded himself and was now struggling to keep his head above water. In order to catch up, he was coming home every weekend to work with a tutor. His grades were improving, but he missed hanging out with his friends at the dorm. Dillon and Austin looked at each other dumbfounded. They could not believe Joshua Martin, who had always made straight A's, was now struggling in college.

"Dude, I knew you were trying to do too much!" Austin exclaimed.

"Yeah, well…now I'm working my tail off to get back on track, but I'll do it. You watch. I am not going down."

"I'd say so with a tutor that looks like Maddie," Austin teased, and Dillon laughed.

Not knowing how Austin learned Maddie was his tutor, Joshua tried to cover his embarrassment and joke about it.

"Come on, guys. We're just friends, and besides she is waaay older than me."

"Hear that Dillon, Josh got himself an older woman." The teasing continued, and his friends showed no mercy. If the situation was reversed, Joshua wouldn't be cutting them any slack either.

As the three talked about school, it was now Joshua that couldn't believe what he was hearing. Dillon was carrying a full load and involved in only one extra activity. Austin's plan of action fell somewhere in the middle of too much work and too much play. Joshua was not upset with his friends teasing him, but he wasn't thrilled they knew he was being tutored.

Without ever saying it out loud, Maddie wished Nathan was coming. When she saw Meagan and Ryan and no Nathan, she was disappointed, but couldn't let that show no matter how heavy her heart felt. She let out a big sigh and continued to walk toward her friends. Caroline saw Maddie coming and met her.

"Glad you're here. How's the tutoring going?"

"Fine. He's doing fine. It isn't going to take him long to get back on track."

"Great! I'm so glad to hear that. Now, how are *you* doing?" Maddie looked at her knowing full well what she meant without having to ask.

"I'm okay. Right now, I'm not sure whom I'm angry at most: Ethan for what he did, or me for not seeing from the start the jerk he really is. Meagan saw from the beginning. Why didn't I? Why didn't I listen to her when she tried to tell me? And if being a jerk wasn't enough, he had to steal from my employer and make it look like I did it!" Looking off into the distance, she went on. "I thought he cared about me."

Caroline put her arm around her young friend. "First of all, Brian and Richard never believed you were the one who stole from them. And second, Ethan wasn't the one for you. Trust me. You'll find that special young man one day. Be glad you found out about him now before it was too late. It would have been much harder if you were engaged or married."

"Oh, that would have never happened. I mean I cared for him, but I'm not...I wasn't in love with him. I just thought he cared for me too."

Their conversation had to be cut short as the guests began to mingle closer to them. But as they went separate ways, she promised herself she would keep Maddie in her prayers. That was for sure.

With lunch finished, everyone was setting up to play volleyball when Meagan, seeing Nathan pulling up, nudged Ryan. He at once located Nathan's truck and walked across the grass waving so he could see where they were. Ryan had received a text from Nathan telling him if he could get there, he would be late.

"Look who made it," Meagan announced.

Turning her head, Maddie saw Nathan walking toward them. The sight of him made her smile inside. He wore a Nashville Predators t-shirt and gym shorts, and surprisingly his hair was down. She watched him until he was nearly upon them.

After the teams were selected, Maddie found herself on the opposite side of the net from Nathan. She was glad she had sunglasses on because she could not take her eyes off of his hair. As the match began, they were mirroring each other from opposite sides of the net.

"You're goin' down, Baxter,"

"Oh, a little smack talk. Think again, Abbott. You got a belly full of food; can't jump high with a belly full of hamburgers."

After a few sets, he pulled his hair back like he normally wore it. *I guess it gets in his way.* Forcing herself to focus on the game and not Nathan's hair, she made an aggressive play resulting in an added point for her team.

They chatted a little through the net, joking mostly. Was he trying to distract her or was he just being himself? She needed Meagan's help, but she was on Nathan's team and too involved in the game to notice.

It was a hot day. After finishing the match, both teams headed toward the cooler for something cold to drink. Joshua and his friends stood next to her guzzling their soft drinks when Maddie asked him if he needed a ride back to his house. "Before I go back to your house, I'm going to mine to shower.

"Okay, I'll ride back with Austin and Dillon."

Nathan was standing near her drinking his Pepsi, but at a more reasonable rate than Joshua's crew.

"You play well. I thought your team had us beat for most of the game," he admitted.

"Well, you know, never call it over, until it's over."

He chuckled at her comment. "I hear you're doing some tutoring?"

"Yes, a friend needs help," she volunteered freely. Then suddenly, she was aware of the fact she didn't have to explain her comings and goings to anyone anymore. The realization gave her a new sense of freedom, which was something else that Ethan had slowly taken from her. At first his jealousy was flattering, but soon it became a problem. She was angry at herself for letting him treat her the way he did. Their relationship was not serious enough to compel her to give an account to him, and that made her furious. *Never again.*

"See ya at church tomorrow?" she asked as they walked back to their cars.

"Maybe."

As she neared her car she spoke again. "Nathan, I'm glad you came today."

He winked at her then unlocked his truck, got in and drove off.

Later that night Nathan lay in bed thinking about the afternoon. He enjoyed spending it with Maddie but was unsure if her feelings for him were the same. She had been deeply hurt and needed time to sort through it all. He told himself he would wait, but for how long? How much would she need to put it all behind her? He would be devastated if someone else came along while he was giving her space. *This is a waste of time. I'll never fall asleep just laying here thinking about this.* He threw off the covers and walked to the kitchen for a late night snack.

Sitting at the kitchen table eating milk and cookies, he checked his phone and played a game hoping to relax his mind so he could go to sleep. He heard muffled voices but was unsure where they were coming from. As they got louder and more clear, he realized it was Ethan having a heated conversation with someone on his phone. Nathan attempted to ignore it, but it couldn't be prevented as Ethan walked toward the kitchen.

He paused in his conversation when he noticed Nathan sitting at the table, and neither one said a word.

It was a hectic Monday at the shop for Nathan; he was busy from the minute he arrived. He had replaced a set of brakes, a couple of starters and was currently up to his elbows in a transmission. On top of that, he also had three 'drop offs' to be looked over and given a diagnosis. At one-thirty he stopped what he was working on to eat his lunch and call Ryan.

"Yo, Coop, what are your plans this week?"

"Mostly working. What's up?"

"Dude, I gotta find myself a new place to live. It's too weird living in the same house with Ethan. I just want to punch that guy in the face every time I look at him."

"Sorry I don't know of any places for rent, but you can crash here tonight if you want."

"Thanks, man, I think I'll take you up on that."

"Talk to ya later."

After ending his call, he looked on Google for apartments in the area in his price range. There were a few possibilities, but he needed to get back to work. His search would have to wait until after five.

As she walked in the door of her apartment, Maddie sighed. *Another evening alone; just me and the TV.* She was feeling down and didn't know why. Date nights with Ethan were sporadic at best, so an evening alone like this wasn't out of the ordinary. She knew her Saturdays would be taken up with tutoring

Joshua, which she enjoyed, but she longed to do something fun this evening.

Maddie heard the knock at the door knowing it was Ryan. He and Meagan had a date. As Meagan slipped into her shoes, she asked Maddie about her plans, but immediately, she regretted asking.

"You can help Nate find an apartment," Ryan teasingly suggested. Everyone agreed it was a good idea for him to move out, but it also reminded them of why. They all tried to avoid talking about Ethan, but there were times when it couldn't be avoided. It appeared that Maddie had put it all behind her, or at least on the surface, but her friends didn't want to make things harder by continuing to talk about it.

At seven o'clock, Maddie was sitting in front of the TV eating her burger and fries. As she mindlessly watched a DVD, she found herself searching for apartments on her computer, although she had no idea why.

Thirteen

Joshua was committed to bringing his GPA up to where it needed to be and had been working hard with Maddie's help in doing so. In order to accomplish this painful task, he needed to cut out a few extra activities to make time to study. Even now after a few weeks of making progress, he was still surprised that he gotten into this predicament in the first place. He was realizing that he couldn't just float and have fun in college. He had to learn how to prioritize, maintaining his grades before he could be involved in more fun stuff. Right now though, his belly was telling him he desperately needed a snack. Looking at his cell and seeing that nearly two hours had gone by, he politely told Maddie he was taking a break.

While Joshua raided the fridge, Maddie took the opportunity to make a phone call. Finally getting up the nerve to call Nathan, she was actually relieved when he didn't answer. She left a message about a few apartments she had seen online. *What am I doing? He's going to think I'm nuts.* Her focus quickly changed, causing her to laugh when Joshua came back in the room carrying a large bag of chips, a full sandwich and a tall mug of Pepsi.

"Hungry, buddy?"

"Yes. Are you sure you don't want anything? I can make you a sandwich."

"No, the iced tea is enough."

With his mouth around a bite of sandwich, Joshua asked, "Maddie, I'm thinkin' of letting my hair grow out...like Nathan's. What do you think?"

His question caught her off-guard. "Aah, why?" Her brain went in overdrive trying to ignore the mental pictures of Nathan that kept flashing through her head.

"I don't know. There are a few guys at school who wear their hair like that, and the girls seem to like it."

"So, it's to get girls?" she teased.

"Noooo. That's a plus, but not the only reason."

"The question here is what will your mother say?"

"Yeeeeah that could be a problem...but what about you? Do you like guys who wear their hair like that?"

"Aah... I think we should get back to work," Maddie said with a chuckle, needing to drop the subject.

<hr />

Turning down Joshua's invitation to go with him and his friends to grab a pizza, Maddie got in her car and headed home. Her stomach reminded her it was time to eat, but didn't know what that was going to be. As she pulled into her parking space at her apartment, her phone rang. It was Nathan. Having no clue what she was going to say or how she would explain the message she left on his phone, she took a deep breath before she answered and let it out slowly.

"Hello."

"Hey, Maddie, I got your message. So tell me about these apartments you saw online."

Sounding calmer than she felt, she told him what she had found and where they were located. The first apartment building was not far from where he worked. Since she didn't drive that direction for anything, she silently prayed he would not ask her how she found it.

"I think I will go by there and take a look. Are you busy? Want to go with me?" He surprised himself. The words just flew out of his mouth, even though asking her out had been on his mind a lot.

"Aah, sure. Want me to meet you there, or..."

"I'm actually not far from your place now. I'll drive by and pick you up."

"Okay, I guess I'll see you in a few minutes."

Taking stock of herself, her clothes and her hair, she frantically rummaged through her purse for gum and a hair brush. *What am I doing? I can go inside,* she scolded herself.

Running to her bedroom, she quickly changed her blouse into something a little less comfortable, then hurried to the bathroom to brush her teeth and fix her hair. She heard a soft knock on the door as she set the hair brush down on the counter. Walking slowly to the door, she calmly opened it as if she had been ready all along.

As he steered out of her complex, she gave him the addresses. He casually mentioned he had not eaten. Neither had she, but she wasn't going to say anything. As hungry as she was, she had forgotten all about food the minute they ended their call.

"What about you? Have you eaten?"

"No. But we really should go by the apartment first in case someone is still at the office."

"Oh, yeah, you're right."

As they drove up to the building, it looked old and in need of many repairs. "The picture online looked a lot better, really it did," she apologized.

"Well, I don't think there's a need to go in. Let's drive to the next place."

The next place looked a lot better. "I think we can take a look at this one. Let's see if the office manager is still here."

Nathan introduced himself and told the man he was looking for a one bedroom apartment. He instantly went into his sales pitch. "I think the two of you will like living here. It's quiet and people won't bother you."

"Oh, we're not together. I mean, the apartment is just for me."

"I'm so sorry. I just assumed."

Maddie stood there trying to hide a grin. It was entertaining to watch Nathan squirm.

The manager showed them the one empty apartment available. As soon as they stepped inside, they were greeted by a smell that was an unpleasant mixture of animals and cigarettes. The carpets were worn, and Maddie was confident that's where the odor was coming from.

"This apartment has just been vacated, so I haven't had time to have the carpets cleaned, but I assure you they will be," the man promised.

Nathan continued to look around as the manager talked. He noticed the lock on the front door needed a few new screws, and the ceiling in the bedroom had a brown stain from someone smoking in bed.

After seeing the entire apartment, the three of them walked toward the door. "Thank you for your time. I have a few other places to look at before I make my final decision," Nathan politely stated, offering his hand.

Sitting at Steak 'n Shake eating burgers and fries, Maddie asked Nathan about the apartments he had seen so far.

"That was my fifth one," he chuckled. "I didn't know this would be so hard. I either find ones that have every luxury you could think of in them and are totally out of my budget, or ones like we just saw. I gotta find something soon."

"I have an idea that may help," she said, pulling out a pen and piece of paper from her purse. "Let's make a list of what you're looking for, starting with the area you need to be in. Then we'll move on to things you want to make sure the apartment has, and that might narrow it down some."

"Now, why didn't I think of that?" he asked before putting several fries in his mouth.

It didn't take him long to fill out the list, and since she lived in an apartment, she knew through firsthand experience that he needed to add a few things to his list, such as a dishwasher and good lighting.

"Are amenities important to you? You know, like a pool or a gym?"

"I haven't thought of that either. To be honest, I could care less about a pool, but a gym would be nice. Does your apartment complex have those things?"

"We have a pool and a laundry room, but not a gym, which brings another thought: laundry."

Clearly there was more to apartment hunting than he was aware of.

"I am so glad you're helping me. Other than the dishwasher, those things have never crossed my mind."

Talk about apartment details eventually faded. Now they sat sipping milk shakes and just enjoying each other's company. They began to learn more about one other, like finding out where they went to school and how many they had in their family. Looking around the restaurant, she noticed only one other customer. "I think we're the only ones here again." They both laughed out loud.

Neither really wanted to leave, but knew they should go. It was well after one o'clock when he drove her home, and being the gentleman that he was, he walked her to the door.

"Thanks for helping me…I didn't know apartment hunting could be so fun."

"Me neither. And you're welcome. If I find anything else, I'll let you know."

"Good night, Maddie."

Sunday morning came all too quickly. Maddie hit the snooze button one time too many. She woke abruptly, and once she saw the clock, she knew it was impossible to make it to Sunday School. She laid there for another fifteen minutes then stumbled into the kitchen for a bite of breakfast.

Walking in ten minutes before the service started, she found herself looking for Nathan. Seeing Meagan instead, she sat beside her.

"Why didn't you wake me?"

"I tried. You moaned something back at me then went back to sleep."

Meagan noticed her friend looking around. "I don't think he's here."

"Who? What are you talking about?"

Meagan chuckled out loud. "Right."

Nathan didn't make it to church that day because he too had overslept. Guilt engulfed him as he remembered his conversation with the Lord about getting back into church. Even if he left right now, he would never make it on time. He squashed his guilt and turned his focus toward finding a new place to live. He grabbed the Sunday paper from Kroger and a doughnut from Krispy Kreme and started his search, again.

"Yo, Nate, I got news man! There's an apartment in my complex that's about to be available," Ryan conveyed on the other end of his phone. "The guy lives on the opposite side of the breezeway from me, and I saw him moving his stuff so I asked him about it."

"Awww, Coop, that's great. Is the office manager in today?"

"I have no idea."

Nathan chanced it and drove there anyway. The manager was not only there, but let him see an empty apartment that he had just rented. Keeping Maddie's list in mind, he liked what he saw. He then filled out the necessary paperwork and felt confident he would be getting the place. When he mentioned Ryan as a reference, the manager all but promised him the apartment. When Nathan told Ryan they were going to be neighbors, they reacted like little boys going camping with their best friends.

Nathan only owned bedroom furniture and a television, which wasn't a problem since the apartment was small. He would ask his parents if they had anything they could donate to the cause. Maddie also had suggested he look at Goodwill and yard sales for some good deals. Not only was it a good suggestion, but it was another way to spend the day with her, so he gave her a call.

It didn't take long to learn that shopping was one of Maddie's favorite things to do. She knew exactly where to go for the items he needed. She joked that a person could find more than cars on the internet, which is where they found a small kitchen table with two chairs. From his parents, he got an old coffee table that was in the attic and his father's old recliner that was being replaced with a new one. To Nathan he had all he needed. Being a female, of course, Maddie knew otherwise. Before the day was over, they had also found him a bookshelf and floor lamp.

⁕ ⟶ ◦ ⟵ ⁃

Looking at the sky, rain was on its way. Loading his truck Nathan didn't think he could get to the new apartment before the weather moved in. His biggest concern was keeping his mattress and TV dry, so he doubled-timed it. He had spent the previous weekend painting the apartment, an agreement he made with the manager. The two worked out a deal if the complex supplied the paint, he would paint it himself, which would be discounted off the first month's rent and allow him to move in sooner. The apartment manager had never made a deal like that, but he could see the desperation on his future tenant's face. Additionally it was advantageous for both, so he couldn't lose.

"Alright, Coop, you get that end and I'll get this one." The guys quickly hauled his full-size mattress, big screen TV, and its stand up two flights of stairs. With help from Meagan and Maddie, they managed to get everything inside about five minutes before the November sky opened up and large, cold drops started falling.

"Thanks, guys, I couldn't have done this without your help."

"No problem, Nate. Hey, I thought your mom gave you a recliner."

"She did, but my Dad's still sittin' in it. Their new one gets delivered next week."

Maddie just sat back and silently thanked the Lord for placing these three in her life. As she gazed at them joking around and being themselves, she was grateful for how much help they had given her and how willingly they helped each other. Watching Nathan warmed her heart. She so enjoyed being around him. He was fun, smart and handsome. She could not ignore the respectful way he treated her, like she meant something to him. She tried to control her feelings for Nathan, but each time she was around him they became stronger.

"Hey, guys, how about we call in a pizza? I'm starved," Ryan suggested. Everyone agreed, and after they ordered, Ryan and Meagan left to buy soft drinks leaving the other two to wait for the delivery. They soon realized there weren't any glasses in the kitchen when they tried to get something to drink.

"Yo, Coop, get some cups will ya?"

"And paper plates," Maddie said loud enough to be heard from the background.

⸭————⟡————⸭

Maddie stayed awhile longer at Nathan's apartment after Meagan and Ryan had left again. She didn't have any plans for the evening, so he had invited her to stay. She didn't like sitting still knowing that more things could be done, so she offered to organize his kitchen which he gladly accepted.

Over the past several weeks, they had spent a lot of time together talking and laughing. His gorgeous smile kept her attention. She never thought she'd go for a guy who kept a three-day beard and had hair longer than hers, but she could no longer deny she found him attractive.

The day was long since over when she drove home. She remembered the night at the Sonic when she first saw him. She really didn't notice any of his features then, just that he was being a little rude. Of course another scene from that night came into her mind as well, when she fumbled with his change, rattling her initially, and then later their embarrassing fiasco with her Pepsi and candy that made her so angry. *No one can see clearly through angry eyes.* But now, months later, she sees a very different person. She notices everything about him, right down to his muscular hands. Turning down the covers well after midnight, Nathan still lingered in her mind.

The next weekend Joshua was home again with his nose in a book, trying to get caught up. He was tired of that routine and missed his free time. Continuing on, he promised himself he would not let this happen ever again.

When Maddie walked into the Dunnings's home Saturday afternoon, Joshua's long face spoke volumes. The arrangement was that she would come over Saturdays and Sunday afternoons to help him, so her being there was no surprise. She asked if it would be better if they skipped today's tutoring.

"No, everything's fine. I'm just tired that's all."

"Maddie, help yourself to something to drink or eat. I'll be in the other room with Richard. He's watching a ballgame," Caroline stated. "It isn't a game I'm interested in so I'll sit near him and read my book while he watches. It's known as spending time together."

Maddie laughed at her comment. She then turned to Joshua and contemplated his mood.

"Are you okay? You ready to get started?"

Taking a deep breath and letting it out slowly he grumbled, "I guess."

"Hey, before we get started, let's play that video game you showed me the other day." This seemed to cheer him up a little.

"I gotta tell ya, Maddie, I will get back on top of my grades, and this will not happen again."

"Keep that attitude, my friend." She patted him on the shoulder as she took the controller out of his hand and began the game.

Joshua was doing well, and she had no doubt after this semester he would not need her help anymore. But today he needed more than just tutoring; he needed support and a friend.

On her way home, Maddie remembered they were out of milk. Knowing she would come out with more than milk, she grabbed a hand basket and went toward the dairy case. Picking up what she needed, she quickly turned to leave when she almost ran into another person...and of all people.

"Excuse..." They stood there for the briefest of moments that seemed like hours.

"Hi, Maddie, how are you?" Ethan asked.

"I'm fine."

"Good. I'm glad to hear that." Both were silent, and neither seemed to know how to walk away. "I was just in here for some cheese and..."

"Yeah, there's always something needed from the grocery." Anger began to well up in her just at the sight of him.

He looked at her and immediately missed her. He was painfully aware he had lost a valuable jewel, one he could never get back. He wanted nothing more than to make her come back to him, but that would mean telling her everything, and he could not do that.

"Well, it was good seeing you again. Bye, Maddie."

Ethan walked away leaving her standing there. He seemed to always leave her waiting for something, a compliment, an explanation…something. Today was no different. He had cut her to the core, and her feelings toward him had changed. She swiftly made her way to the register to pay for the milk, making sure he was nowhere near her and left.

Within the few minutes it took to pay for her purchase and walk to her car, her anger grew to the point that she almost couldn't think. Deep in her heart she was hoping after all these weeks, he would admit what he had done and apologize to her, but it was not to be. She waited until she had cooled down before starting her car, only her car would not start.

Looking across the parking lot waiting for Meagan to answer her phone, she saw Ethan drive off in his shiny red Camaro. It was if someone had just punched her in the stomach.

"Meagan, I'm at the Kroger parking lot, and my car won't start. Can you come and get me?"

"I can. I'll be there in about forty minutes."

"Meagan, where are you?"

"I'm at the office. I had to work this afternoon, remember?"

"Oh…I forgot. Don't come. I'll call someone else. You stay and get your work done."

"Are you sure? I'll come get you, or…you could call Nathan."

"I know. I'll call you back if I can't get anyone else to come."

The truth was she didn't want Nathan to see her like this. *Joshua, maybe I can catch him.*

"Sure, Maddie. I'll be there in a few minutes." He quickly agreed to come to her rescue.

Now it was Joshua's turn to help her. He pulled up to Maddie's car thinking it probably just needed a jump, but that wasn't the case. He knew enough about engines to get by, but today he had no clue why the motor refused to turn over.

"Looks like you'll need it towed in somewhere."

He tried again making adjustments and listening to the moan it made when turning the key.

"Sorry, Maddie, I tried. Let me give you a ride home."

Maddie's mood was much lighter when Joshua dropped her off despite the fact that she would spend the rest of the evening trying to figure out what to do about her car.

Meagan walked through the door around seven. "I see you made it home. Who did you call?" she asked dropping her purse on a nearby chair.

"Joshua."

"Did he get it started?"

"No, it's still at the Kroger parking lot."

"Did you call Nathan?"

"No, I'm afraid he'll think I'm taking advantage of our friendship."

Meagan looked at her friend mockingly. "Oh honey, I think this little thing you two are denying is more than a friendship," she stated as she chuckled. "If you called him right now, he would drop everything and come runnin'."

Who was she trying to kid? Shaking her head at her own words, she picked up her phone.

"Hi, Nathan."

She continued on with explaining what happened and included Joshua's prognosis.

"Okay, I'll come pick you up and take a look at it."

The last time Nathan was under the hood of Maddie's car he had it running within ten minutes, unfortunately that wasn't the story today.

Standing up and wiping off his hands, he broke the news. "It looks like you've blown a head gasket, and the radiator is pretty much done. I believe it's time to make that purchase Mr. Dunning was teasing you about."

"Are you serious? My car is totally broken?"

"DOA is more like it. I'll have a truck come get it. but you'll be out more money getting it fixed than you will to buy a newer one. I can help you look for one."

Maddie was devastated. She loved her little beat-up car, her first and only car. "Thanks, Nathan. I appreciate your help."

"Hey don't worry. We'll find you a car, and I can get you to and from work until you find one."

"Oh, Nathan, that will be a lot of trouble. I can call Mr. Dunning and get a ride with him on his way in."

"You mean you would rather drive to work with a seventy year old man than me? I'm hurt, Maddie, hurt deep," he teased.

She laughed out loud at his banter. He could make her laugh like no one else. "Okay, you can take me to work."

"And?"

"And take me home," she laughed again.

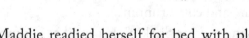

Maddie readied herself for bed with plans of looking over her finances; the incident with Ethan at the grocery was now totally forgotten. She should be upset about her car being out of commission, but wasn't since spending the evening with Nathan was fresh on her mind. With checkbook and laptop in hand, she pulled the covers back and crawled in. "Let's take a look at the ole budget," she said to herself.

Since working for the Dunnings' for the past several months, her bank account was in the best shape it had been in her life. She had lived on a shoe-string budget for so long it had become normal to her and she never adjusted her spending. When she finished updating her budget, she learned she had enough for a decent car, not a new one but a nice used one. And who better to help with that than a mechanic? The idea of buying a new car excited her. She didn't know what she was looking for, but she liked having a choice. She fell asleep after midnight with visions of cars flashing in her head.

Fourteen

Richard planned to enjoy his day off watching college basketball. He loved all sports throughout the year, but his absolute favorite was basketball. Caroline often sat in the room with him reading or on her computer while he watched other sports but she was a true basketball fan herself. She grew up watching games with her dad and brother, and during basketball season, she could be found sitting right next to her husband cheering for her favorite team.

It was busy around the Dunning household today. Despite it being his day off, Richard didn't mind the activity. He actually liked being around it. Seeing Joshua study so intently reminded him of his college years. Like him, he spent too much time goofing off resulting in last minute cramming for the tests.

Maddie had arrived mid-morning and did her usual routine, but today she particularly didn't want to waste any time. She had been invited along with a few others by Caroline to come over and watch the big game, and she was looking forward to it.

"We cannot goof off today, Joshua. Belmont plays Lipscomb this afternoon, and I'm watching it, so let's get busy," Maddie instructed.

"Who are you rooting for?"

"Belmont."

"So am I. Richard is for Lipscomb. It's gonna be a good game."

"It always is," she responded.

Joshua worked straight through stopping only for a short break and a trip to the bathroom. As he returned from one, Maddie laughed out loud when he came back with three pieces of leftover pizza and a soft drink.

"What?" he said with his mouth full. She just smiled.

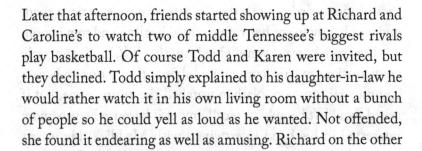

Later that afternoon, friends started showing up at Richard and Caroline's to watch two of middle Tennessee's biggest rivals play basketball. Of course Todd and Karen were invited, but they declined. Todd simply explained to his daughter-in-law he would rather watch it in his own living room without a bunch of people so he could yell as loud as he wanted. Not offended, she found it endearing as well as amusing. Richard on the other hand was rather envious of his father.

The guest list included Melissa and her husband Alex along with Adam Garrett, Richard's best bud, and his wife Sabrina. They also invited the single young adults from their church. Ryan's response when Meagan asked was, "Great, now I can see it on a big screen and in HD!" In asking Nathan, Maddie was still a little skeptical, but his answer melted her heart.

"That depends. Are you going to be there? If not, then no thank you. If yes, then may I pick you up and we ride together?"

By tip-off, fifteen people were sitting around the TV eating snacks in Caroline and Richard's living room. She and Melissa had stock piled soft drinks in the fridge and prepared finger foods for the game including Richard's favorite tortilla chips and cheese dip.

It was a fun reason to get everyone together. At times this crowd became loud and rowdy while watching such a close game. Richard would've preferred it was just him and his wife, but today he didn't mind the extra people enjoying the game with him. Nathan and Maddie sat on the couch next to one another. Even with the score tied at the end of the first half, he hardly watched because her hand was so close to his own. He inched his fingers closer, but paused, unsure of himself. *What if she pulls away?* His mind was getting the best of him. *Get a grip, Baxter. Be a man.* Heart pounding, he reached for her hand. Instead of pulling away like he feared, she entwined their fingers stirring both their hearts. Caroline noticed them and was happy to see her young friend healing and moving on.

Everyone's eyes were glued to the TV, and the only conversations were comments about the game when a commercial came on. Nathan watched the entire game, but if asked wouldn't be able to recall any of it because he was more interested in his hand intertwined with Maddie's. He wasn't sure where this was going or what it meant, but he loved how their hands fit together.

Sunday morning, Maddie saw Caroline after class and asked if she had some free time to talk. Caroline was more than happy to give time to this sweet girl. What she had to say was not a surprise to her. She had been keeping an eye on her from a distance after the issue with Ethan. For reasons she could not explain, she sensed the urge to protect the young ladies in her class like a lioness guarding her baby cubs.

"I don't get it, Caroline. Why did I spend all that time with someone like Ethan when I could have been spending it with Nathan? Am I that dense?"

"No, of course not." Caroline allowed her young friend to talk, getting everything that was bothering her out. "Now, Nathan and I are starting to get close and…well, he is all I think about. Some days I can't get much done. I'm afraid of moving too fast and getting hurt again. To be honest, I can't understand why Ethan hurt me so badly because I wasn't in love with him. I certainly didn't think about him like I do Nathan. He was my friend. I cared about him…but I wasn't in love with him." She paused and looked earnestly at Caroline for wisdom and answers. "So, why did I get so hurt and why am I so afraid now?"

Maddie seemed to have one difficult question after another, so Caroline weighed her words carefully. Before the conversation began she had prayed silently to be of help to her, and now this young woman looked to her for answers that she really could not give.

"At that time, it may not have been God's timing for you and Nathan to begin a relationship. If I remember correctly, you said your first meeting was not a good one. God works in ways we cannot understand, but as far as Ethan goes, it could be there was a lesson for you to learn from that experience." Maddie listened intently as Caroline continued, "Maybe it was for you to be a light in Ethan's world for a specific time. It could even have been you were out of God's will on this one, and He protected you from making a major mistake. Of course, I don't know that. I'm just giving you something to think about. If you are serious about wanting to know the answers to your questions, sit down in a quiet place and pour your heart out to the Lord, ask him those questions, and ask him to reveal what

He wants you to know." Maddie stared at the floor taking in what Caroline had just told her. "Also, you may want to ask Him about Nathan."

Her head swam from popping up so quickly. "What do you mean?"

"Ask Him if a relationship with Nathan is His will for you."

"Ooh...yeah I should, shouldn't I?" Caroline smiled and nodded her head.

"You were wounded because Ethan was your friend and you trusted him, and he betrayed that trust. Even though you didn't care about him in that way, he was your boyfriend, someone you spent a lot of personal time with. The deeper the hurt the longer it takes to get over it. But don't let his hurting you have a permanent place in your heart. The Lord protected you in that relationship, and now you need to let the Lord heal your hurt... He can, you know."

"Yes, I know," she replied softly.

"And don't think Ethan is getting off scot-free. The Lord knows all about this situation and He will deal with Ethan in His timing." Everything Caroline was saying made total sense to her. She felt silly for not thinking of it on her own. "And while you are having this heart to heart with the Lord, tell on Ethan." She noticed a strange look coming from Maddie. "Yes, tell on him. Tell the Lord everything he did to hurt you, even though He already knows. Then turn it completely over to Him, and if you are like me, you will need to ask Him to help you not to take it back."

The more Caroline spoke, the more Maddie's spirit lifted and her pain lessened.

"You'll be wise to not move too fast in this new relationship... that is where a lot of couples get into trouble. Take it slow and enjoy the chase. Oh, and if you and Nathan go too slowly, come back and we'll have another talk." Their laughter carried beyond where they were standing.

Caroline's words proved helpful. Even though Maddie considered herself a fool for getting involved with Ethan in the first place, she thanked the Lord for His protection and for giving her a second chance with Nathan.

Todd usually got to the office early, often being the one who unlocked the door. Though retired, he still liked coming in to spend time with his sons and the employees and to help out if needed. When Katie had been their receptionist, Todd would cover for her while she went and picked the kids up from school. He missed Katie working in the office.

His first order of business was to look around to make sure all was in order. Once satisfied, then he headed for the coffee pot. When Maddie and Nathan came in, they found him in his usual spot reading the paper and drinking a cup of coffee. As he looked over the top of his paper, a grin lit up his face when he saw them together as they exchanged greetings.

"Nate, how's it goin'?"

"Well, Mr. Dunning, it looks like I'm going to be Maddie's personal driver until she gets a new car," he said with a sparkle in his eye.

"Good man. Maddie, what kind of car are you looking for?"

"One I can afford."

Chuckling at her response, "I'll check around and see what I can find for you. And I'm sure Nate has some connections. All mechanics have car connections, don't they, Nate?"

"We have a few."

Nathan followed her to her desk watching her walk behind it and set her purse down. He leaned across towards her with his face very close to hers and spoke so that she only heard. Todd pretended to notice nothing, but he was laughing on the inside.

After dropping Maddie off, Nathan went to work and was all thumbs. If he dropped a tool once, he dropped it a dozen times. His boss noticed and withheld his laughter.

"Having one of those days are ya?"

"Yeah, I think I'm going to take a break for a minute, that is if I can get myself a cold drink without dropping it."

Nathan's boss John was a good guy. He didn't hound his employees. He gave them their space to work, but if one of them started to take advantage, they were out of there. He and Nathan got along well and were more like friends rather than boss and employee. He had on occasion invited Nathan to come over to his house and help him as he restored an old heap back to its former glory.

Nathan had given Maddie time and space to get past Ethan and his garbage. He wanted her to know his intentions, but he was afraid she would run like a scared rabbit. They were at the handholding stage so it was time and he didn't want to hold back any longer.

"John, do you know of anyone who has a car for sale?" he asked as John put coins in the drink machine.

"What're ya looking for?"

After Nathan gave him some details, he offered a list of options he thought would be a good fit for Maddie and in her price range. Car guys had their favorite places to find a good

A Second Chance

buy. If they couldn't find one, it wouldn't be long until one would find them, and John had a knack for it. His heart was in repairing and restoring, not selling, but he helped his friends out when he could.

"No, but I'll check around for ya."

John was an outright, easy-going, good ol' boy. No one would ever accuse John of wasting his words because he said what was needed and that was it. Nathan assumed that was one of the reasons they worked so well together. A year or so ago, John had to let an employee go because he wasn't that good of a mechanic. Over time too many cars had returned to the shop to be reworked due to this guy's oversight or lack of know-how. But another reason which had nothing to do with his skills was that he constantly talked and it got on John's nerves.

After lunch Nathan was more settled down, and for the remainder of the day he dropped his tools less. Somewhere between his ham sandwich and his cookies he made his mind up that it was time to define his and Maddie's relationship. He prayed they were both on the same page; he certainly didn't want to be in love alone.

---◦◦◦---

Caroline usually had supper on the table at the same time each day. If she didn't, Richard didn't make a fuss, but it meant she either had a rough day or something had gone on to shift her schedule. Stepping into the kitchen from the backdoor, Richard's nose immediately identified the aroma of chicken and dumplings floating in the room. "Mmm smells good," he said as he gave her a peck on the cheek.

"Thank you. If you'll wash up, we'll sit down."

After the blessing, Richard began updating her on the new budding romance between Nathan and Maddie.

"I know."

"What do you mean you know?"

"Honey, it's been going on for a while. Have you not noticed them at church and at the picnic? Then here watching the ballgame holding hands?"

The fact that his exciting news wasn't actually news at all left Richard feeling a little deflated.

"Oh, by the way, we are going over to your parents this evening for dessert and coffee."

Todd and Karen were essentially having the same conversation at their dinner table too. Karen listened to her husband without much interruption about what he saw in the office. It was strange and so unlike him to get involved in other people's affairs, especially those of the heart. Her feelings around this were split between worry and amusement.

As they finished, she told him Richard and Caroline were coming over after supper for dessert and coffee, and then changed the topic to what was really on her mind. While she had his full attention, she suggested it was time to do some refurbishing to the house. Her news didn't go down as smoothly as the meal she prepared. His reaction was more like a piece of meat lodged in his throat, which didn't truly surprise her.

"Our cabinets are outdated and warped. And the counter tops have nicks on the edges. Todd, we haven't done anything to this kitchen in twenty plus years, and I think it's time we did."

"But, honey, there isn't anything wrong with the kitchen. Do you know how much work that will be, not to mention the cost?"

"I know dear, but I'm not asking for anything that is not necessary."

Todd was a typical man. He could live in the same house for twenty years and never notice the need for any changes. He was also a man who didn't buy unnecessary things, and to him new kitchen cabinets were unnecessary. He kept his yard and garage in tip-top shape, but when it came to more domestic areas like buying new furniture, decorating or replacing things that were old and worn out, he just didn't take notice. Karen wasn't a woman to constantly be purchasing new stuff, but when things were worn out or broken she wanted to replace them. When she went shopping with one good friend in particular, almost without fail her friend would spend well over a hundred dollars on foolishness. Knowing how Todd would respond to that, she would always spend carefully on those trips.

Karen had made Todd's favorite dessert, red velvet cake, not only because Richard and Caroline were coming, but also to help butter him up to the idea of a new kitchen. She always made sure there was at least one of his favorite foods on the table every meal, her way of showing her love to him. She was hoping he would reciprocate his love with a new kitchen.

"Your mother doesn't understand how much work goes into remodeling a house...and money," he grumbled as he and Richard sat in the living room drinking coffee.

"Well, Dad, you and Mom have lived in this house a lot of years, and not to be taking sides, it could use a little facelift. You know me and Brian could help, and I know some guys who do this type of work. We could hire them, maybe do some trading."

"Trading?...of what?"

"Some plumbing work for some remodeling work."

It was as if a light just came on. "You know, that might not be a bad idea." Rubbing his fingers over his past five o'clock shadowed chin, he replied, "Son, you find some fellas we can work and trade with and we'll make a deal."

"Karen! Come in here, please."

Getting up from the table with her iced tea, she and Caroline went into the living room where their husbands sat.

"Our son here has an idea of how we can get this kitchen work done."

Karen was shocked that Todd had agreed to the remodel so quickly. He usually made her wait for months before considering such things. *Was it the cake or their son?* Either way she was thankful. She and Caroline returned to the kitchen and began chatting about the different ideas she had. They discussed styles, designs and eventually color. Finding just the right look was not an easy task and was going to require research. Karen kept up with technology as much as the next person her age, and starting tomorrow she would go online to search for ideas. As they left, Karen kissed her son and thanked him for his help.

Later that night turning down the bed covers, Karen was still a little stunned at what had happened here this evening. She had known Todd Dunning most of her life. He was her man, and she knew him like the back of her hand. After forty years of marriage, she could interpret his moods, determine his likes and dislikes and predict how he would react about certain things. But this evening he had thrown her a curve ball.

After arriving back at their place, Richard and Caroline too settled in for the night. As they laid in bed, they chatted as they did most nights. "That was a great thing you did for your mom this evening."

"I hope so. Big projects like that are stressful on people." Richard's mind took him back to a time in his childhood when his parents had a big renovation project. His father wanted to add a back patio and was determined to do most of the work himself. Todd, wanting to teach his sons how to work with tools and do things themselves, he made them help where they could. For what seemed like endless Saturdays they worked out in the hot sun digging, sawing, hammering and pouring concrete on what eventually became a patio. The frustration grew as the project took longer and cost more than expected. The memory of this event caused a small smile to come across his face as he remembered how Brian had played a trick on him and put wet cement in his shoe. Of course such an act called for retaliation. One night after Brian was sound asleep, Richard took duct tape and taped him to the bed. The next morning when he awoke, the look on his face was priceless.

Richard tossed his truck keys to Maddie so she could go make the bank deposit. She really didn't like driving someone else's vehicle, but she had no choice right now. She refused to act like a baby and tell him she was afraid of wrecking it or that his truck was too big, although both statements were true. Thinking she had to look like a little kid playing in their daddy's truck, she was glad no one was around to watch her climb into the cab. To her, the steering wheel looked like it belonged on a semi. If the truck was a manual, she would have a real excuse not to drive it. Closing the door she settled herself behind the wheel, fastened her seat belt and put the key in the ignition. It started right up. This was a man's truck alright, and she had to drive it. *Just go slow,* she told herself.

She made it to the bank without mishap. She desperately wanted to stop at Sonic for a large soft drink, but pulling this big vehicle into the stall made her shudder. Instead, she went straight back to the office to park this thing, relieved the task was over and done. Pulling into Richard's parking space, she blew out a long breath. Never had she experienced such a serious drive. Stopping at Richard's office, she gave him back his keys. He was on the phone so she mouthed the words thank you and left. Since the ordeal was over and she had indeed survived, she stopped by the vending machine to reward herself. Hearing the coins slide down the machine, she knew it would only be seconds until her peanuts would appear. Add that with her cold Pepsi and she was a happy gal.

The afternoon flew by as Maddie worked to get her list of things done. Todd had left a few hours ago, so her area was quiet. She was so engrossed in her work that she didn't notice someone standing at her desk.

"Aa-humm."

"Oh, hi… oh my, what time is it?" she asked rubbing her neck. Looking at the clock, she saw it was just past quitting time.

Nathan stood there smiling at her. "Take your time. I'm in no hurry."

He sat down in Todd's chair and enjoyed the view. There was no doubt about it. He could sit and stare at Maddie all day. She shut down her computer, locked up the filing cabinets, and wrapped up several other end-of the-day tasks. After she was finished, she turned his way and flashed a big smile at him. It was the best part of his day.

"Do you have to get right home?"

"No, I don't have any plans."

"Would you like to stop at Sonic for a snack?"

"That sounds wonderful."

"Great." Pulling into the Sonic, he ordered soft drinks and a large fry. He was too nervous to eat, but needed something to do with his hands.

She unfastened her seat belt and turned sideways to look at him.

"How was your day?"

She didn't respond, and he smiled wondering what she was thinking.

He has the most handsome face. "Hmm, oh I'm sorry, what did you say?"

She told him about her day and driving Richard's truck. He laughed softly at the mental picture of this petite woman driving a full-sized heavy duty Chevy truck. He loved listening to her talk, and he wanted to spend the rest of his life hearing that voice telling him about every part of her day.

When she asked him the same question, she was thrilled to know she had someone looking for a vehicle on her behalf. "With two people looking, maybe I will find something soon. Todd said he would ask around too."

"I figured he would. He thinks a lot of you."

"What makes you say that?"

Looking at her, Nathan realized she was serious. Was she that unassuming or did she really think she wasn't special to anyone? The carhop rolled up before he could answer her question.

Nathan said the blessing for their snack, something he never did before. Now that he had gotten back in church and was spending time with Maddie, he was becoming more comfortable doing it. He so wanted to share what was on his mind, but wasn't sure how she would respond. Wherever they were in their relationship he certainly didn't want to mess that up.

"You know, Nathan, I truly enjoy being with you."

He responded with a small smile. She kept talking a bit more than usual, just random chatter which made him wonder if she sensed what he was about to say. He had friends, mostly female friends, who were nervous talkers, but he had never seen Maddie do this before. As they ate, their conversation covered a lot of ground going in many different directions. In no time the fries and soft drinks were finished, and she needed to get home. He wanted to kick himself right now for not just blurting out what was in his heart.

Fifteen

Nathan questioned himself for the hundredth time and now at the point of no return, he feared Maddie's reaction. He had worn his hair long for the past five years. The chair at the salon was somewhat comfortable, and the clipping sound of the scissors echoed in his ears; he could hear each individual strand being cut. He wasn't sure where Maddie stood with long hair on men, especially on one who was interested in her. However, he had caught her staring more than once when he wore it down along with some people at church, but they didn't matter to him. The stylist braided the first section and cut it with sharp scissors, then laid it down on a clean, white towel to put with the rest of his hair that would be given to Locks of Love. This was not his first donation to this organization. Before his junior year in high school, he and several other students had grown their hair out for that reason alone...well, almost that reason alone. He and the two other guys did it to impress the girls they had their eyes on at the time, and it worked. He and his buddies wound up dating those girls and then going to the junior prom with them.

"Remember you can always grow it back," she consoled after the majority of it had been cut. She finished the whole process including styling it in about forty-five minutes. It was short for him and definitely a different look, but to the average eye, not terribly so. The stylist blew it dry and put some gel on it, which he never used, and didn't care for it now. His new hair style was at his neck line with the bangs having a messy look. Not wanting to throw himself nor Maddie into too much shock, he kept the short beard.

"I have to tell you, you have the most beautiful head of hair I have ever seen on a man. It's full and has just enough body to make any woman jealous. It's healthy, no split ends…I'm telling ya, women would kill for a head of hair like this. What do you use on your hair?" she asked as she continued to style.

"Shampoo and conditioner," he replied.

"Wow." There was no need for her to try and upsell this customer on hair products. "Well, how do you like it?" she asked giving him a hand mirror to see the back.

"Looks good, thanks."

Running up the flight of stairs and gently knocking on the door, he wondered what was taking Ryan so long to answer.

"Sorry man I was in the showw…Dude, you got a haircut."

"Yeah, just now."

"It's been awhile since you had it that short." Taking another glance, Ryan gave his approval. "Looks good. Has Maddie seen it yet?" he asked putting on his T-shirt.

"No, not yet."

That was the end of their conversation about his hair. If it were any longer, they would both have had to hand over their man cards.

Nathan showed up at Maddie's apartment at the usual time to take her to work. He waited in the truck and answered his cell phone. It was John with news about a car he had found.

A little breathless from her walk out to his car, she greeted him. "Good morning, Nathan. Sorry you had to wait on me. It took longer to fix my lunch than usual, and you cut your hair."

"So, what do you think? I can always grow it back and I will. I always do."

"It looks nice, really it does." She was honest and surprised that she was a little sad. "I gotta ask. Why did you have it cut?" The words sounded silly in her ears. His hair, after all, was past his shoulder blades.

"You really don't like it, do you?"

"No, I do. I was just wondering why?"

"Back in high school, me and some guys grew our hair out along with some girls and donated it to Locks of Love. And I don't know, ever since I've grown it long to donate it. It's just something I've done for the past I don't know how many years."

Maddie's heart overflowed with emotion after hearing his words. This guy was so considerate of others. "I think that is the most wonderful thing. You're a good person, Nathan Baxter."

"Well, whatever," he replied embarrassed. He quickly changed the subject to his recent phone call. "Oh, by the way, John called while I was waiting for you to come out, and he said he found a car that you might like."

"Oh goodie!" she cheered, grinning ear to ear like a child being given a reward for some good deed.

Todd wasn't in the office like usual. Maddie inquired about him as Richard walked by. "Where is Todd today?"

"My parents are picking out new kitchen cabinets today."

"Oh, that sounds like fun," she responded. He laughed out loud and told her that his father was most definitely not having fun.

Maddie was distracted today. She had made several small errors and mentally scolded herself. When Todd arrived midmorning, he sat down with a cup of coffee and saw her sitting at her computer looking off into space.

"Hey there, Maddie." She continued to stare. "Me and the Missus just robbed a bank. That's why I'm just now getting here." Nothing.

Jerking at the sound of sharp snapping, she turned and saw Todd standing on the other side of her desk.

"Oh, Mr. Dunning, you're here. How did the cabinet shopping go?"

"As well as it could I guess. So what's on your mind today?'

"Oh nothing. Just working."

He laughed out loud knowing full well that was not true.

Richard walked out of his office looking for his father to let him know a contractor friend would be coming by after work to talk to him about the remodel.

"So I need you to stick around, okay?"

"Alright I'll call your mother and let her know I'll be late for supper. You've already talked to him about a trade?"

"Yes, sir. That's part of what he is coming to talk about."

<hr/>

With John standing nearby, Nathan walked around the car lightly running his fingers all around the exterior, then opened the doors and looked at the panels. Next, he tested the motor. Cutting the engine, John began sharing the details around the car's owner.

"A friend of mine bought it for his daughter when she was learning how to drive. The daughter recently bought a new one, and they want to get rid of this one."

Selling a car privately instead of trading it at a dealership was always more profitable, but came with more risk. With the lead coming from John, he felt the car was a good buy after he had looked it over. He took a few pictures with his phone and sent them to Maddie after hearing the price. It was a nine year old Mazda, and he could tell by the condition it had been well cared for. Oil change receipts and maintenance records were in the glove box along with the owner's manual.

Hearing her phone ding indicating she had a message, she stopped to look at the screen. She answered Nathan's text and then tried to focus on her work which had been difficult all day. He would be there to pick her up in less than half an hour and her workload was as big as it was earlier that morning. "I really should stay late and get this done," she said, inadvertently out loud, quickly learning Todd had rounded the corner and heard her.

"Talking to yourself again, Maddie? You know that is a sign of losing your mind or old age. Being of sound mind and a middle-aged man, I never talk to myself," he chuckled at his own joke.

She couldn't help but laugh out loud. Todd was such a sweet man, and he always made her laugh. "I'm losing my mind. You usually leave around three-thirty. Why are you still here?" she added.

Todd explained the trade he was working out with Richard's contractor friend who was coming by after the shop closed. She then told him about the car she might be getting. Just as she finished, Nathan walked through the door, and the twinkle in her eye couldn't be missed.

As soon as Todd saw Nathan, he noticed his haircut. If he didn't comment on his new look, then he wouldn't be Todd Dunning.

"Well, I see you found some scissors," he joked shaking Nathan's hand. They both had a good laugh, and Maddie explained about him donating his hair. "I never understood why you wore your hair like my old school teacher," Todd continued causing everyone to laugh. Shifting the conversation back to Maddie's potential new car, he looked to Nathan. "So you looked at this car, and it's safe and at a good price?" For unexplainable reasons, Todd felt protective of Maddie, especially after her situation with Ethan.

"Yes, sir. I looked it over from bumper to bumper, and drove it a few blocks. It's been taken good care of, has a few nicks around the hood, but that's normal for any car that's been driven very long. I think it's a good buy."

Todd trusted Nathan when it came to cars. All the Dunnings did, and he also trusted him with Maddie's heart.

"Maddie, this is John, my boss and good friend. He's actually the one who found the car."

John and Maddie exchanged hellos, and then Nathan opened the car door and let her sit inside.

"Oh my goodness, this is so much nicer than my other car! How much are they asking?" she inquired a bit nervously.

"Twenty-six hundred, but I think I can get him down a little," John responded.

She had the money, but it would be a big hit to her account. She would let John do his thing and pray it would all work out. She listened to the two guys talk their car talk. It sounded like a different language. No missing it, these two had a passion for automobiles. Before they left, their conversation turned to restoring vintage cars, and John invited her to the back bay to see what he was currently working on.

"It's a 1965 Mustang. I found it in a junk yard, paid nine hundred for it. Don't look like much right now, but when I'm done, it'll look like this," he said handing her a magazine opened to a page displaying a candy apple red Mustang with chrome bumpers and white interior. He continued, "There are a few original things I can keep like the steering wheel, door handles and most of the knobs, but they need a lot of work. This whole car needs a lot of work." This piqued her interest.

"So, after you're finished restoring it, what will you do? Drive it or just look at it?"

"Sell it."

"Really?"

"Yes. It's the chase. I love restoring old things back to new." He took her over to his desk and showed her a photo album of vehicles that he had restored. "See this one. It's a 1955 Chevy truck. I paid a thousand for it. Ole Nate here helped me with some of the work. I took it to a car show last year and sold it for twenty-eight thousand."

Nathan laughed at the memory of working on that old beat-up truck. Maddie on the other hand could not believe her ears. This man bought old beat-up vehicles that were virtually worthless and turned them into expensive collectibles.

"John, what do you drive?"

"I drive a 1977 Chevy pickup."

"Did you restore that too?"

"Yes, ma'am," he responded with delight. Walking to the door, he led her outside to show her his pride and joy.

"This was my Dad's. I bought it from him, didn't think he would ever sell it. It wasn't in bad shape, just old…it's actually the first one I restored."

Maddie was enjoying this peek into Nathan's world. She had never restored anything, but found it all fascinating.

———⚬———

When they got back to her place, she invited Nathan in. They hadn't intended to stay at John's talking for so long, but she totally enjoyed herself. He took a seat at the kitchen table as she began to scurry around the kitchen. Dropping a handful of spaghetti in a pot of water, she turned and spoke. "You will stay for supper, won't you?" How could he resist.

Watching her move between the stove, the fridge and the cabinets, the words he'd been trying to find for weeks finally came spilling out. His mouth spoke without checking in with his brain. "Maddie, I've been wanting to tell you something, and I hope you don't mind what I'm about to say. But I really would like it if we made it official and became a couple." The words didn't come out just right, but when the brain is left out of the mix, that was bound to happen.

She turned towards him with a grin. "I think I would like that very much."

Letting out a huge sigh of relief, he quickly wrapped his arms around her.

There was a rustling at the door and the sound of keys being fumbled. As the door opened, Meagan caught a glimpse of Nathan and Maddie quickly separating. Meagan felt her face grow warm as she said hello and walked quickly to her own room giving the two lovebirds some privacy.

Hearing the soft knock on her bedroom door, Meagan opened it part way.

"I'm making spaghetti, would you like to join us? You could call Ryan and invite him over. It's not too late to add more pasta to the pot."

She had talked to Ryan only ten minutes earlier, and they had planned to grab a quick meal out. Truth was she really didn't want to go out this evening. Her day had been busy and hectic. She just wanted to take her shoes off, put on a comfy pair of jeans and old T-shirt and relax. But she also didn't want to intrude on Maddie's evening with Nathan.

"I'll call Ryan and see what he says."

A few minutes later, she let Maddie know to add two place settings and that Ryan would be bringing the dessert.

During their meal, the four covered a variety of topics. As she swallowed her last bite of dessert, Maddie thought about how they had become so comfortable around each other and how much she loved spending time with this group.

"So what was the decision on the car?"

"John is going to talk to the owner and see if he will come down any. I can't wait to find out." No one could miss the excitement in her voice.

"Hey, what color is it?" Meagan wanted to know.

"I don't know the car term, but in laymen's terms it's burgundy." They all laughed at the way she answered the simple question.

"I have a friend in the insurance business, and she told me that people who drive red cars get pulled over more often and get more speeding tickets," Meagan explained.

"Seriously?" Ryan asked in disbelief.

"Yes, seriously."

"That makes me want to go out and buy a red car and prove that person wrong."

"You do that, Coop." Laughter filled the room.

While Maddie searched for something to watch on the TV, Meagan and Ryan loaded the dishwasher which wasn't usually the case. The system in their apartment was the one who cooked did not have to do the clean-up. Maddie unfortunately was not that good of a cook, so she usually had dish duty most nights.

"Wow, that's some DVD collection."

"Thanks, you like cars. Well…I have a serious DVD collection," she replied thumbing through the stack, "but I can't find one of my *NCIS* DVDs. Meagan, have you seen my *NCIS* season eight DVD?"

Coming out of the kitchen, Meagan answered. "No. Are you sure it isn't in all…that?" she asked waving her hand toward the overfilled case.

"No, they are all here except season eight." Maddie let the matter drop, for now. "We'll just watch something else."

The two couples decided to watch *Psych* instead. Ryan had his arm around Meagan while Nathan sat with Maddie snuggled at his side. Even though this was her favorite show, Maddie found herself too distracted by the missing DVD to really enjoy it.

Ryan and Nathan left around ten o'clock since they all had work to get up early for the next day. When the door shut, Maddie's question took Meagan totally by surprise.

"Can I borrow your car?"

"Where are you going?"

"To get my DVD back." Meagan saw the intensity in her roommate's eyes and was quite sure what was about to happen.

"I'll drive you."

Pounding on the door, she heard voices from the TV. The door opened and there he stood dressed in the same dress clothes he worked in, minus his shoes. Ethan was just as shocked to see her as she was to spontaneously be there.

Pushing her way in, he had no choice but to step aside. Her aggressive actions surprised her as well as Meagan, who stood just outside the door watching the memorable scene play out.

"You have taken something from me, and I want it back, *now*. So either hand it over or, I promise you, I will start ripping this place apart," she warned taking a quick glance around the room.

"Excuse me!" He had been caught. What he didn't know was how she had figured it out. He knew there was no way anyone could prove he took the money. Taking the few steps it took to cross to the living room to where the entertainment center stood, she started rummaging like a hunting dog on a hot scent. She flung stuff in all directions making sure she tore the room up like he had torn up her world.

"Hey! What do you think you're doing?" he demanded while dodging a flying DVD.

"Getting what belongs to me," she hissed through gritted teeth holding up the DVD in question. "And let me tell you something, Ethan Price. Every time there is something in my apartment missing, you can bet I will come back here to find it!" On those words, she left him standing in the middle of his living room in his sock feet with his mouth hanging open, relieved it wasn't what he feared.

Meagan didn't know Maddie could slam a door that hard, but she believed she heard the siding rattle when it did. Pulling out onto the street, Meagan broke the silence.

"Whoa! Were you awesome or what?! I have never seen you act like that before…and to be honest, for a few minutes I was a little scared."

Maddie's heart was pounding way too hard to speak, but shot her friend a half-smile. The truth was she had never done such a thing in her life. As her adrenalin slowed and her heartbeat returned to normal, she was proud of herself. For the past few months, she had walked around being a victim of a thief. The item retrieved was small, but her victory was huge.

Sixteen

The first day of December John handed Maddie the keys to her new car. She was beside herself with joy, "Come on, Nathan. Let's go for a ride," she giggled.

Pulling out onto the street, Maddie loved the new car feel. Even though it was not brand new, it was new to her. Finally, she got to experience the fruits of her labor. They rode around for about half an hour. It was a beautiful evening, the moon not yet full. While they were stopped at an intersection she noticed the shiny light reflections on the hood of her new car.

"Wanna stop in at Steak 'n Shake? I'm buying," she declared.

"Yeah, I never turn down a free shake."

The Steak 'n Shake seemed to have become 'their place'. The waitresses were starting to ask if they wanted their usual.

When the shakes arrived, Maddie took a long draw from her straw, her eyes closed in contentment.

"I don't think I have ever met anyone who loves a chocolate shake like you do," Nathan commented with a hint of laughter.

"What can I say, it's delicious."

"I, on the other hand, am an equal opportunity milkshake lover. I don't play favorites," he stated after taking a drink of his peanut butter shake. She couldn't contain her laughter.

"Ahh, you may not have a favorite, but you do have one that you order a bit more often." He was intrigued. Did she really know that much about him? Had she noticed such a small thing, something he wasn't aware of himself? Learning this warmed his heart.

"So tell me, what flavor do I order more often?"

Holding back her answer, she kept him in suspense until she could not contain her amusement any longer. "Strawberry."

"Really?" he questioned slightly skeptical.

Chuckling out loud, she asked, "How could you not know that was your favorite?"

"I don't know. I guess because I don't always order it."

"I wonder if you have any other favorite things you're not aware of...favorite jeans, t-shirt?"

"I don't know. You'll have to pay more attention and let me know." Swallowing another long swig of his shake, he added, "There is one favorite I have that *you* may not be aware of." Her curiosity was now piqued. Playing with the straw in his glass, he continued. "You have become my favorite person."

Her smile said it all.

"I got you back in one piece," she teased slowly pulling into the parking area of John's shop. "Thanks, Nathan. I really appreciate all you did to make this possible."

He took her hand. "You're welcome. I would do anything for you, Maddie. I hope you know that." Pulling her closer, he gave her a tender kiss, then walked toward his own vehicle.

As Maddie drove back to her apartment passing an empty school bus, she was reminded of her previous career. She recalled this time last year how unhappy she was working at North Side Christian Academy. She had not missed the classroom at all since she had quit her job there. *What does that mean?* She had no answer. *All that time and money I've invested in a career as a teacher. Do I just throw it all away?* Another question without an answer. Truthfully she had clocked a lot of hours, but not in the way she had hoped, which were to prepare her for her own classroom. Instead those hours were spent mostly being an errand girl. She loved the children, but didn't like putting in extra hours without being compensated. When her day was done, she wanted to go home versus staying late for round two of the school day. She then thought of her current job. A calm peacefulness came over her. Her work was interesting, and at times she was given more responsibilities, which was exciting. She loved the people at Dunning Plumbing and the thought of not working there made her sad. Pulling into her usual parking spot in her new car gave her a sense of achievement. Her job at Dunning Plumbing was a blessing from the Lord, no doubt.

Still excited from the day, Maddie welcomed the coziness of her bed and anticipated the added comfort of fresh sheets. Finding that perfect spot, she let out a contented sigh, and within ten minutes the day began to drift away. Her thoughts became fuzzy as sleep was attempting to claim her. Just as she was about to drift off, she was suddenly startled by a noise outside her window. Listening but not hearing the sound again, she turned over waiting for sleep to return. Her mind was now running in different directions until it settled on her career. Questions raced through her mind one after the other before she could even come up with an answer. After tossing and turning for almost an hour, Maddie left her bed and went to the kitchen for something to drink. She found Meagan sitting at the table having cookies and milk while reading a book.

"Can't sleep?"

"No, I figured I would get a little something to eat, maybe that would help. Why can't you sleep?" Meagan asked before biting into a cookie.

"My mind won't stop racing."

The two sat at the small kitchen table eating chocolate chip cookies and sipping milk when Maddie broke the silence.

"Meagan, can I ask you a question?"

"I think you just did." Noticing her friend's face, she apologized.

"Did you always want to work in a lawyer's office?"

"No, when I was in high school I was determined to get my degree in cinematography. Then my freshman year at college I decided I wanted to work in a lawyer's office, but I didn't want to be a lawyer. Waaay too much work and stress. Why?"

"I'm not sure I want to be a teacher anymore."

Meagan stopped chewing and looked at her friend.

"I mean I've wanted that for as long as I can remember, but after being in the system and seeing it from the other side and being paid so little to do so much, I'm not sure anymore. And especially now that I have a good paying job that I really do love, I don't think I want to go back to teaching."

"Is this something you have to decide right now?"

"No, but on the way home this evening, I saw a school bus and it dawned on me. I don't miss being in the classroom. I don't miss teaching, the challenge...any of it. I must say, I enjoyed tutoring Joshua, but that was different. I wasn't teaching I was...helping."

"Hmm. What do you want to do?"

Maddie nibbled her cookie and looked out into space.

Turning back to her friend with solemn eyes, she confided, "Maybe I wasn't meant to be a teacher after all. For the first time ever, I can say I really like my job and the people I work for...*and* the pay and benefits are a lot better than what I made working as a teacher's aide." Maddie sighed. "Somewhere along the way to becoming a teacher, which I have yet to be, I lost my passion for it. Meagan, when I think of going back to the classroom it depresses me. There are a few little faces I've wondered about this year, but that's it. I have no desire to go back."

"Then I guess you should keep doing what you're enjoying and leave the teaching to someone with that desire and passion."

Meagan's timing with words was impeccable. She seemed to always say just the right thing in a way that cleared up all confusion. Maddie suddenly had clarity. No one was making her leave the job she loved and go back to teaching, nor did she need to explain herself to anyone. It was her choice and hers alone, and unless the Lord changed her mind or the Dunnings no longer wanted her, she would stay at Dunning Plumbing as their receptionist.

Swallowing the last of her milk, she placed her glass in the sink. "Thanks, Meagan. I think I'll go to bed now." Meagan sat longer having a few more cookies and went back to her reading.

Caroline looked at her calendar to see how many games she had left before the schools went on their Christmas break. "One more," she said out loud to no one. She and Richard had been trying to plan a Christmas party for the single adults, but finding a time to do so had become a challenge. She called her husband's phone and waited for him to answer.

"Hi, gotta minute?"

"For you I have forever." His response melted her heart.

"I'm looking for a time to have a party for the singles, but I can't seem to find a date where you and I both are available. I'm looking at the calendar and somehow it has quickly filled up. Either you need to cancel your hunting trip with Brian and your Dad, or I'm going to have to cancel dinner with my parents, or we change the office Christmas party to a New Year's party instead."

"Don't fret over it. When I get home, we'll get our schedules together and work something out."

"Easy for you to say," she teased.

Hanging up, she heard a noise outside and knew after a moment it was Joshua home from work. "I wasn't expecting you for another couple of hours."

"I was only scheduled to work five hours today, but the rest of the week I'm working eight hour shifts. For the rest of today I'm a free man," Joshua announced.

"Okay," she chuckled. "I'm off to the grocery. That was on my agenda for tomorrow, but I really need to go today. I'm sure there's something here for you to snack on."

"I'll find something," he assured her on his way to the kitchen.

Joshua sat at the table eating a dinner serving size bowl of cereal, and with his mouth full, he tapped in Maddie's number on his phone then waited for her to answer.

"Hey, Madds, you busy?"

"For you? Are you kidding? What's up?"

"Your help really paid off." Using his grades as an excuse to call her, "I got one B and the rest A's on my finals."

"Congratulations!"

"I couldn't have done it without your help, Maddie, really, thanks."

"You're welcome my friend. Any time."

"If you don't have any plans tonight, me and some friends are heading to Pizza Perfect. You're welcome to join us."

"Thanks, Joshua. If you don't mind Nathan coming along with me that would be great."

"Nate, oh yeah, he can come."

After months of working together, the two had become close friends, and his crush on her had faded. She was proud of her student. To her that was what being a teacher was about, helping someone learn and accomplish their goals. She freely offered her help if he ever needed it again; he only needed to ask.

Opening the fridge to get the milk for his Rice Krispies, Richard only found a vacant spot it once occupied, but when he looked over his shoulder, he saw the empty jug sitting on the counter where Joshua had left it the night before.

"Sorry, dear, I'm running a bit behind this morning. What would you like for breakfast?"

"I was going to just have a bowl of cereal, but there isn't any milk. Weren't you at the store yesterday?"

"Yes, but I forgot to buy milk. Just sit down and I'll make your breakfast." Within minutes, she poured him a cup of hot coffee as he glanced over the newspaper while he waited.

Setting a plate of scrambled eggs and toast in front of him, his mouth watered simply from the delightful aroma. He gladly laid the paper to one side. "Now that our calendar of events for this month is settled, I can move on to other things," she said letting out a breath. "The days fly by faster when there are too many activities in the month. Oh goodness! Speaking of time flying, I need to get moving. I have a hair appointment in twenty minutes." Caroline got up from the table, kissed her husband, grabbed her purse and keys and headed out the door. Richard picked up the paper and continued to read while he finished his breakfast.

Three hours later, Caroline walked in the house carrying a bag of groceries in both hands. As she set the bags down her phone beeped letting her know she had a text message. It was Melissa asking if she was free to go shopping tomorrow. Caroline kept most Saturdays free to spend with Richard, but tomorrow he would be helping his father and brother with kitchen renovations. After making plans with Melissa, she decided to make some lunch and then get started on her household chores.

Joshua was getting ready to leave for work. Before he walked out the door Caroline called out to him, "Son, what are your plans for tomorrow?"

"I'm helping Papaw and Uncle Curt clear off some land. Why?"

"I plan to be out all day tomorrow with Melissa, and I was just wondering what your plans were."

Caroline's older brother Curt lived not too far from her on a large piece of property. He had been wanting to build a new garage for his tractor and other equipment for over a year. The project was more than he could handle and needed help. Since Joshua needed money and had some building skills, it was a win-win for both.

Along with his father Zachary's assistance, he had confidence they could finish the job quickly. Joshua's uncle had stepped up as a mentor and father figure and taught him things only a man could. Since his father died in military action when he was very young, Caroline's brother devoted a lot time to Joshua. After accepting his offer to help, Joshua was looking forward to working with tools outside again even though the chilly winter air was closing in.

"What time does he want you there?"

"He said he wanted to start by seven. I don't know why we can't start later, like nine or so." Caroline just grinned at her son's comment.

"Uncle Curt can't be there until early in the afternoon, so Papaw and I are starting without him. I hope he lets me drive the Bobcat this time," he spoke with a gleam in his eye.

——•———•◦•———•——

Joshua pulled up to his uncle Curt's house at seven o'clock in the morning. His papaw was already there discussing the day's plan with Curt on his phone. Joshua was assigned to Bobcat duty to clear the area where the building foundation would be laid. This ultimately made it worth getting up early. His papaw's heart was filled with joy seeing his grandson's thrilled reaction.

With a fist punch in the air, he followed with an enthusiastic "Yes!" He couldn't wait to climb in and start her up. After about an hour, Joshua was like an old pro with the Bobcat. He drove it without any jerking motions and even made his turns as if he had been doing it for years, which made his papaw proud.

Zachary waved his hand to his grandson to signal him to stop. "Time to break for lunch!" he called out. Joshua had been so focused on his work he had forgotten about his stomach. They sat down on the back porch of Curt's house and ate. As Zachary opened his sandwich and took a bite, he glanced over seeing his grandson's lunch and could not contain his grin.

"Looks like you got enough food for several people there."

"No, just me, but I'll share with you, Papaw, if Mamaw didn't pack you enough."

Zachary laughed out loud, "Thank you, Joshua. I may take you up on that." Zachary always took time to talk to his children and grandchildren when the opportunity arose. He valued staying connected with his family no matter what and where they were in their lives. He figured he could not be helpful to them if he didn't know what was going on in their world. As they finished their lunch, he asked Joshua about school, his summer plans and anything else that came to mind. Also Zachary never passed up an opportunity to tease either. "So, what pretty little girl are you running after? Or do you have one running after you?"

"Papaw," he said half embarrassed.

By the afternoon, they had cleared the entire section marked off for the building and were now feeding the limbs and brush into the chipper. Zachary's plan was to have both done in one day, but it didn't happen. The two worked until five when Zachary called it quitting time.

Richard came through the back door dirty after working on his father's kitchen all day. He kissed his wife and then washed up while Caroline put their supper on the table. The aroma of beef pot pie hovered in the kitchen and drifted throughout the house making his mouth water and stomach growl. After the blessing had been said, Richard broke the news to his wife that they needed to change the schedule they had agreed on, again. He had a business conflict that he could not get out of on the eighteenth.

"Are you serious? Richard, we are just going to have to cancel that activity. There is just no way we can do it all."

"No...Let me handle it. I can fix this."

"I'm going to do just that because I'm done. I'm done with calendars and schedules for the month of December."

The words were barely out of her mouth when her phone rang. Richard really didn't like being disturbed by the phone at mealtime. Caroline looked to see if she recognized the number and had to take the call.

Walking out of the room she spoke, "Hi, Mike, how are you?"

"Fine, thanks, Caroline. I hope I'm not interrupting anything, but I just found out we are going to need you to referee a game on the eighteenth. Carl broke his ankle this afternoon and will be out for several weeks. I've gone down the line, and everyone is either already calling a game that night or out of town. Can you call in his place?"

"Let me check." Hearing her husband's recent words echo in her head, she immediately answered, "Yes, I'm available. Where and what time?" She hated to say yes since the month was full already, but Mike was a good friend and in a bind, not to mention her plans for that night had just been canceled. Mike gave her the necessary information, and she wrote it all down in her date book.

"Great, you'll be with me so you know it'll be a fun evening." Laughing at his own words, he thanked her again then ended their call.

She returned to the table and explained about the call as she continued her meal. "Good thing that night became available."

As Richard chewed his food, an idea was forming in his mind, but he dared not say anything in fear of his plan not working.

Joshua dragged himself home bone-tired. He perked up when he smelled food as he walked through the door. Homemade beef pot pie was the right cure for a tired body.

Just as he finished his supper, he received a phone call and somehow Joshua's exhaustion faded. He got up and walked to his room for privacy.

Caroline noticed Joshua's hair was getting a little long, but said nothing. Her son was an adult, and the way he wore his hair was his decision whether she liked it or not.

The hour was getting late, and Caroline was turning out the lights when she noticed Joshua's light was still on. As she walked by his room, she could hear his muffled voice. *For someone who was so tired at the supper table, he sure is staying up late.* Continuing to her own room, she was ready for the day to be done. Although her to-do list wasn't complete, she did enjoy spending the day with Melissa. She and Caroline hadn't talked as much these past couple of weeks, and she missed that. As she lay in the quiet listening to her husband's even breathing, she recalled her day with her dear friend and what she had shared with her while shopping.

Seventeen

The month of December could not fly by any faster, Caroline was sure of it. She had run around getting her Christmas shopping mostly done. She hated shopping alone, but Melissa was not available to go with her these days. She and Richard had been to two Christmas parties already and another coming up, plus a big family Christmas at her parents' home. Her momma Anna always said the only gift she wanted was a Christmas meal with her entire family. Before the actual holiday they would gather together to share a traditional Christmas dinner with all of her family's favorites. She spent many hours preparing for and fixing this meal in advance. Anna and Zachary enjoyed watching their kids and grandkids open the presents they gave them. But most of all, she treasured being around the people she loved most in this world. To her, that was a gift money could not buy.

Richard fixed the scheduling problem as promised with the young adults from church. His new plan was to forego the party and simply go to the ballgame Caroline was calling instead. "It will be great, and all so easy," he told her. "Everybody will meet at the game, and afterwards go out to eat. We'll have entertainment and food without any of the hassle," he explained as if he had just come up with the most brilliant idea ever known to man. She happily agreed. Richard then contacted everyone about the new non-party plan. Her stress immediately lifted seconds after he explained the details to her.

While Richard and Joshua were out, Melissa had dropped in to see Caroline. The two had a long conversation over glasses of Dr. Pepper. Melissa could tell her best friend anything, but this time she stumbled putting it into words. Eventually she told her why she and Alex were going through a rough spot.

"I won't try to give you advice since you have way more years of marital experience than I do, but know that I'm here for you. I will always be here for you, Melissa. Just like you have always been there for me."

She smiled at her friend. "I know, Caroline. It's good to be reminded though."

⁕ ⁕ ⁕

Caroline and Mike stood at the scorer's table talking as they waited for the buzzer to start the game. They would ref both girls' and boys' varsity games tonight. The Lighthouse Lions and the Franklin Road Minutemen were long time rivals. At Christian school sporting events, the fans usually didn't get too rowdy, but at times a fan who was a little too passionate and competitive would go over the top and have to be asked to leave the premises. For this game, she was glad to not have any family or friends from either school. Caroline missed seeing anyone come in from the church group, but she did see Joshua and a few of his friends at the ticket table. After paying and entering the gym, he gave her a wave as he walked past on his way to his seat.

As the tip-off grew closer, the crowd began filling up the bleachers. Maddie, Meagan, Nathan and Ryan drove to the game together. Caroline's parents were seated near them as well even though they weren't necessarily for either team. She wasn't sure if they were there to support her or because her dad loved a good basketball game. Either way these rivals were sure to provide an exciting game. Joshua saw his grandparents and moved to sit between Zachary and Maddie.

Caroline held the ball ready to toss it for the opening jump. At six on the dot, she blew the whistle to start the game. The Lighthouse ladies jumped out to a quick lead and went into halftime ahead by ten points. Early in the second half, the Franklin Road ladies hit a pair of three pointers to cut the lead to four. From there, the game went back and forth, the crowd for each team cheering and gasping with every basket and missed shot from their players. In the final minute, the Franklin Road girls began fouling as a strategy to win the game, but Lighthouse foiled their efforts and pulled away by hitting six of eight free throws.

When the girls' game finished and they left the court after shaking hands, both boys teams raced out onto the floor and began moving through their warm-up drills. Mike and Caroline grabbed their water bottles with little conversation while keeping an eye on the teams. This was going to be a serious game between these two teams with more physical activity than the girls' game. Both refs and players would make more trips up and down the court, but they were prepared for it. Caroline was in shape and confident she could keep up with the players.

The gym was packed as new fans were still arriving right up to the tip-off. As expected, the boy's game was very close, neither team getting a big lead the entire first half. Late in the second quarter, the leading scorer for Franklin Road picked up his second foul trying to block a shot by the Lions' big man. Usually, a second foul in the first half earned a player a seat on the bench, but the Minutemen's coach took a chance and left his star in the game hoping to get another bucket before halftime to take the lead. However, on the play, the boy passed up an open jump shot and drove toward the basket. He collided with one of the Lions before putting up his shot. Caroline quickly blew the whistle and called him for a charge, his third foul, waving off the basket. This brought a chorus of disagreement from the Franklin Road fan section. One man in particular who was sitting just below Joshua in the stands directed a couple of loud comments towards the call and to Caroline personally, but Joshua ignored it.

The second half opened to a quick pair of baskets by Franklin Road to take the lead. For the remainder of the third quarter, the teams traded baskets and free throws. Fans for both teams got louder after each score, and as it sometimes happens, there were a few who bordered on being rude or obnoxious by cheering too loudly or verbally disagreeing with every call made by the referees. The man sitting in front of Joshua made an unkind comment about how women referees clearly don't understand the rules of a man's game. At the break before the fourth quarter, Mike and Caroline requested the School Administrator make an announcement over the PA reminding the fans that personal attacks on the referees and their decisions were not acceptable behavior and could result in their removal from the gym and premises.

The fourth quarter was filled with back and forth, up and down action. With less than thirty seconds to go, the Franklin Road star scored to give them a two-point lead. The man, who clearly was the star's father, screamed at Caroline questioning her eyesight for not also calling a foul on the play. Joshua could ignore him no longer and started to respond when Zachary firmly touched his arm. Quickly, Lighthouse moved the ball up court and called a timeout. During the timeout, Mike walked over toward the man and reminded him that he had been warned, and one more comment would get him removed from the gym and escorted off the premises. The man didn't take him too seriously.

Coming out of the timeout, the Lions ran a play freeing up one of their forwards for the shot that tied the game sending it into overtime. On the first possession in overtime, the Lions' big man turned to shoot the ball and was hacked on the arm by the Minutemen's star. Whistles blew as both referees signaled a foul on the Franklin Road player, his fifth and final foul. In the stands, the boy's father jumped up and screamed his opinion of the call. This was the last straw, and Mike signaled for the School Administrator to eject the man from the gymnasium. After he was led from the gym, play resumed. Both of the free throws were made, and on the next inbound pass, the Lions stole the ball and laid it in to take a four-point lead which the Minutemen could not overcome.

After the game, Caroline quickly left the gym to meet Richard and the others at a nearby restaurant. As she got behind the wheel, her phone rang.

"I'm not far from the restaurant, and unless I get stuck in the traffic I should be there in about ten minutes."

Caroline waited in her car for Richard to arrive so they could walk in together. As they walked in, a man came up behind her and spoke.

"Excuse me, ma'am."

Caroline turned to see who was speaking to her.

"I just want to apologize for the way I acted at the ballgame. I love basketball, and sometimes I get too carried away. I really am sorry."

"Oh, that's okay. It's no problem, but thank you."

"What was that all about?" Richard inquired as they walked away.

"I'll tell you later, honey," Caroline whispered as they arrived at the table.

"Wow, Mom, that was one of the most exciting high school basketball games I have been to in a long time. I love having a referee for a mom!" Joshua joyfully exclaimed.

"It usually is between these two schools. They have been rivals for years. I thought for sure there was going to be a serious problem with that guy. Oh, and by the way, he just saw me in the parking lot while we were walking in and apologized for his actions. Someone said it was one of the player's fathers. It was a poor example to the kids."

"Well, I almost was a poor example. I was about to go punch that guy out for saying those things to you. Papaw held me back. He said, 'Son, you don't want to do that here'." They laughed at his attempt to imitate his grandfather.

"Caroline, that was some game! I've never seen anyone thrown out of a game, well, not a fan that is." Nathan added.

She chuckled. "To be honest, I've only had to eject someone from a game a few times. Usually everyone watches and enjoys themselves, and you always have a few that get louder and take it more seriously than others. But trust me, there are occasions when it has to be done. It was about five years ago, and this man would not stop yelling at us refs and some of the players. He was asked to stop or he would be asked to leave, but he continued so I stopped the game and told the principal to escort him out of the gym and off the property. That man was so mad. I can still remember his angry face."

"Wow." Maddie had always found Caroline to be a very interesting person, but now, she had a brand new respect for her.

On their way home, Caroline thanked Richard for organizing the evening's activities. Even though she was tired, she had fun. She wasn't sure if it was due to the good company, good food or the fact that she didn't have to lift a finger for any of it.

"You're welcome. I told you I could fix this," he laughed. Nothing more was said about the game or the man which was fine with her. Caroline was glad that it was the last game until after New Year's Day. They rode the rest of the way home in silence.

<hr />

Joshua's Christmas break was coming to an end too fast. He along with his pawpaw, uncle, and a few other guys had finished the building. Now he had two days left before he went back to school, and he was going to enjoy every moment. Besides working for his uncle Curt, he also put in some hours at a nearby pizza place and had earned enough money to cover his college needs for the next semester that his scholarship didn't. He was tired but relieved he had accomplished his goal.

While sitting at Pizza Perfect with Dillon and a few other friends, Maddie and Meagan walked in and spotted them right away. It was Meagan's night to cook, and it was slim pickings in their kitchen since neither one had been to the grocery in about three weeks. Meagan suggested pizza, and Maddie quickly agreed.

"Well, if it isn't my old pal Joshua."

He stood up and gave her a hug. "Hi, guys, want to sit with us?"

"Sure, why not? But we need to order first," Maddie replied.

The two returned to the table with Joshua and the others. While they waited, she took a few minutes to catch up with him and couldn't help but notice his hair.

"Looks like you're about to need a haircut there, bud," she smiled touching his hair remembering his interest in growing it long.

"I'm seriously thinking of letting it grow."

She let out a little chuckle. "How long?"

"I don't know. Just letting it grow for now."

After finishing their pizza, Maddie and Meagan noticed the time and began to gather their things to leave. "Where you going? Stick around."

"We have jobs to get up for in the morning, and some of us have to be up earlier than others," Meagan answered.

"Well, if you must. See ya around, Madds."

"See ya, Joshua. Hey, don't leave for school without saying goodbye."

"I won't." He gave her a hug bye and went back to the conversation with his friends. Dillon jumped on him immediately to tease him about having a *thaaang* for an older woman.

"Jealous." Joshua responded straight-faced.

On their way home, Meagan mentioned the same thing. "I think Joshua has a bit of a crush on you, Maddie. You might want to be careful."

"Whaaat? That's silly, we're just friends, good friends. I helped him pass a few of his classes. You are totally off base on this one."

"Oookaaay. If you say so."

"I say so."

Maddie changed into an oversized t-shirt, and just slipped under the covers when her phone buzzed. Picking it up, it was

Nathan. The only light in the room shone from her cell. She loved talking to him at night alone in her room and having his voice be the last one she heard before going to sleep.

"It's midnight, so I guess I need to let you go and get some sleep," Nathan suggested after a lengthy conversation.

"Yeah, I guess so. You may want to call it a night as well. Wouldn't want you falling in an engine or anything." He laughed at her comment.

"Yeah, we wouldn't want that."

Maddie was not only in his head, she was in his heart. Not having to say goodnight over the phone or at the door was now in his head more often than not. He just wasn't sure if she had the same feelings toward him.

Pulling into her parking space, Maddie turned off the motor and gathered her things before opening the door. She gasped at the sudden sight of someone standing next to her car.

"Hi, Maddie, how are you?"

"Ethan, you scared the daylights out of me! What are you doing here?"

"I came to see you. Just wanted to see how you were doing, that's all."

"I'm fine. Now if you will excuse me, I need to get inside, or I will be late for work."

Her response appeared to irritate him. "You're always punctual, aren't you? Everyone can always count on Maddie."

"Ethan, what do you want? I don't have time for this."

"Would you have dinner with me this evening?"

"No, I will not, not this evening or any evening." She began to walk away, but he sidestepped and blocked her path.

"Ethan, don't do this."

"Come on, Maddie. We used to have such good times together. I miss you. Come on. What do you say? We can just grab a burger like we used to." She could hear a hint of desperation in his voice.

"No, Ethan, I'm sorry, but I don't want to do that," she replied more kindly than she felt. At that moment, Richard pulled up noticing the look on Maddie's face. As Richard climbed out of his truck, Ethan saw him and quickly said his goodbyes and left.

"Maddie, you okay? Wasn't that Ethan Price?"

"Yes, and I am so glad you pulled up."

"Not to be nosey, but what did he want?"

"He wanted to go out with me again. I told him no, but he continued to ask."

"If he keeps pestering you, you let me know, okay?"

"Okay, thanks, but I don't think he will come around anymore."

———————•◦(•)◦•———————

Nathan sat in the snack room eating peanuts and drinking a Pepsi. It was cold and hit the right spot. Reaching in his pocket, he pulled out his cell phone and made a call.

"Hi, Dad, how's it goin'?"

"Hey, Son, what's up?"

"Aah, nothing much. I need to talk to you about something. Do you have some time this weekend?"

"Sure, my weekend is wide open."

"Okay, I'll come by Saturday morning then."

Without ever hinting about what he wanted to talk about, the two spoke a bit longer about their jobs and then ended the call. Nearing the end of the work day he turned his focus on cleaning his work area before leaving for the day. He had finished early and was looking forward to getting home and watching a little TV before Maddie came over.

When he walked into his apartment, he realized TV time wasn't happening with things looking as they did. Without changing his clothes, he began collecting dirty dishes from the living room and taking them straight to the dishwasher until it was full. He then filled the sink with warm soapy water for the remaining dishes while he ran the vacuum. Looking around he was pleased with his efforts until he walked into the bathroom. When he had roommates who shared cleaning duties, he had done better at keeping his space clean and tidy, but now that he had the whole apartment to himself, he had become a bit of a slob.

"If Maddie sees this, she will run screaming, and I can't say I'd blame her," he said as he scanned the mess in front of him.

Within an hour he had cleaned his entire apartment making it livable again. The last order of business was him. Looking down at his dirty work clothes, he hurriedly headed to the shower.

Waiting for Maddie, he plopped on the couch and clicked on the TV. Unknown to him, he had fallen asleep. Awakened by a noise he couldn't place as it grew louder and more persistent he realized what it was. Seeing his sleepy face when he opened the door, Maddie smiled knowing what had happened.

"Hey, I was beginning to wonder if you were home."

"Aaah, I think I dozed off for a minute," he groggily admitted as he stepped aside to let her in.

Nathan had ordered Chinese food which they both loved. They chatted easily about various topics as they ate, but one subject took on a more serious tone.

"Okay, if you think it's time we do this, then let's do it. I'll call my mom tomorrow and see when a good time for us to come by will be. They're usually not very busy...and you will do the same, right?"

"Actually, I sort of already have. They both are looking forward to meeting you, and so are my siblings." Maddie's nerves suddenly went into overdrive, and Nathan noticed the strange look on her face.

"Is there a problem?"

"No, no problem."

"You have told your parents about us, haven't you?"

"Yes, sort of."

"What do you mean by sort of?" He had no clue what that could mean.

"Well, they know I've been seeing someone, and they know your name, but I haven't told them too much." Seeing his reaction, she tried to explain. "I've just been afraid of mentioning too much, that's all. After everything with Ethan...once bitten twice shy I guess."

Nathan was beginning to see the problem: Ethan. He was getting tired of that guy still lurking in the background. He assured her everything would be fine, but his words were for him as much as they were for her.

"At this stage of our relationship, I think it's good to meet each other's family, don't you?" he asked mostly to encourage himself.

"Yeah, I do too. I'm just nervous about meeting yours. I mean, you have a big family. And mine, well, it's just the four of us."

"I don't see us as a big family."

"Exactly what do you call a big family?" she asked confused.

"I don't know...never gave it any thought."

"I assure you when there are six kids, it's a big family."

After the meal, Maddie cleared the table and Nathan threw the empty containers in the trash, and then put the *Psych* DVD in the player. During the show, they became more interested in each other than the craziness of the Santa Monica police department.

Epilogue

The room full of guests sat around beautifully decorated tables after their satisfying meal. She sighed. "I guess I will need to find a new roommate now. Who knew they would get married this soon? Don't get me wrong, I'm happy for both of them. It's encouraging to see two people who are so right for each other making the big commitment and getting married."

Lifting his glass of melted ice water, he just listened and nodded his head. The party was still going on as it should be. It was a warm early summer evening, and everyone was in a cheerful mood. The couple's happiness overflowed freely, and it was infectious. All around them couples were dancing and laughing.

"Care to join me again on the dance floor?" he asked holding his hand out toward her.

Smiling at him, she gently took his hand, and while the music played softly, Nathan held Maddie close and spoke for her ears only.

"I must say Coop dresses up right nice, and Meagan is very beautiful, but not as beautiful as you will be on our wedding day." He kissed her gently.

About the Author

Reba Stanley grew up in Muhlenberg County, Kentucky, where she developed a life-long love of the arts and first came to know her Savior, Jesus Christ. Reba is also a professional artist who has worked in various mediums of paint and color. She says her visual artwork is, and always will be in her blood, but writing is the form of art she has found to be most rewarding. With her writing, she conveys a variety of fictional stories, but the one unchanging truth that guides her story telling is her love for and dependence upon her Lord and Savior, Jesus Christ.

Reba and her husband of more than thirty years reside in beautiful Brentwood Tennessee. They have four children, and four grandchildren (and counting). While the Lord has taken them to live in other areas of the country, Tennessee is her home.

"Because your love is better than life,
my lips shall glorify you."
Psalms 66:3 NIV

Other books by Reba Stanley:

The Garland Series
Storms
The Rancher
Where My Heart Lies
The Dunning Series
A Promise Kept

Please visit my website at www.rebastanley.com to view each book and to make your purchase. I would love to have you sign up for my newsletter and to join me on Facebook, Twitter, Pinterest and Goodreads.

Dear Reader:

If there were such a thing as a time machine, would you want to travel back a few days, years or even your entire life for a do over? Most of us would answer yes. I personally would.

If you are feeling unloved, unwanted and alone in this big crowded world, again, you are not alone. Though it is true there is no such machine and we cannot go back in time, we can however, have a better life; we can have forgiveness, peace and a start over.

If you are wondering, "how can I achieve such a major goal?" please allow me a few minutes of your time to explain how easy you can start your life all over.

God so loved the world that he gave his only begotten Son, that whosoever [you too] believeth in him should not perish, [die] but have everlasting life. *John 3:16*

But God commended his love toward us, in that, while we were yet sinners, Christ died for us. *Romans 5:8*

Everyone who enters this world is a sinner and in need of God's salvation: For all have sinned, and come short of the glory of God: *Romans 3:23*

Dear reader, Jesus is our only way into heaven. Jesus saith unto him, I am the way, the truth, and the life; no man cometh unto the Father, but by me. *John 14:6*

For the wages of sin is death; but the gift of God is eternal life through Jesus Christ our Lord. *Romans 6:23*

We are all sinners. As it is written, there is none righteous, no not one: [not you or me]. *Romans 3:10*

That if thou [you] shall confess with thy [your] mouth [speak out loud] the Lord Jesus, and shall believe in thine [your] heart that God hath raised him from the dead, thou [you] shall be saved. *Romans 10:9*

For whosoever [you too] shall call upon the name of the Lord shall be saved. *Romans 10:13*

He doesn't turn anyone away. Behold, I stand at the door, and knock; if any man [any person] hear my voice, and open the door, I will come in to him, and will sup [eat] with him and he with me. *Revelation 3:20*

This dear reader is how you start your life over: through Jesus. Jesus invites you to come to him. He is waiting to receive you (no matter what you've done or what your life is like). If you will receive Jesus Christ right now, here is a simple prayer to guide you in what to say as you pray to receive Jesus as your Savior.

Dear Jesus, I now know that I am a sinner. I believe you are the son of God and died for me, will you please forgive me of my sins? Will you please save me? Thank you, dear Jesus, for saving me and coming into my heart to live forever. Your word tells me that I am now yours and never will be lost again, and one day I will live with you for eternity in your heaven. ~Amen

If you prayed this prayer or something similar and meant it, this is the first day of your new life, and your name is now written down in God's book of life never to be erased.

Thank you for allowing me to share Jesus with you.

~ Reba

Acknowledgements

Editors: T.B.M., and M.M. Smith
Research Consultants: M.D.B., S. Pack, and J. H. Fortney
Biblical quotations from the KJV and NIV

To my family: David, Tara, Christopher, Marisha, Nicholas, Brad, Lenae and Momma. Thank you for your love, support and patience during this project, each of you were a help in some way. I love you more than words could ever express.

David: I fell deeply in love with you over thirty years ago, and I'm still in deep. 1-4-3.

Printed in the United States
By Bookmasters